W9-DEV-850

THE JUNGLE

TOR BOOKS BY DAVID DRAKE

Birds of Prey

Bridgehead

Cross the Stars

The Dragon Lord

The Forlorn Hope

Fortress

From the Heart of Darkness

Killer (with Karl Edward Wagner)

Skyripper

Time Safari

DAVID DRAKE

THE JUNGLE

WITH

CLASH BY NIGHT

BY HENRY KUTTNER

A TOM DOHERTY ASSOCIATES BOOK
NEW YORK

THE JUNGLE

CLASH BY NIGHT

A Tor Book
Published by Tom Doherty Associates, Inc.
49 West 24th Street
New York, N.Y. 10010

Library of Congress Cataloging-in-Publication Data

Drake, David.
The jungle / David Drake.
p. cm.
ISBN 0-312-85197-9
I. Title.
PS3554.R196J86 1991
813'.54—dc20 *91-19055*
CIP

Book Design by Fearn Cutler

First edition: September 1991

Printed in the United States of America

0 9 8 7 6 5 4 3 2 1

CONTENTS

DAVID DRAKE

THE JUNGLE

To the Memory of
Petty Officer 2nd Class Philip Jessie (Jay) Thomas
Americans have been giving their lives for their country for a long time. That doesn't make the latest loss any easier to take.

I

May 17, Year 382 AS (After Settlement). 1047 hours.

There was an instant of silence as the second salvo of 8-inch shells drowned their freight-train roar in the shallow water off the port side of Air Cushion Torpedoboat K67. When the shells exploded, their three blasts erupted together from the sea in a spout of sand and water. Toothed lifeforms snapped and tore at one another even as they seared to death in the sunlight which burned through the clouds of Venus.

"—to Orange Leader," Ensign Brainard shouted into his commo helmet. "For God's sake, Holman, we can't hold this heading! Over."

They had to veer to seaward or reverse course. They had to do *something,* and do it quick or it wouldn't matter.

When shells had begun to fall unexpectedly on their two-ship scouting element, Lieutenant Holman had ordered K67 and his own K70 to skim the shallow embayment of one of the nameless islands of Gehenna Archipelago. At first, the order had seemed a good idea to Brainard also. The island's central peak, wrapped in festering vegetation, should confuse the radar of the cruiser targeting the two hovercraft.

But radar was never trustworthy on Venus. Solar radiation and magnetic fields twisted radio beams into corkscrews which might or might not bounce back to the receiving antenna. This time the cruiser's luck was good, and Brainard's luck—

The shockwave hammered them.

Brainard commanded one of the smallest vessels in Wysocki's Herd—Hafner's Herd originally, but a 16-inch shell had retired Cinc Hafner. Brainard gripped the cockpit coaming and glared at the waterspout, as though his eyes could force a response from Lieutenant Holman when a laser communicator could not.

K70, their sister-ship and the patrol leader, rocked out from behind the shellbursts, holding course. Instead of taking station ahead or astern of K67, Holman held his vessel 200 yards to seaward. That might be why the cruiser was still getting a Doppler echo separated from the shore—and an aiming point.

The sky screamed with another salvo. Ahead, the further cape of the embayment approached through the haze at K67's flat-out speed of 90 knots.

"Orange Two to Orange Leader!" Brainard shouted, knowing the volume of his voice wouldn't help carry the words to K70 if the laser communicator didn't function . . . and if Lieutenant Holman didn't want to hear. "Sheer off, for God's sake! Over!"

Newton, the coxswain, steadied K67 against the airborne shockwave and the surge of water humping over the shallows to pound the hovercraft's skirts. A ten-foot ribbonfish, all teeth and iridescence, swept up on the narrow deck, then slid into the roiling sea again. The fish had locked its jaws onto something round and spiny. In its determination to kill, it seemed oblivious to the notch some other creature had bitten from its belly.

Despite the oncoming shells and the onrushing land, Newton seemed as stolid as the ribbonfish. Perhaps he was. Newton made an excellent coxswain, but Brainard sometimes suspected that the seaman was too stupid to realize there was anything to be afraid of. He would hold course as ordered, even though he knew running up on the island's jagged shore at 90 knots would rip K67's skirts off and strand her crew in the middle of Hell.

The 8-inch salvo burst squarely between the two torpedoboats, hiding K70 momentarily in another deafening uprush of water. The cruiser was firing armorpiercing shells. Its radar must be treating the paired echoes as a return from a single large vessel. When K67 adjusted course to port as they must do in a moment—*must* do!—they would be squarely in the footprint of the next trio of shells.

There was another salvo on the way. Brainard could hear the howl over the intake roar of the fans pressurizing the bubble of air which filled K67's plenum, driving her across the surface by thrust vectored through the skirts.

The starboard forward fan was running hot. Technician 2nd Class Leaf, the motorman, was half inside its nacelle ahead of the gun tub.

He glanced back toward Brainard. The opaque helmet visor hid Leaf's face, but Brainard could imagine the panic in the motorman's eyes. The same terror stared back at Brainard whenever he looked into his soul—so he didn't do that, he concentrated on his instruments and his duty and to *hell* with Lieutenant Holman.

"Coxswain," Brainard ordered on his helmet's interphone channel, "drop twenty knots and adjust course ten degrees to seaward."

That would clear the jaws of land, barely, and avoid their consort—if she held her course. If Holman chopped K70's throttles also, the high-speed collision of the two flimsy craft would do as thorough a job as the 8-inch shells could have desired.

Officer-Trainee Wilding looked up from his navigation/ electronic countermeasures console on the other side of the coxswain. "Sir," Wilding's voice crackled over the interphone, "I've tracked the shells back, and it isn't the Battlestars firing—"

Wilding had a reporting capsule ready to go, a laser communicator which would transmit its message program when it rose high enough to achieve line of sight with the Herd's main fleet. There was no point in releasing the capsule now. The 90-knot windspeed would shred the ascender balloon before the capsule released from its cradle.

Newton adjusted his throttles and helm. K67 took his input, but her slow response was almost lost in the thunderous vibration of the incoming shells. The cloud cover, lighted a translucent white by the sun only 67 million miles away, quivered with the sound.

These weren't shells fired by a cruiser. This was a main-gun salvo from a dreadnought. The cruiser's rounds had not taken effect, so she had passed her radar target to a battleship.

"Hang on!" said Ensign Brainard, but he was only clinging to the cockpit rim with his left hand himself. He threw himself back into his seat; the shock harness gripped him.

Brainard's right hand checked the key on his commo helmet. He had to make sure that it was clicked forward to interphone so the crew could hear him. If he filled his mind with duty to his crew there was no room left for fear.

Shells lifted the sea off K67's port bow. Sand, corals, and innumerable forms of life bulged up and outward in a man-made volcano. The bursting charges released fluorescent green marker dye so that a spotter could differentiate the fall of shot among multiple ships in a fleet engagement.

K67 bucked as the tidal wave swept across her track, but

the hovercraft lifted instead of being overwhelmed by the circular chaos. All the world was the white pressure of the shockwave, the simultaneous detonation of several 18-inch shells.

Brainard was weightless. Only the touch of his left hand on the coaming connected him to his vessel. For an instant, he thought that they were safe, that K67 had ridden out even *this* cataclysmic fury—

Then he realized that the hovercraft was dropping off the back side of the wave. When the skirts lifted, they braked K67 like a parachute—but not enough, and their direction was now a vector of their initial course and the 90° side-thrust from the shockwave. K67 was about to slam down on a jagged shoreline at a speed that would rip through the armored belly of a dreadnought, much less a hovercraft's flexible skirts.

Brainard realized one other thing as well. The Battlestars didn't bother with marker dye in their shells. One of the Herd's screening cruisers had seen a big-ship echo where the Herd had no major fleet units. The cruiser had taken the target under fire, then passed the target to a battleship.

From the color of the dye, K67 had just been destroyed by the *Elephant*, the flagship of Brainard's own fleet.

May 10, 382 AS. 2334 hours.

As Brainard and his momentary consort sauntered up the circular ramp, he glanced down through a haze of alcohol at the ballroom's panorama of metal and jewels and the fabrics which shimmered brightest of all.

He'd seen parties like this one before, but he'd never been present in person. Every Keep's holonews focused on the glittering celebrations that the founding families and their retainers held, on festival days or whenever a special event arose.

This time the event was the imminent war between Wyoming Keep and Asturias Keep. The Callahans, whom Officer-Trainee Wilding said were the most powerful of the Twelve Families directing the affairs of Wyoming, had risen to the occasion. A gathering this splendid would occupy the holoscreens until battle news arrived to entertain the mass of the population.

The common people had their own celebrations in every bar and club throughout Wyoming Keep—and Asturias as well, no doubt. Those parties Brainard *had* seen, as officer-trainee and as civilian, for as far back as he could remember.

Because mercenaries—the surface fleets of the Free Companies—did the actual fighting, war was only an economic risk to the populace of the domed keeps beneath the seas of Venus. If the Battlestars, the Free Company employed by Asturias, defeated Wysocki's Herd, the leading families of Wyoming Keep—the folk here in this ballroom—would manage to insulate themselves from the worst effects of reparations payments. The common people had so little to begin with that less would not significantly degrade their manner of life.

Civilians celebrated because battles were exciting. Mercenaries—and there were ten or a dozen at this gathering besides Brainard, the others mostly high officers—caroused because they might be about to die.

The woman on Brainard's arm drew herself possessively closer to him. What *was* her name? He couldn't remember.

The ramp to the chambers on the high second level was

designed to permit those on it to see and be seen by the crowd in the ballroom itself. It was broad and sloped gently, making a full circuit of the big room in its ascent.

Two couples were coming down together as Brainard and his companion went up. The women were strikingly beautiful in jumpsuits of pastel chiffon. The fabric was almost transparent.

The men wore lieutenant-commander's braids on the blue-and-silver dress uniforms of Wysocki's Herd.

"Oh, Lieutenant Brainard!" bubbled the woman in chartreuse as she fumbled to take the ensign's free hand. The other three strangers carried drinks, but this woman's expression was brighter than alcohol alone would paint it. "I'm so glad to see you! Prince Hal—Hal Wilding, *you* know—promised to introduce me to you!"

The woman in pink let her half-empty glass fall and said, "Prince Hal is a *very* dear friend of mine!" She tried to insert herself between Brainard and the other woman, but Chartreuse had a surprising amount of muscle in her plump arms. "Would you like me to show you over the house?"

Brainard stared at the two men. Their uniforms were real. Their complexions probably resulted from makeup, but the men had the deep mahogany tans which high-energy rays penetrating the cloud layers burned into the exposed skin of Free Companions on the surface.

But the eyes were wrong. The men were phonies, rich civilians in costume, and they turned away from the expression they saw on Brainard's face.

The woman on Brainard's arm gave Pink and Chartreuse a look as cold as the ensign's own. "Dearests . . . ," she said, drawing out the sibilants into a hiss. "I'm going to show Ensign Brainard the house myself. After all, dearests . . . . it *is* my family's house, isn't it?"

Drink buzzed in Brainard's mind. He supposed his consort was a Callahan.

She must have done something with her dress when she saw rivals approaching. Now it was formed of two slitted layers instead of a single piece of fabric. She smiled at Brainard and shifted her stance, so that her erect pink nipples peeked out at him.

The two couples passed on down the ramp, snarling among themselves in low voices. From across the ballroom, Officer-Trainee Wilding, surrounded by his own harem and the cameras of a holonews team, glanced up and met Brainard's eyes.

The ensign saluted sardonically. Prince Hal, was it? He'd known that K67's new second-in-command was a member of the Twelve Families; that was how he'd gotten Brainard an invitation to this party, after all. But Brainard hadn't been born in Wyoming Keep, so he'd had no idea that Wilding was prominent even within his class.

A footman in magenta livery with buff facings knelt to pick up the dropped glass. The tail of the servant's coat brushed Brainard's leg. His consort noticed the contact. She squealed and lashed out with her foot, displaying a slender leg and a line of blond fuzz from her pubic wedge to her navel.

Brainard caught her so that the kick missed its target. The footman scuttled away without looking back.

"We had to lay on extra help for the party," the woman said pettishly. "Some of them are worse than useless."

She hugged herself close to the ensign again. "Come along," she said. She giggled. "But not *too* fast."

Brainard's face did not change. They resumed their

stately progress up the ramp. His consort wanted everyone to see that she had snagged a certified combat hero for the evening. Well, that was all right with him. . . .

The ballroom's high ceiling was a holographic projection of the terraforming and settlement of Venus. In the opening scenes of the loop, huge cylinders arrived, filled with bacteria gene-tailored to live and grow in the Venerian atmosphere. The waste products of bacterial growth included oxygen and water vapor. Rain fell in torrents that finally, as the atmosphere cleared, reached and pooled in oceans over most of the planetary surface.

The terraformers' centuries-long work continued. Later cylinders spewed the seeds and eggs of multicelled lifeforms onto the newly receptive planet. Trees of myriad species; vines, grasses and epiphytes; *all* the diversity of Earth, plus multiple mutations for every original species. Through the burgeoning jungles stalked beasts—insects, arachnids, crustaceans; even the forms of backboned life which were simple enough that the young did not require parental care. All were genetically tailored to the new environment.

The terraformers' success was beyond plan—almost beyond comprehension. Human-engineered changes to gene plasm had coupled eagerly with the virgin environment and the high level of ionizing radiation penetrating the clouds of water vapor. The result was a hell of aggressive mutations like nothing ever seen on Earth. Perhaps the artificial ecosystem was unique in the universe.

The new conditions changed but did not force the abandonment of plans for the human colonization of Venus. Now the holographic views showed how the planners set up their first colonies in undersea domes at the edges of continental shelves, as nearly barren—and therefore safe—

as any region of the planet. Colonization of the surface, turgid with ragingly lethal lifeforms, would come later—when the domed keeps could themselves support the effort.

But before that day came, Earth had destroyed itself in a nuclear holocaust which turned the atmosphere's welcoming blue into a hideous white companion star for the sun.

Human life continued in the Keeps of Venus, but the Venerian surface was reserved for the Free Companies and their proxy wars. Holographic dreadnoughts flashed at one another in the final scene of the ceiling decoration—and the looped image reverted to the lifeless chaos which preceded terraforming.

In the ballroom below, couples danced and drank and laughed in brilliant, tinkling voices.

The ramp ended at the balcony which gave access to fifty upper-level rooms. Most of the rooms near the ramp were already marked by the discreet In Use notations which appeared when the inner lock was turned. A few doors were open. Within, servants in livery changed washable couch-covers, disposed of used glasses and drug paraphernalia, and occasionally removed the torn or forgotten undergarments of previous temporary occupants.

"There's an empty bed further along," Brainard's consort said.

The ensign's brain was foggy with alcohol. The woman's pleasant, contralto voice came from a blur of warm flesh, not a form.

She chuckled. "But the night's still young. They'll be lining up before daybreak."

Though there were toilet facilities just off the dance floor, there were others set at 90° and 270° from where the ramp joined this level. Brainard and his consort were nearing the men's room. Male guests stood near the door, lounging against the balcony or wall; chatting and looking idly about.

There were empty stalls inside. These folk were held by ennui or inertia, not need. All were civilians. Their faces quivered with various shades of envy as they eyed Brainard and the woman.

A mercenary officer stepped out of the men's room—Lieutenant Cabot Holman, Brainard's immediate superior. He was a forceful, blocky man, not as tall as the ensign but heavier in a muscular way. At the moment, he was flushed with drink.

Brainard nodded with minimal politeness. He stepped closer to the rail so that Holman could pretend to ignore him if he so desired. The two officers would never have been friends, even if it hadn't been for Holman's younger brother. . . .

Holman looked up, saw Brainard, and let his gaze glance aside like an arrow sparking away from rock.

Holman froze. His red face went livid, then white. Brainard blinked at him, wondering if the lieutenant was about to have a seizure from something he had consumed in the name of entertainment.

"Stephanie, you slut!" Holman shouted. He looked queasy.

It took Brainard's dazed mind a moment to remember that his consort had introduced herself as, "*Stephanie—Stephanie Callahan, dear one.*"

"And with the bastard who killed Ted, too!" bellowed Holman.

People stared. Doors opened around the second level;

folk in the ballroom below craned their necks for a better view.

"I didn't kill your brother!" Brainard said. He'd drunk too much. His tone was more of a snarl than his conscious mind had intended.

Holman punched him in the mouth. It felt like being too close to the breech of a recoiling cannon.

Brainard staggered, numb all over. The balcony rail was against the small of his back. The wide arc to his front was a blur of screams and faces filled with wolfish glee.

Another door slammed open. Captain Glenn, Officer in Charge of the Herd's screening forces, stepped onto the balcony. Glenn was stark naked except for his flat uniform hat, covered with gold braid.

"What in the hell is going on out here?" the captain bellowed. Two girls peeked out of the doorway behind him. Neither of them seemed more than pubescent.

Holman knelt on the balcony and put his hands to his face. The knuckles of his right hand were bloody.

"He killed my brother Ted," Holman sobbed; then he vomited onto the floor.

On the ballroom ceiling, the holographic display again formed itself into a ravening jungle.

2

MAY 17, 382 AS. 1051 HOURS.

Leaf's mind split into a part that understood what was happening and another part that still believed he could survive. He'd unlatched the access plate to # 2 fan and was sprawled within the nacelle when he felt the torpedo boat lift onto her last crest. Air boomed with the braking effect of the skirts.

Leaf's left hand gripped the fan mount while his leg muscles locked his boots against K67's starboard rail and the lip of the nacelle opening. His right hand held the multitool with which he had just loosened the journals of the fan's back bearing and squirted in microsphere lubricant. The bitch'd shake herself to shrapnel in forty minutes, but that was half an hour longer than she'd last before burning if the motorman did nothing.

Leaf had had to disconnect the hose feeding cool, dry air to his environmental suit before he crawled into the nacelle. The suit's impermeable membrane trapped his sweat and body heat, steaming him like a shrimp dinner.

The climate wouldn't have time to be fatal, though, because Leaf had also unsnapped his safety line.

Leaf dropped his multitool to grip another handful of

rim. The spring lanyard spooled the tool up snugly beneath his right arm. *It* would come through the next few seconds just fine.

The hovercraft dropped, touched a solid surface, and spun with the momentum of more than 40 knots times her mass.

Leaf's existence was a montage in which serial time no longer ruled:

The barrels of the twin machine-guns in the gun tub cut an arc to port, then to starboard, against the white sky. Yee, strapped into the gunner's seat, swung between the weapons like a participant on a carnival ride.

Ensign Brainard sat like a statue, his head visible through the cockpit windscreen. He was shouting something into the interphone, but Leaf could only hear the timbre of the CO's voice in a universal roar too great for even the circuitry of his commo helmet to sort out.

A palm fought with a blackberry at the edge of the jungle. Thorns probed deep into the palm's hard tissues, but its wounds wept a binary sap which smoldered as its chemicals oozed onto the bramble.

K67's starboard quarter struck hard enough to compress #4 fan against a coral head. The blades exploded upward, through the guards and housing. If that fan had been running hot instead of #2, Leaf would be lunchmeat.

The sea was a huge spout of vivid green against the sky. The dismembered head of something reptilian slammed its jaws on another fragment of its body.

Tools, cups, and the holographic image of a naked woman flew from the torpedohouse aft the cockpit. Tech 2 Caffey, the torpedoman, and his striker were harnessed safely into their seats.

Unlike Leaf.

Instinct anticipated the shocks where intellect would have been overwhelmed.

Right boot shifts, right side tight against the edge of the access port—God! it hurt, but if he'd been flung sideways the three inches of a moment before, the lip would have broken his pelvis.

Down, chest flat against the mesh guards and the fan still howling at full revs. Inertia slams down a thousand times harder, bulging the mesh and crushing the breath from the motorman's lungs.

Forward—his arms take the strain and he screams but they *take* the strain. Right side, *again,* and *worse,* but alive. He's still all right. Not great; the inside of his visor is speckled with what looks like mud but is blood from when he banged his nose. Broken bones or just pulled muscles? But . . . alive.

K67 slammed down squarely, compressed what was left of her skirts, and sprang three feet into the air before coming to rest. Leaf had nothing to brace him against the last shock. He flew out of the nacelle like a bomb from the tube of a mortar.

He tumbled in the air. He'd lost his helmet, though he didn't know how: the chin strap was supposed to be strong enough to tow a destroyer. Slime and water splashed to envelope him. It was a moment before Leaf realized that he was no longer moving.

And that he was alive.

Leaf gasped a lungful of air. He screamed it back out because of the pain in his ribs. He lay on his back in a pool, floating easily because of the air trapped in his environmental suit.

There was ten feet of open water in every direction he

could see. Jointed reeds grew from the margins of the pond. They bent their spiky tips toward him slowly.

Leaf tried to turn his body. He screamed again and his head bobbed under water. When he came up, eyes bulging with fear, he saw the quick flick-flicker of a tongue through the reeds to his right.

The snake eased the remainder of its head into view.

Leaf heard nervous human voices nearby. The wrecked hovercraft must be close, though he couldn't see it the way he lay in the water. "Guys?" he called softly.

The snake's head was wedge-shaped and the size of a barrel; there must be at least a hundred feet of gray-brown body behind it. A nictitating membrane swept sideways across the one glittering eye that fixed on the motorman.

"Help!" Leaf shouted.

"Good God, man!" Brainard shouted back. "Don't move!"

That was when Leaf saw the spider peering with its eight tiny eyes from the reeds to his left.

The spider extended its long forelegs cautiously, spanning two yards. Their tips were brushes of fine hair which dimpled the surface of the black water but did not sink through it.

Leaf tried to hug himself in fear, but his head started to sink again as soon as his arms moved. He froze, unwilling to close his eyes but terrified by what he saw through them.

He wasn't carrying a sidearm. The multitool could be pressed into service as a weapon, but he'd be underwater sure if he tried to draw it down from its take-up spool.

The snake cocked its head further to the side, interested in the spider's stealthy movement. The forked tongue lapped the air for a taste of its potential rival. The arachnid poised, more still than the gently lapping water, while the reed tops bent above it.

Men talked behind him, but Leaf couldn't make out the words. They spoke softly, as if to avoid drawing the attention of the two monsters away from Leaf. He heard a squeal as the gun tub was cranked around by hand. The hovercraft's motors must have shut down during the crash.

Neither of the beasts would die easily. If one was shot, both would go berserk. They'd finish Leaf in their death throes, even if a stray bullet didn't get him first.

The motorman's body stuttered in a sequence of trembles, then tensed with pain. Both spasmodic movements were beyond his conscious control.

"Leaf," Ensign Brainard repeated, "whatever you do, don't move. Do you understand?"

"Yessir." His voice was a cracked whisper, but perhaps they saw his lips move.

The rifle shot startled him. The high-velocity bullet missed *everything.* It lifted a column of spray from the far edge of the pool.

God, he's missed!

The snake struck at the water spout. The spider leaped from the other side of the pool to sink its fangs into the reptile's neck, and the gun tub's twin .75-caliber machine-guns laced both creatures with high explosive.

Something wriggled through the air to the motorman. He shouted in fear before he realized what it was—a safety line—and grabbed with both hands. A firm pull dragged him toward land.

Explosive bullets had blown the spider's abdomen away from its cephalothorax, but its mandibles continued to worry the snake's neck. A long burst from Yee's revolver-breech machine-guns walked down the snake's body.

Something clung to Leaf's legs, then slipped away from the smooth fabric of his environmental suit. The water around the blasted, still battling, monsters blurred, then turned pale.

A hand gripped Leaf's hands. He lunged convulsively to the shore, where Officer-Trainee Wilding knelt to spread his weight better over the liquescent bog.

Leaf glanced over his shoulder. A membrane as pink as the inside of a stomach had risen through the water. It enfolded the snake and spider. The torn bodies, still thrashing, dissolved into pink slime which the membrane sucked in.

May 11, 382 AS. 0109 hours.

Leaf sat on a crate of empty bottles, ignoring the whore who tried to entice him by brushing his face with her pink tits. His back leaned against the brothel's piccolo as it blared out—for the twentieth time in a row—a song that had been popular when Leaf was a kid. He could barely hear the words, but he mouthed them by memory: "*. . . Tennessee. . . . Tee for Thelma, She made a fool outa me. . . .*"

Leaf closed his eyes. His glass was empty, but he was too drunk to get up and buy another drink. The bottle rims stabbed his buttocks like a bed of blunt needles, but they were a better seat than the slimy floor, and he wasn't sure he was able to stand just now.

The Año Nuevo's ground-floor reception area was stiff with sound. The orders sailors bawled to the tapster behind the semicircular bar were more often than not misheard, but at this time of night it didn't make any difference. Men drank whatever was put before them.

The separate staircases down to the basement and sub-basement were on either side of a low stage. The sub-basement was a credit cheaper, but it was damp and stank like a sewer; if you cared, which most of the Año Nuevo's customers didn't. The evening's floor show was over. The huge holonews display on the wall behind the stage was tuned to a party thrown by the local upper crust.

"Gonna buy me a shotgun wif a great big shiny bar'l. . . ."

The brothel's star turn was a black-haired, black-eyed minx named Susie. She was a tall woman compressed into five feet of height: large breasts and broad hips, but with a distinct waist separating them. She was a looker by local standards, though that wasn't the main reason for her popularity.

Every evening, the girls collected a half- or quarter-credit from each of the customers to pay for Susie's time, and some lucky guy got a freebie on the stage. Tonight, Susie's choice—a sailor from the dreadnought *Elephant*—had already been too drunk to perform effectively. That made the entertainment even better for the half of the brothel's clientele who weren't battleship sailors.

"Gonna shoot that Thelma . . . ," Leaf sang.

Two couples on the stage now were giving a pretty good informal show of their own. If the sailors thought they were going to save a room charge, they were wrong. Above them, glittering party-goers smirked through interviews on the holographic display, their words lost in the general racket.

". . . just to see her jump an' fall."

The music, a vibration through the motorman's spine, ended as the piccolo shut off. Leaf sighed with his eyes closed and fumbled in the pocket of his tunic. He still had a few half-credit coins left. He slipped one out and raised it toward the slot above and behind him, moving by practiced reflex.

"Tee for Texas," he mouthed. *"Tee for Tennessee . . ."*

A hand closed over Leaf's groping hand.

"Go away, honey," he muttered tiredly. "I'm fucked out, believe me."

"I said, are you gonna shut that noise off or am I gonna bust your head?" a voice shouted in his ear.

Leaf's eyes flashed open. He wasn't drunk any more, but his skin was very cold.

The whore had gone to plow more useful fields. Another sailor bent close to the motorman's face. The tally around his cap read *Elephant,* not a big surprise. He was a young fellow, six inches taller than Leaf and muscular. His flush was drink or anger or both.

Almost certainly both.

"Got a problem with something, sonny?" Leaf said as he rose smoothly to his feet. Leaf wasn't shouting, but the general volume of noise had dropped enough that most of those in the reception room could hear him. He let the coin drop to free his hand. "Can't get your dick stiff, maybe?"

This wasn't the sailor from the floor show, but he'd heard the story. He reacted without hesitation, punching Leaf in the face.

Leaf had ten years in the Herd and a lot of bar fights behind him. He shifted his head so that the fist glanced along his jawbone. It would leave a bruise, but for the moment Leaf scarcely noticed it against the rush of alcohol and adrenaline.

He flung himself backward into the piccolo as though the punch had caught him squarely, then sprawled on the floor. If the other sailor was smart, he'd try to put the boot in—and then it was going to get interesting.

He wasn't smart. "And *leave* it off!" the battleship sailor shouted as he turned toward the bar instead of finishing what he'd started. "Flitterboat pussies!"

Leaf came off the floor. The crate of bottles was in his hands, swinging in a sideways arc.

Shouted warnings started the kid's head rotating to see what was happening behind him, but it was already too late. The crate hit him at the center of mass. Bottles flew out. The impact smashed ribs and flung the victim over the bar. He caromed off the tapster who had already jerked down the alarm lever.

It was too late for that as well. Even before the crate landed, battleship sailors and crewmen from smaller vessels began to fight one another all over the reception area.

Some of the girls joined in, shrieking with fury. It wasn't any business of theirs . . . but then, all the sailors were from the same Free Company.

Leaf ran for the stairs to the sub-basement. At the top of the steps he collided with a redhead in a string top which displayed all the little she had. The whore seemed to have lost her client below. She grabbed Leaf with both hands and began mechanically to proposition him.

"Move it, bit'h!" the motorman snarled, realizing that the right side of his jaw was numb. He pulled himself free.

There was an emergency exit from the sub-basement into a drainage tunnel, and this was an emergency by Leaf's standards. In a matter of minutes the Año Nuevo would be full of stormtroopers with truncheons and stun gas, Wyoming Keep's Patrol or the Herd's own shore police. Leaf didn't intend to be around while the authorities sorted out how the fight had started.

The holographic display was still tuned to the upper-crust party. Leaf dived past it, but the voice of the commentator followed him down the stairwell; saying, *"And why is Prince Hal wearing the uniform of a high officer in Wysocki's Herd? Because it's his uniform! Yes, really, darlings, the most eligible bachelor in Wyoming Keep is a Free Companion!"*

3

MAY 17, 382 AS. 1106 HOURS.

"Wilding," said Brainard, extending a hand over the rail to help the officer-trainee back aboard, "see if you can get a response on the radio. I can't raise a thing."

Wilding was barely able to move after boosting Leaf on board. Heat, the weight of his environmental suit, and the boggy soil into which he sank knee-deep at every step combined crushingly. "Sure," he gasped. *How did you explain to a man like Brainard that other people had limits?* "In a minute. Are the balloons okay?"

Radio communication was as undependable as radar imaging in the charged Venerian atmosphere. The alternatives were long-wave communication through the sea itself, and modulated laser. Long wave was slow, and the apparatus was too heavy to be mounted on a hovercraft. Laser commo was fast and virtually proof against interception, but it was line-of-sight only.

The answer was to raise the transmitter a thousand feet or more above the surface by balloon, bringing distant receivers above the horizon.

Brainard shook his head. "Sorry," he said. "All that gear's gone."

Wilding was exhausted, but the man he had rescued moved like a zombie in a suit twice the proper size. Bozman, the assistant motorman, supported Leaf's bulging body to his station just aft the torpedo controls.

"I got the auxiliary running, chief," Bozman chattered. "We'll have you plugged into the air conditioning soonest."

Leaf's suit dribbled pools of slime on the deck as the motorman moved. "How's the main motors?" he asked.

Wilding found the motorman's words remarkable both for their huskiness and for the fact that they were directed at his regular duties.

"They're fucked," said Caffey in a grim voice. "The commo's fucked. And we're fucked."

The torpedoman had clipped a light machine-gun—his personal weapon, since they weren't stock issue for hovercraft—to the seaward rail. The gun tub was rotated inland, covering the pool fifty feet away where the giant snake and spider had hunted, but no direction was safe.

Brainard glanced at Caffey without speaking. The torpedoman grimaced, then broke eye contact by calling to his striker, "Wheelwright! Bring another drum of ammo."

Wilding slid into the cockpit and reconnected the hose to his environmental suit. The seepage of cool, dry air through the suit's lining steadied his mind before it could make any practical difference to his body.

Brainard had brought the console displays up as soon as the auxiliary drive provided power for them. The radio transmitted an any-station emergency signal; K67's main computer would key the crewmen's commo helmets if there were a response.

There wasn't a damn thing else to do, except check the balloon ascender gear. The console had a scarlet Not Ready message under that heading.

A glance astern showed why. K67 had been inverted at some point as she spun ashore. The last five feet of the deck had been scraped, carrying away two decoy launchers and the long-range communications apparatus.

For the first time since a cruiser invisible over the horizon began to shell them, Wilding had leisure to consider their situation. Caffey was right. They didn't have a prayer.

K67 lay in a salt marsh inside this nameless island's outer barrier of coral. The coral had shredded the hovercraft's skirts, but that was probably the reason any of them were still alive. A rigid-hulled vessel would have disintegrated on impact, but the tough, flexible skirts had scrubbed away K67's velocity as they abraded.

Air-cushion torpedoboats hung their pair of primary weapons in the plenum chamber. Both torpedoes had been torn from their mountings as K67 bellied into the bog. Their safety mechanisms kept them inert despite the shock.

The torpedoes lay like a pair of broken sticks in the path the hovercraft had torn through the vegetation. The body of one had been crushed like a pinched grassblade, while the warhead of the other lay askew with half its attachment lugs stripped. Hungry reeds nuzzled the weapons in vain.

The warheads contained a nominal thousand pounds of barakite explosive. Their blast was designed to penetrate the main armor belt of a superdreadnought. If either weapon had detonated during the crash, there would have been nothing left of K67 and her crew.

Inshore, the jungle ascended in terraces of dark green toward the peak that the hovercraft's database indicated was a thousand feet above mean sea level. Mist and the foliage bulging from the slopes prevented Wilding from checking the accuracy of the charts.

Far to seaward, a storm or the broadsides of massed battlefleets thundered. The jungle responded with a fluting cry that seemed even more terrible because of its supernal beauty. Wilding shivered.

"I could maybe get Number One fan spinning, sir," said Leaf. "The blades are dinged, that's all. But we can't pressurize the plenum chamber with just one fan."

"You've studied this stuff, haven't you?" Brainard said.

"There aren't any skirts left to patch, anyhow," Caffey said morosely. He massaged his chest where the crash harness had held him during the multiple impacts. The gesture reminded Wilding of how much his own ribs hurt.

"Where's Holman?" Newton asked. "When's he comin' back for us?"

The coxswain sounded curious rather than aggrieved. He stared out to sea.

There was no sign of K67's consort, but the surface boiled in a natural frenzy. Living things devoured one other and the flesh of creatures the salvos had killed.

"Wilding!" Brainard snapped. "You studied surface life, didn't you? Your file says you did."

Wilding turned around, blinking in surprise. *The CO* had *been talking to him. . . .*

Brainard's face was hard. Not angry, but lacking any sign of weakness or mercy. The ensign was three calendar years younger than Wilding himself, but Brainard had been born with a soul as solid as the planetary mantle. He belonged here, and maybe the other crewmen did as well; but Hal Wilding would vanish in this environment as swiftly as the tags of bloody froth where the sharks fed.

"Yessir, that's right," Wilding said aloud. He heard with horror the crisp insouciance with which he clothed his words. It was the only protection he had, and it was no protection at all. "I have some course work in ecology."

Brainard wasn't one of his Twelve Family acquaintances, before whom Prince Hal needed to conceal serious endeavor. "Ah, I completed a degree program, as a matter of fact."

Wilding looked up at the jungle humping into the white sky behind them. "I don't have a great deal of specific knowledge, though. The rate of mutation here is so high that new data is generally obsolete by the time it's catalogued."

"I'll tell you where that bastard Holman is," Caffey muttered to the coxswain. "He's left us here because he's too chickenshit to risk coming ashore to take a look for us."

Brainard turned and pointed his right index finger at the torpedoman. "Drop that," he said quietly. "Nobody's been abandoned."

"That last salvo may have been right on top of them," Wilding suggested. He tried to remember the moments in which the manmade waterspout swelled to engulf K67. "They were—"

"Drop that!" Brainard repeated, the syllables sharp as gunshots. Wilding's tongue and heart froze.

"We aren't K70's problem," Brainard continued softly. "We're *our* problem. We're alive, we've got our equipment. So we're going to make things all right."

"We got fuel for three months, just running the auxiliary," Leaf said. His voice was surprisingly perky considering the shape he'd been in minutes before.

"If the auxiliary don't pack it in, you mean," retorted Caffey.

"We should be all right for food," Wilding said, pretending that he didn't believe the torpedoman's gloom was a realistic assessment of their chances. "We can supplement emergency rations with the flesh of most of the animals. Maybe even a few plants."

"The laser communicator can double as a portable," Brainard said, ignoring everyone else's comments. "Is it still functioning?"

"Look, Fish," Leaf said to the torpedoman, "the auxiliary'll still be running after you 'n me 're fertilizer. Anyway, I could rig Number One motor to power the air system."

Wilding unlatched the laser unit and lifted it so that the prongs feeding power were free of the jack on the bottom of the chassis. The self-contained module had its own sighting and stabilization apparatus. It was supposed to be capable of an hour's continuous operation on its integral batteries.

Wilding switched the unit on. It ran its self-test program without hesitation. "Checks out," he said and lowered it into its cradle again. A weight of fifteen pounds made the module portable, but not exactly handy.

"Hey!" shouted Yee from the gun tub. *"Hey!"*

Everyone turned to follow the line the twin guns pointed to starboard. Thirty feet from K67, a bubble of methane rose to the surface of the bog and plopped.

Twenty feet beyond, in line with the wrecked torpedoboat, a six-foot dimple in the marsh marked the spot a previous bubble had burst.

Yee fired a short burst. The muzzle blasts flattened a broad arc of the nearest vegetation. Explosive bullets cracked into the reed tops with dazzling flashes. The gun tub would not depress low enough to rake the semi-solid ground.

"Cease fire!" Brainard ordered. "Cease fire! Everybody get sidearms. We'll wait by the rail for it to surface!"

Reeds smoldered where the bursting charges had ignited them. The air was bitter with the mingled stench of explosives and burning foliage. A gray haze drifted away from the torpedoboat.

Another bubble broke surface ten feet closer.

Caffey struggled to unclamp his machine-gun from the port rail. Leaf, moving without wasted effort, unclipped an automatic rifle from the motormen's station and tossed it to his striker. The short blade clicked from his multitool. Newton and Wheelwright scrambled for their personal weapons. The CO was already pointing his rifle over the rail at a 60° angle.

Wilding wore a pistol as part of his uniform. He knew from his several attempts at qualification firing that the weapon might as well be back at the Herd's shore installation for all the good he could accomplish with it. He ran to the bow, skirting Caffey in a tense pirouette as the torpedoman freed his machine-gun and turned with it.

Wilding's air line disconnected and reeled itself back into the cockpit. The suit's impermeable outer skin slapped him like a wet sandbag. The two decoy dispensers forward had come through K67's grounding without damage. They were simply spigot mortars from which small propellant charges would lob the decoys.

"Look," one of the crewmen cried, "he's running!"

Wilding wasn't running. There was no place to run.

Each decoy was a bomb-shaped projectile weighing about fifty pounds. At the first dispenser, Wilding broke the safety wire which locked the fuze until the dispenser fired. He spun the miniature propeller on the projectile's nose to complete the arming procedure. The decoy was not supposed to burst until it was at least thirty feet from the vessel launching it. . . .

The propeller came off in Wilding's hands and tinkled to the deck, arming the decoy. He lifted the decoy in a bear hug and staggered to the starboard rail with it. He couldn't see past the bulky cylinder.

"Get b—!" he shouted and slammed into the starboard rail. The impact knocked the breath out of his body and tipped the projectile nose-first into the bog.

Brainard grabbed a handful of Wilding's suit and jerked the officer-trainee back to safety as the decoy fell.

The nose of the decoy sank into the soft ground before the bursting charge went off with a *whump!* and drove a pair of binary chemicals together. The mixture expanded as a bubble of heavy gas formed a skin with the moisture in the air and ground.

The gas was a brilliant purple-gray and so hot that it blistered the hovercraft's refractory plastic hull. At sea the decoy would skitter over the tops of the waves, drawing enemy fire and attention until it cooled and flattened into an iridescent slick. Here—

K67's crew stumbled to the vessel's port side, driven by heat from the swelling decoy. A claw eighteen inches long drove through the glowing boundary layer of decoy and atmosphere, clacked twice, and then withdrew on its jointed arm. The muscles within the crustacean's translucent exoskeleton had already been boiled a bright pink.

Five guns dimpled the decoy's opaque surface with automatic fire.

"Cease fire!" Ensign Brainard ordered again. "We'll need the ammo soon enough."

Wilding got his breath back. He straightened. Brainard released him. The decoy began to ooze sluggishly away from the torpedo boat. It seared a broad track into the reeds behind it.

"All right," said Brainard without emotion. "This boat's shot. That's too bad, but we're still okay ourselves."

He looked from one crewman to the next, his eyes hard and certain. Wilding held his breath while Brainard's glance rested on him. "We're going to need more height in order to lase a signal to somebody who can rescue us. Since we don't have the ascender apparatus any more, we're going to climb that mountain."

He nodded in the direction of the island's hidden peak.

"God almighty, sir!" Caffey gasped. "We can't march through that jungle. Nobody could!"

Brainard looked at the torpedoman. The ensign's face was as calm as the sea, now that the feeding frenzy had burned itself out.

"No, Fish," Brainard said. "We're going to do it. Because that's what we have to do to survive."

November 6, 381 AS. 1500 hours.

"I don't think," said the Callahan, a man of fifty whose features were as smooth and handsome as the blade of a dress dagger, "that we need wait for the others."

His finger brushed a control hidden in a tabletop carved from a single mother-of-pearl sheet. The chamber's armored door slid shut, separating the Council of the Twelve Families from the crowd of servants in the anteroom.

The panel staggered as it mated with the slot inlet in the jamb. The machinery made a grunching sound.

Hal Wilding looked around the council chamber, cloaking his disgust beneath his usual sardonic smile. Nine of the twelve chairs around the circular table were occupied, but in three cases the occupant was only physically present.

The McLain was senile.

After a series of brutal tongue-lashings by the Callahan, the Hinson had learned to keep his mouth shut during council meetings; a success of some degree for a man with an IQ of 70, but a dog could have been trained more easily.

The Platt had mixed recreational drugs in an unfortunate combination. For the past ten years he had had little more brain activity than a wax dummy. His family continued to send him to council meetings, because if they removed their titular head, they would be faced with an internal struggle for succession.

The Wilding's seat was filled by the eldest son of the House. . . .

"I called this meeting when I saw the catch projections for the next twelve months," said the Callahan with his usual lack of ceremony. "They can be expected to drop to sixty percent of their current levels in that time—and current levels are already a third down on really satisfactory quantities."

The Galbraith frowned and fluffed his lace shirt out from beneath the sleeves of his frock coat. "Can't we build more netters and bring in more food, then?" he asked.

"That's the problem, you see, Galbraith," Wilding said. "We're already overfishing our grounds. That's the main reason the stocks have crashed."

The Callahan nodded. "Yes, that's correct," he said. "The problem is with empty holds, not lack of netting capacity."

Whenever the Callahan looked at Wilding, it was with

cool appraisal for a potential rival. Wilding understood the attitude very well.

Wilding smiled coldly. With the rate of mutation and adaptive radiation on this planet, it was easy to imagine the appearance of life forms able to prey upon even the huge submarine netters which supplied the keeps with fish.

"Well, it's not as though anybody's going to starve, is it?" the Penrose said. "There'll still be plenty of vegetable protein."

"It's not starvation we need to worry about, it's riots," said the Callahan.

"You'd riot too, Penrose, if you had nothing to eat but processed algae," gibed the Galbraith.

The Penrose chuckled and patted the vest over his swollen belly. "No, no," he said. "We certainly can't permit that. What's the alternative?" He was looking at the Callahan.

Wilding interjected crisply, "We could colonize the land. *That* would provide additional resources." Wilding felt cold. He hadn't been aware of what he was going to say until the words were out of his mouth. As soon as he spoke, he realized that the sub-strata of his mind had planned the statement from the moment he decided to attend the council meeting.

He wasn't sure what response he expected. What he got was averted faces from everyone in the room except the Callahan.

The Callahan said in an icy voice, "Master Wilding, if you wish to dance through life, that is your right. You do *not* have the right to interfere with those of us who are keeping the system going."

The two men stared at one another. At last, Wilding shot his cuff, withdrew a snuffbox carved from a block of turquoise, and snorted a pinch from the crease of his hand and thumb.

"I believe the best course is to send our netters into the grounds of Asturias Keep," the Callahan resumed. "That will mean war within six months, so I suggest we start negotiations with one of the mercenary companies at once."

"Wysocki's Herd did a good job for us three years ago," the Galbraith said. "Shall we try them again?"

"I'm not sure six months is soon enough," said the Penrose, frowning. "The shortages will be obvious well before then. Perhaps we ought to speed matters up by leaking our plans directly to Asturias, rather than letting them learn when our netters are spotted."

"Oh, I believe the time frame should be adequate," said the Callahan. "We'll just need to inflate all their initial statements before we release them to the public. Say, three months before Asturias realizes what we're doing, and another three months of drawing out negotiations before it comes to war."

The Dahlgren was by far the eldest of the functional council members, but he lacked the drive that made the Callahan a leader. He nodded and said, "Yes, that's the better course. Twice the effect for the cost, very practical."

"I fail to see the practicality," said Wilding in tones of chilled steel, "since Asturias Keep has almost certainly overfished its own grounds as badly as we have ours. We need to expand our sources of sup—"

"I'm afraid you've missed the point, *boy,*" said the Callahan. "The war emergency will take the mob's attention off the shortages. Shortages will be expected, in fact. Then, in the six months or so that our grounds go uncropped, the stocks will rebuild—whether or not the netters bring an ounce of protein from Asturias's grounds."

"I thought in past years," said Wilding, enunciating perfectly and locking his glare with that of the Callahan, "that Wyoming Keep's apparent lack of direction was because I heard council decisions filtered through my father's perceptions." He sniffed. "Or lack of perceptions. But I now realize that he was perfectly accurate. If this is an example of the policy of the Twelve Families, then the policy of the Twelve Families is bankrupt. Manipulating the common people to accept wretched conditions is pointless when we could be improving those conditions."

"You know, *boy* . . . ," the Callahan snarled.

All eyes in the council chamber were on Wilding. Some expressions were hot, some cold; all were full of hatred.

". . . when I was informed that you would be representing your family, I was pleased." The Callahan nodded around the table. "Yes, pleased. Because I foolishly thought that you might be turning over a new leaf. I see now that I was wrong. You're simply a destructive dilettante, looking for something new to smash."

"You should let your father come in the future," said the Penrose. "After all, all the Wilding did was drool—and that was easy enough for the servants to clean up after the meetings."

Wilding stood. His whole body was trembling. He could not have spoken, even if he could think of something to say.

"You know, Prince Hal," said the Galbraith, "if you're so concerned about injustice to the common people, you should give up your perquisites and join them. Once you acclimate, I suspect you'll find the mob's round of drink, drugs, and sex much the same as that of your own circle."

Wilding began walking toward the door. He could not see for the red blur blindfolding him, but he heard the groan of the armored panel opening.

On the threshold, with his back to the council, Wilding paused to shake imaginary dust from the tails of his frock coat.

4

MAY 17, 382 AS. 1117 HOURS.

From the deck Brainard looked at the wall of jungle beyond the tide-swept marsh. Vines, branches, and flowers like bright sucking mouths entwined in twisted agony.

There was movement. A stand of slender, black-trunked trees quivered back instead of leaning toward the humans over the salt-resistant reeds.

"What's happening with them?" said Wheelwright. "The trees."

That was the question that Brainard was afraid to ask. Brainard didn't know anything about the situation—except that he was terrified of having to think beyond the immediate next step.

"Morning stars," said OT Wilding coolly. "Plants can't normally move as fast as animals, even here, but these store energy by drawing back their trunks like springs. When we come within fifty feet, they'll snap forward and grab us with the spikes in their branches."

"The edge of the jungle is worse than anything we'll find inside it," Brainard said. "It's like a warship's armor. Once we penetrate the shell, we'll be all right."

To build and maintain their bases, the Herd and other Free Companies fought a constant war against nature. There had been lectures on surface life-forms during training, but Brainard had pretty much dozed through them.

Active duty hadn't given him any practical experience, either. Large vessels, dreadnoughts and cruisers, provided the perimeter guards who battled the jungle's attempts to retake Base Hafner.

The line Brainard parroted was the only thing he remembered from the lectures. The words sounded empty.

Leaf frowned in puzzlement. A scar trailed up the little motorman's left cheek and into his hair where it continued as a streak of white. "How can we get through that, sir? We got two cutting bars and our knives."

He wasn't arguing. He just wanted an explanation of a plan that his mind couldn't make practicable.

"We can burn it," said Caffey unexpectedly.

"Go on, Fish," Brainard said. His face was expressionless; his mind was empty of useful ideas.

"It takes a fuze to make barakite explode," the torpedoman said. "If you just light a wad of it, it burns like the fires of Hell. And we've got a ton of the stuff we can take outa them two." He thumbed in the direction of the crumpled torpedoes.

Brainard nodded. "Right," he said. "Caffey and Wheelwright, begin removing the warheads. Newton—no, I'll guard you myself. Wilding—"

"Sir, we can't carry much, just the two of us," Wheelwright blurted.

"Boz and me'll lift a deck panel," Leaf volunteered. His boot tapped the ribbed sheets of radar-absorbent plastic which covered the hovercraft's upper surfaces. "We'll bend the end up and make a skid. You can dump the stuff on that."

"Wait," Brainard said. He thought for a moment. Barakite explosive was a white, doughy substance, as seemingly harmless as so much taffy. He'd seen what happened to a warship when a barakite torpedo exploded in her belly, though. . . .

"Just take the backplate off one of the warheads," he said. "The casing'll direct the flames out, like a flamethrower."

"Jeez, we better make sure we unscrew the fuze first!" Wheelwright gasped.

"Yes, you had better," said OT Wilding with a twist of his lips.

"Wilding," Brainard continued, "take charge of loading useful items into packs. Weapons, ammunition, food if you think we'll need it. You're the environmental expert. Remember that we'll carry loose barakite from the other warhead. We may need it farther along." He swallowed. "I'll take the communicator myself," he said.

The laser communicator was their one hope of rescue. With that solid security in his hands, Brainard thought he might be able to get through the hours until they reached the peak. Might.

Everybody looked at him. "Caffey, what are you waiting for?" he snapped. "Let's move!"

The two torpedomen swung immediately to the hovercraft's rail. Caffey snubbed up at the end of the hose connected to his environmental suit and paused. He looked back at Brainard.

Next problem. One at a time. "Until we're through the, the frontal wall of the jungle," Brainard said, "you can wear your suits or not as you choose. After that, they'll be too heavy and confining. We'll leave them."

They all *stared* at him. The tough suits were armor, real armor against the lethal surface environment, but men wearing them couldn't carry a load as much as a hundred yards with the air hoses disconnected.

"I'm going to take mine off now," said Brainard. His body began to obey his mouth, opening the catches and taking the direct shock of heat and saturated humidity. His mind watched the events as if they were taking place on the holonews.

Caffey unclipped his hose and clambered over the rail, followed by his striker. For the grace period Brainard had offered them, the discomfort of a disconnected suit was more bearable than facing the surface unprotected.

Leaf knelt and began cutting the tack welds with his multitool. The motorman directed Bozman as if his assistant were a barely sentient tool himself.

Wilding gave orders in a clear, precise voice, separating into manageable loads the objects that would keep the crew alive during its trek. Everything was under control.

Brainard stepped out of his suit. He felt naked and afraid. He jumped quickly from the deck before he could lose his nerve.

Stupid. He sank to mid-calf in the muck. Wheelwright glanced back. Men were looking at him from deck also.

"Get on with—" Brainard called.

A leech the length of Brainard's arm rose from the mud. It twisted toward his face. It was green with white stripes the length of its body, and its mouth was a black pit.

Brainard tried to scream but his tongue stuck to the roof of his mouth. He thrust out with the rifle in his hands. The creature engulfed the weapon's muzzle in a hideous sexual parody.

Brainard pulled the trigger and nothing happened, *nothing happened!* He jerked the rifle upward convulsively. The leech clung for a moment, then slipped off, and writhed through an arc over the marsh. A tube worm shot from its armored housing near the shore and snatched the leech while it was still in the air.

Brainard stared at his rifle. The selector was still on Safe. He rotated it to Automatic and began to drag his legs forward. He was almost blind from fear. He knew that unless he moved at once, he would be unable to move ever again.

"Newton," ordered Wilding, "I told you to bring the remaining bandoliers from the arms locker. Get moving!"

It was a good thing they had Wilding along. He'd been born to lead. Most officer-trainees were kids who went blind with fear in a crisis. . . .

JULY 12, 381 AS. 0933 HOURS.

"I've brought your new XO, Tonello," Lieutenant Holman called to the officer bent over in the cockpit of the hovercraft docked on a shallowly submerged platform.

Holman prodded Officer-Trainee Brainard between the shoulder blades. Brainard, his hard-copy files clutched in his hands, hopped convulsively from the quay to the vessel. The gray deck shivered beneath his sudden weight. The hovercraft was 60 feet long and 28 feet across the beam, but her mass was deceptively slight because most of the volume was the empty plenum chamber.

Lieutenant Tonello straightened with an engaging smile and extended his hand out of the cockpit well. He was a lanky man several inches taller than Brainard's own five-foot-eleven. "Welcome aboard K67—" his eyes read the name tape sewn over the left breast pocket of Brainard's utilities "—Brainard. You had three months aboard the *Kudu,* I believe?"

Tonello's grip was firm, but he didn't play finger-crushing games the way Lieutenant Holman had done half an hour earlier. Brainard handed his new CO his file with some embarrassment. "Ah, no sir," he said. "I'm straight out of training school."

"That was Officer-Trainee Suchert," Holman said from the quay. "Suchert, ah, went to K44 instead."

A score of small craft, both air-cushion and hydrofoils, were moored to either side of the quay. No combat aircraft could survive in the environment created by the beam weapons and railguns mounted on capital ships. High-speed torpedo craft could blend closely enough against the sea to remain effective. They carried out the reconnaissance and light-attack duties which would once have been detailed to aircraft.

It was a dangerous job—but war is risk, and no man is immortal.

A head watched Brainard from K67's gun tub, and another popped out of a hatch forward that must give access to the plenum chamber. Enlisted members of the hovercraft's crew were sizing up the new junior officer.

Lieutenant Tonello riffled through Brainard's file, then glanced up at Holman with a thin smile. "Wanted somebody with experience to hold your brother's hand, did you, Holman? Well, that's all right with me. Brainard here's got two years of technical school behind him. Just the sort a flitterboat needs."

Holman's chin lifted. "Ted doesn't need anybody to hold his hand," he snapped.

"I didn't say he did," Tonello remarked, looking down as if he were going through Brainard's file more carefully. "*I* didn't say it."

Holman spun on his heel. He strode down the quay to where K44 was moored. The scar-faced man looking from the plenum chamber grinned at Brainard, turned his head, and spit into the oil-rainbowed water of Herd Harbor.

Tonello dropped Brainard's file on a console and grinned again. "What do you know about hovercraft, Brainard?" he asked.

"Not much, sir," Brainard said, wishing there were some way he could lie and expect to get away with it. He'd assumed his first assignment would be to a ship whose scores or hundreds of crewmen could cover for his own inexperience. "Just that you've got eight-man crews."

"And two torpedoes, Brainard," the lieutenant said. He was still smiling, but his lips now had the hard curve of a fighting axe. "Don't forget those. Because if we do our jobs right, the other side won't forget them." Tonello's expression softened again. "No problem. I'll give you the grand tour." He gestured forward. "That's Yee at the gun tub," he explained. "If a mission goes perfectly, we'll get in unobserved and he won't fire a shot."

"Fat chance," remarked one of the men who had risen from the scuttle aft the cockpit.

"If things don't go perfectly," Tonello continued in an equable voice, "then nobody *likes* a faceful of tracer fired from twin seventy-fives. If our problem's with a boat more or less our size, Yee may well settle matters."

Tonello turned to indicate the man who had just spoken. "That's Tech Two Caffey," he said, "our torpedoman. If I do my job, the fish'll track to their target by themselves. Caffey and his striker are there in case I'm not perfect. Their station's got imaging and control along fiber-optics cables, so they can thread the torpedoes through the eye of a needle if they've got to."

"A big fucking needle," the torpedoman grunted, but he was obviously pleased.

"And that's Tech Two Leaf," the lieutenant said, turning toward the scarred fellow looking out of the plenum chamber. "When he's on duty, he's the best motorman in the Herd—"

Leaf grinned.

"—and when he's off duty, he's my worst discipline problem," Tonello continued—and the motorman continued to grin. "What are you working on, Leaf?"

"Replacing the impeller on Number One fan, sir," Leaf said. "I got Newton and Bozman in the water wearing suits, while I tighten fittings." He waved a multitool. "RHIP."

"You remember that when you go on leave, Leaf," Tonello said. "Because the next time you're caught in a bar fight, you'll have neither rank nor privileges. I promise."

Leaf gave a mocking salute with his multitool, then ducked out of sight.

Quietly, so that none of the enlisted men could hear, Tonello said, "We've got four fans to float us on a bubble of air and drive us. If one goes out, we can still maneuver, but we're sluggish and a target for anybody with so much as a popgun." He nodded forward. "In the eighteen months Leaf has been motorman, K67 has never lost a fan to maintenance problems." Tonello continued in a normal voice, "Your station's here, Brainard." He pointed to the left of the three seats across the cockpit. "In action, your primary responsibilities are navigation and electronic countermeasures, but you may be called on to do *any* job on the vessel, so you have to know every man's duties."

The lieutenant gave his axe-blade smile again. "In particular," he said, "you may have to command the vessel if something happens to your commanding officer. So stay alert, hey?"

He clasped Brainard's wrist and gave it a gentle shake for emphasis.

Brainard would have swallowed, but the lump in his throat was too big.

5

MAY 17, 382 AS. 1610 HOURS.

Leaf had known plenty of brave men—

"Keep her moving!" ordered Ensign Brainard, darting quick glances in all directions as he walked ahead of the six-man crew at the draglines. Leaf was the man nearest the skid on the left side. "Don't lose your momentum!"

—but he'd never met somebody as willing to hang his balls on the wall as Brainard. *Don't waste ammo,* he says, so when a leech goes for *him,* he don't even bother to shoot it, just swats it away.

"Sir, should I . . . ?" Yee called from behind them, in K67's gun tub.

Leaf looked up. Sweat blurred his vision, but if those morning stars weren't within the fifty feet Wilding gave as their trigger range, they were sure damned close to it.

Only thing was, Brainard was out in front.

"Not yet!" the CO said.

They were using safety lines as drag ropes for the skid. Reeds flattened into the slippery ooze, creating a perfectly lubricated surface over which to pull the massive warhead—but the same muck gave piss-poor traction to the boots of the men tugged the skid toward the wall of jungle.

Leaf wheezed and staggered in the discomfort of his heavy suit. It didn't seem to him that he was pulling his weight, but somebody among the six of them must be doing the job. The skid moved, and the twisted trees were goddam close.

At least they hadn't had problems with large animals. Leaf had been raised in Block 81 of Wisconsin Keep, a slum; he understood territories. The snake and spider he'd attracted had kept this stretch of marsh to themselves. There hadn't been enough time since the local bosses got the chop for replacements to take over.

The crew gave the pond itself a wide berth. Whatever lived on its bottom had been given a big enough meal to occupy it for a while, anyhow.

"Mr Brainard?" gasped Wilding, on the far end of Leaf's rope. "I think—"

Brainard had offered to take a rope and let Wilding control the operation. The officer-trainee refused, saying he'd be useless as a guard because he couldn't shoot. Leaf didn't figure a pansy like Wilding'd do much good on the line, either; but at least he was trying.

"Right," ordered Brainard. "Everybody down. Yee!"

Leaf flattened. He clapped his hands over his ears and opened his mouth. The man beside him, Newton, was still upright. He either hadn't heard the order or—more likely with Newton—hadn't understood it.

Leaf grabbed the butt of the coxswain's slung rifle and

tugged it hard. Wilding must have been pulling from the other side, because Newton flopped down an instant before Yee's twin seventy-fives cut loose over their heads.

Even fifty feet away, the big guns' muzzle blasts punished bare skin and stabbed agony through the ear Leaf had uncovered to save Newton. The ballistic crack of the supersonic bullets snapping just overhead was worse for the motorman's nerves.

These rounds were aimed high deliberately. Too often in Leaf's small-boat service, a *snap!snap!snap!* meant the enemy was about to correct his sight picture and put his next burst through your hull.

Ropes of brilliant scarlet tracers raked the edge of the jungle, concentrating as planned on the copse of morning stars. The explosive bullets went off with white flashes against the black bark, hurling bits of wood in all directions.

The explosions released tension within the trunks. Sawed-off boles leaped into the air. Their spiky branches slashed at one another during the moments it took them to fall.

The guns scythed a 10° arc through the living barrier, then stuttered into silence. Yee had shot off the entire contents of his ammo drums. Powder gases, explosive residues, and the thick smoke of green vegetation burning hung in the air. A beetle the size of a cheap apartment stepped into the cut, then rushed away through a path it tore for itself.

"Come on!" Brainard shouted. His voice chimed through the ringing in the motorman's left ear. "Move! Move! Move!"

Leaf got up. For an instant he thought he was having difficulty because he was exhausted; then he noticed that during the time he hugged the ground, reeds had grown about him. Their tips probed at the folds of the environmental suit. He swore and tore himself free.

"Come on!" the CO repeated, reaching back to grip the upturned front of the skid. "Before something else moves in!"

Leaf threw his weight against the rope. The skid had begun to sink into the marsh. They got it moving again, somehow. The warhead's weight had one advantage: it dimpled the plastic decking into a cradle, so there was no risk that the burden would roll off the skid.

Ten feet. Twenty feet. A shrapnel-pithed frog, three feet long with lips of saw-edged bone, flopped in a ragged circle at the edge of the jungle in front of them. A dozen blood-sucking insects gripped it. An ilex tree stabbed a branch down from the canopy, harpooned the frog, and withdrew more slowly with its prey.

If the frog had not been there—

"That's enough!" Brainard ordered. "Go back, get your packs, and prepare to move out. Watch yourselves!"

He looked at the motorman. "Leaf, light the warhead. But *don't* get in the way."

In order to give himself a moment to catch his breath, Leaf deliberately fumbled with the multitool slung beneath his armpit. The hot, humid air his lungs dragged in wasn't much help. The suit suffocated him, but it was his only hope of staying alive. . . .

The warhead was a black steel dome twenty-three inches in diameter. It lay sideways on the skid with its flat base pointing in the direction of the jungle. Caffey and Wheelwright had unbolted the thin baseplate, exposing the cream-colored barakite.

They'd also removed the fuze from its pocket in the nose.

Heat alone wouldn't set off barakite. Heat *would* set off the booster charge in the fuze, and *that* would detonate the unburned portion of the barakite. The blast would kick what was left of the hovercraft back out to sea, let alone what it did to the crew.

The motorman's powered multitool was a compact assortment of grippers, drivers, cutters—and an arc welder. Leaf snapped the arc live and touched it to the upper surface of the exposed barakite.

The white spark went blue. A puff of vapor spurted from the explosive. Leaf stepped aside.

Not far enough. Ensign Brainard grabbed his shoulder and pulled him, just in time.

A billow of flame with a blue heart roared outward in all directions. The barakite burned back until the casing could direct the blaze. After a moment, it steadied into a forward-rushing jet. Combustion products from the explosive and the plasticizer which made it malleable boiled outward in a vast white cloud.

"Don't breathe that!" the CO shouted from a vast distance. He released Leaf's shoulder and strode back toward the packs waiting on the torpedo boat's deck.

Leaf didn't move. He had sucked in a double lungful of the poisonous vapors. He viewed his world from multiple viewpoints.

The initial gush of fire baked a wide fan of marsh to the consistency of a cracked brick. The reeds had vanished. Now that the flames had steadied, green tendrils were already breaking their way to the surface at the fringes of the cleared area.

The warhead was designed to release all its energy in a

microsecond flash, shattering battleship armor and sending a spout of seawater a thousand feet in the air. When the barakite was ignited instead of being detonated, the energy release spread over a minute of furious burning—but there was just as much energy involved.

A twenty-three-inch hose of blue-white flame roared into the jungle. It vaporized everything in its direct path and shriveled vegetation ten feet to either side.

Leaf watched:

A man-sized salamander lunged up as the concealing leaf mold burned away. It bit at the gout of flame as though it were a quivering serpent. The salamander's head vanished in the 2,000° heat, but the tail and body writhed away.

Reeds, stunned by the fire's temperature, recovered enough to squirm over Leaf's boots. They were looking for entrance to his flesh as he stood transfixed.

A bright golden reptile sailed from a tree top and performed three consecutive loops. The diameter of the loops increased as the creature's feathery scales burned away. It finally plunged toward the sea, trailing smoke behind it.

Crewmen caught the packs Yee tossed them from the hovercraft's deck. They began to waddle toward the jungle again.

Marshy soil humped a few inches upward in a line that extended toward Leaf at the speed of a slow walk. Reeds bowed aside from the intrusion among their roots.

"Leaf!" Ensign Brainard shouted from the hovercraft. "Are you all right?"

A free-standing walnut tree burned furiously on the side toward the devastation pouring from the warhead. Its branches flailed downward, stabbing the flames with hollow tips through which herbicide squirted. This enemy could not be poisoned. The branches added fuel to the self-devouring blaze.

OT Wilding dropped his pack and began to run toward Leaf. He tugged his pistol awkwardly from its holster.

Most of the barakite had burned. The tongue of flame shrank back and curled, like a tiger clearing away traces of a recent meal.

Leaf's boots had sunk six inches into the muck. The line of raised soil was within a yard of him.

Wilding fired into the ground. He was almost close enough to touch his target. The first bullet splashed mud a hand's breadth from the motorman's ankle; the second round was lost somewhere in the unburned jungle.

The third shot punched through the side of the mound. Six feet of mud slid upward from an iridescent surface. Blunt horns extended from the front end as the creature nuzzled the oozing bullet wound.

Leaf came to in an eyeblink. Suction and the questing reeds gripped his feet firmly. He trigged the welding arc of his multitool and raked it in a long line across the slimy surface of the monster.

Flesh blackened and shriveled, twisting the creature into a writhing knot. A tongue armed with glittering conical teeth extended from the mouth.

Reed-tops touched the body and clung, sucking greedily.

"Mole slug," Wilding wheezed. He grabbed the motorman's shoulder to balance himself. His pistol wavered in a dangerous circle that included the feet of both men. "Ah, are you okay?"

Leaf bent and seared the vegetation away from his boots. "Yeah," he said, "I'm fine. I'm great."

His mouth was dry. He chewed his cheeks and tongue

to release the juices. The warhead had burned out. A breeze carried the remaining fumes toward the jungle.

"I'm as good," Leaf said deliberately, "as I've been since I joined this fucking outfit."

April 1, 372 AS. 2214 hours.

The hand-lettered sign outside the door announced that Enrique's Bar was closed for a private party. One of the neighborhood regulars rattled the latch anyway. His eye appeared at the small triangular window in the door panel. When he saw that the "private party" was a Free Company's recruiting drive, the man vanished as if whipped away by demons.

Inside, the woman who writhed on top of the bar wore nothing. Her hair was blond. It was held in a high, drifting fan by a process that must have cost as much as a drug dealer in Block 81 earned in a week.

The woman's face was aristocratically beautiful, but her eyes were a million miles away. She rotated slowly, ignoring the thirty-odd young men crowded into the room.

The handsome lieutenant wore a row of medal ribbons on the right breast. Over the left pocket was a name tag reading CONGREVE, in blue letters on silver to match the color scheme of his uniform. "Well, I must have made a mistake," he said to the air in a sneering drawl. "I thought there were men here, but *men* wouldn't leave a poor girl in that state."

Congreve leaned against the bar in a pose of false relaxation. An electronic data file was open beside him. He watched everything in the room from beneath drooping eyelids.

Tub Caffey stood up suddenly. His brother-in-law tried

to pull him back to the table. All the guys on that side of the bar ran with the 3d Level gang.

"I'll give the bitch what she needs!" Caffey muttered. He headed straight for the woman. He could have been on the other side of Venus for all the notice she took of him.

Leaf was the only member of the 5th Level gang in the bar tonight. He knew Caffey pretty well. His index finger absently traced the knife scar up his cheek to his hairline.

Lieutenant Congreve stepped between Caffey and the woman. Jessamyn, the senior sergeant who worked the floor with Congreve, moved his big body between the potential recruit and the three friends who had followed him.

"Here you go, lads," Jessamyn said, holding out three puce applicators on the back of his left hand. The knuckles of the clenched fist on which the drugs balanced were a mass of white scar tissue. "Let's all stay happy, shall we?"

Caffey's brother-in-law and the two men who had jumped up at the same time hesitated, then accepted the applicators and sat down again. Jessamyn smiled. His front teeth had been replaced by metal the cold blue-gray of a gun barrel.

Caffey laboriously signed the screen of the data file. The imager built into the lieutenant's signet ring had already snapped the recruit's retinal prints and encoded them into the electronic contract.

Congreve tapped the woman's instep with a finger. "Back room, Kimberly," he said. He opened the bar's swinging gate so that the new recruit could stumble through.

The woman stepped down and walked through the door into what was normally Enrique's private office and storage area. She didn't look behind her.

Caffey collided with the redhead who came out of the back room as the blond entered it. The door closed.

Someone moved close to Leaf. He looked to his side and saw the sergeant. "Here you go," the mercenary said. He offered a three-striped mauve applicator in the middle of his left palm.

Leaf didn't recognize the markings. "What's this?" he demanded.

The redhead mounted the bar and began a slow dance. Her diaphanous garments concealed nothing, but she used the floor-brushing length of her own hair as a curtain to display and reveal alternately.

"Tsk," said Jessamyn. "A good time, lad, that's what it is."

The big noncom touched the applicator to the inside of his left elbow and squeezed, releasing the contents into his bloodstream. He turned his hand palm down, then up again with another applicator on it in a feat of minor legerdemain.

Leaf flushed and took the drug.

The redhead turned her back. Her long-fingered hands now lay on the cheeks of her buttocks, spreading and closing the white flesh. Her fingernails were the color of fresh blood.

"The girls look like they just stepped off a holoscreen," Leaf whispered.

The familiar barroom had a glow over it now. Everything blurred except for the woman at whom he stared. She faced the audience again. Her left hand was behind her back; her right was in front of her. She was manipulating herself with her index fingers.

The woman's pupils were dilated so wide that the color of her irises was indeterminable.

"They've been on the holos, often enough," Jessamyn murmurred. "And at the very best parties, they have. Ashley, there, she's a Callahan from Wyoming Keep, she is. That's one of the best families there."

"Who'll be man enough to give little Ashley what she needs?" Lieutenant Congreve asked in a cajoling tone. "You can see how she's looking forward to meeting a real man."

Jessamyn put a big, gentle hand on Leaf's shoulder. "I can see you're a hard one, lad," the mercenary said. "She likes that, I can tell you. All her sort like that."

There was a tinge of bitter sadness in Jessamyn's voice. Leaf heard the tone, but it didn't matter any more.

He got up. His legs propelled him toward the woman in the center of a rosy haze.

6

MAY 17, 382 AS. 1628 HOURS.

"Let's go, let's go!" Brainard ordered. "Newton, carry your pack, don't try to sling it. You'll be taking off your suit in a hundred feet and you can put the pack on then."

The coxswain blinked at him. He made one last, half-hearted attempt to thrust his arms, doubled in size by the baggy fabric of his environmental suit, through straps which could not possibly hold them.

The walnut tree blazed in the center of the area its poison had cleared. The ferns and bamboo in the warhead's direct line had vanished; those on the edges now smoldered and struggled to pump life into the shriveled foliage before undamaged neighbors strangled them.

Bright green shoots speared up from the devastated swath.

Footlockers, like bunks and air-conditioned quarters, were for the crews of major fleet elements. The personal gear of a crewman aboard a hovercraft was limited to the contents of a .8-cubic foot backpack which could be hung, slung, or stuffed into what little space the flitterboats offered.

Now the packs were stuffed with dried food, ammunition, and wads of doughy barakite scooped from the warhead of the second torpedo. Brainard didn't know how much good the explosive was going to be, but he knew they needed *something.*

"These black balls on the soil," Wilding called. He pointed to a sphere the size of a snooker ball. There were dozens of them, obvious against soil from which all the cover had been burned away. "Leave them alone. *Don't* for any reason touch them!"

Wilding ought to be in charge. He was educated, so he knew the environment. To Brainard, it was all a lethal blur. He was afraid to focus on anything except the peak that was his goal . . . and the peak was invisible, merely something taken on faith from the charts.

K67 hadn't been equipped to support her crew on an overland trek. The rifles and Caffey's slightly heavier machine-gun were the security blankets with which men convinced themselves that they wouldn't be helpless against enemy gunboats if the twin seventy-fives were put out of action.

OT Wilding had only a pistol. Wilding claimed he couldn't hit anything with it, but Brainard had seen the aristocrat nail the slug while he was running to save Leaf.

As for Leaf. . . .

"Leaf, do you want my pistol?" Brainard said aloud. The handgun was part of an officer's insignia of rank, but Brainard had also brought a rifle and bandolier of magazines aboard K67.

The motorman carried his pack at arm's length in one hand and his multitool in the other. He looked at the ensign, his complexion sallow beneath its tan. "Naw, I got this," he said and waved the multitool.

"All right, but you're welcome to something that'll shoot," Brainard said.

Leaf resumed his trudge forward. "This'll do for me," he muttered.

Brainard brought up the rear while OT Wilding led the crew through the flame-cleared corridor. They hadn't discussed the arrangements, it just happened that way. Wilding knew what he was doing . . . and he was a *born* leader, never mind rank.

Brainard stepped around one of the black spheres in the path. A shoot which had broken through the baked surface nearby nuzzled the sphere, preparing to rip through the husk and suck whatever nourishment was within.

The sphere exploded with a puff of steam. Barbed rootlets lashed in all directions. Some of them pierced the earth; others seized the shoot that had triggered the sphere's opening.

"Everything all right?" Wilding called from the front of the line.

"A couple plants trying to eat each other," Brainard shouted back.

He tried to look behind him while he still watched where he put his feet. There were too many things he *had* to see. Even though he'd taken off his environmental suit, his backpack and the laser communicator strapped to his chest restricted his movements.

"Fern spores," Wilding explained. "They get an extra growth spurt from whatever sets them off."

A man's foot would be better a better meal than a bamboo sprout. Sea boots weren't designed to stop steam-driven clusters of needle-sharp roots.

They had to climb to high ground and call for rescue. That was all Brainard knew.

Wilding reached the far end of the flames' hundred-yard path, where the vegetation was seared but not consumed. Just as the lecturer said, the jungle floor was much more open than that of the unpierced wall, where competition for the abundant light created a solid expanse of foliage.

Brainard looked up. The deadly struggle of branch and vine in the canopy hundreds of feet overhead was the best protection available to men in dim corridors among the trunks beneath. Green shapes moved above him, striving to absorb every needle of sunlight before it could benefit the leaves of rivals below.

"All right," Brainard ordered. "Get your suits off, two at a time. Caffey and Leaf."

The chiefs looked at Brainard, then looked away. Caffey began slowly to unseal his protective garment.

"Now!" Brainard snapped. They would collapse in the first half mile if they tried to climb in the heavy suits. They would die, and he would die with them. . . .

"Sir," begged the motorman. "I'll wear mine, okay? It's all that saved me when, when that pond ate the snake and sp-sp-spider."

"What saved you then, sailor," Wilding said in a tone

like a blade of ice, "was obeying your CO's orders to lie still until we could divert your neighbors and pull you clear. You will obey him now—because we can't afford to let you die the way you want to do. *Do* you understand?"

"Fuck," whispered Leaf. "Fuck it all." He released his multitool on its spring lanyard. He began stripping off his suit. His eyes were closed.

Brainard turned, to keep watch and to hide his face. He didn't know what to do, and when he did know they ignored him. They were all going to die because their commanding officer had no business being an officer.

Something moved in the darkness. Brainard aimed his rifle, then relaxed. Ivy rotated toward the crew from the edges of the cleared area. The tendrils moved like corkscrews, growing from the tips rather than being thrust out from the main body of the vine. A collar of barbed thorns sprouted every time a tendril threw out another trio of leaves.

The barakite flame had burned through the boles of several giant trees, opening the canopy and releasing a flood of sunlight to the forest floor. Energized by the light, the ivy grew at the rate of several inches a minute—amazingly fast, but still no risk to the humans. They'd all have changed out of their suits and gone on before the vines reached them.

Caffey saw the motion. "Watch it!" he shouted. He triggered a burst, firing his machine gun from the hip. Bullets plowed the fire-hardened soil. The muzzle blasts made the foliage quiver as if with anticipation.

"Cease fire!" Brainard shouted. *They were never going to make it.* "Cease fire!"

Clear, poisonous sap filled and sealed the nip one bullet

had taken from a tendril. The tip resumed its rotary advance.

"We'll need that ammo," Brainard muttered to himself.

He glanced up into the canopy to avoid meeting Caffey's eyes. Strands of cobweb drifted there. He hadn't seen it when he looked a moment—

The cobweb was drifting down on them. It was a circular blanket ten feet in diameter, as insubstantial as smoke.

"Move!" Brainard shouted. "Run! Run!"

Wilding glanced upward. "This way!" he cried, leading the way deeper into the jungle.

The crew stampeded forward. Bozman dropped his pack. The cobweb banked lazily around the bole of a forest giant and followed. The humans were hindered by grasping foliage, but the blanket moved in open air beneath the mid-canopy. It easily followed its prey.

Brainard stood transfixed. He didn't know what to do. He opened his mouth to call his men back, but Wilding knew about the dangers, and anyway it was too late.

Brainard should—

Brainard should—

He raised his rifle and fired at the creature a hundred feet in the air. He was a good shot. The yellow muzzle flashes hid the cobweb for an instant, but there was a spark of light as a bullet hit something.

He fired again, another short burst, and the creature curved toward him with the grace of a shark moving in for the kill. Fifty feet, thirty. It gleamed like a diffraction grating as a beam of direct sunlight caught it.

Brainard didn't realize his finger had clamped down on the trigger until the rifle butt abruptly ceased to recoil against his shoulder. He threw down the empty weapon and ran for the nearest cover, the burned-off stump of a fern that had been three hundred feet tall.

The cobweb swooped. The edges of gossamer fabric extended like the wings of a bat driving food to the waiting jaws. Brainard saw the glitter in the corners of both his eyes. The stump was too far to—

An ivy tendril caught him. He tripped forward on his face. He flung his hands out, just short of the stump he had hoped would shelter him.

The creature swept over him as a shimmering shadow. It wrapped itself around the stump.

Brainard stared. The crystal fabric humped itself, driving spikes a foot long into the smoldering wood. The holes released spurts of steam which hung for a moment in the saturated atmosphere.

Wilding ran over to him. "You saved us, sir!" he cried. "That was brilliant! You saved us all!"

Brainard gaped at Wilding. He moved his foot in a disconnected attempt at removing it from the ivy's hooked grasp.

JULY 23, 381 AS. 0244 HOURS.

Officer-Trainee Brainard's console was a holographic triptych.

To the right, between Brainard and Watkins, K67's coxswain, the navigation board displayed the Gehenna Archipelago. Tonello's hovercraft and her consort, K44, probed for the Seatiger squadron which Cinc Wysocki believed was lurking there in ambush. Low islands and shallow straits scrolled down the panel of coherent light.

Brainard bent close to the left-hand panel which displayed schematics of the torpedo craft's signatures:

Thermal—

Fan #3's intake glowed 4° above ambient. Brainard touched keys to reroute the overdeck airflow, scattering the warmth in turbulence. Leaf, hunched against the wind, ran toward the drive module to work on the underlying problem.

Electro-optical—

All the hovercraft's emitters were shut down. The blotched gray polymer of K67's hull quivered at between an 83% and 95% match for the surrounding sea in color and albedo. That was a closer copy than stretches of seawater a mile apart could achieve.

The vessel's computer fed low-voltage current through connections to the hull and skirts, modifying the camouflage pattern by the plastic's response to its electrical charge. It didn't require operator input.

Audio—

K67's sonic signature required an act of God to do it any good. There was damn-all Brainard could even attempt now that the CO had called for flank speed. Intake baffles flattened to smooth the path of air howling to feed the fans. Wind rush—over the deck, the gun tub, the cockpit and the crew stations—blended its myriad turbulences into the roar. Exhaust flow, ducted at high velocity to drive the vessel forward, hammered the night.

You couldn't have speed and silence. The best you could do was diffuse the cacophony so that it might come from anywhere in a mile radius instead of giving the enemy a sharp aiming point.

Brainard was doing what he could with the low on-deck air dams. He thought he'd shifted the calculated center of noise starboard and 3° astern, though the sonic ghost-vessel would keep a parallel course. Maybe the line of swampy islands a mile to starboard on the navigation screen would produce a confusing echo, but that was a matter for luck—temperature and air currents, nothing that a hovercraft's electronic countermeasures operator could do.

But something had to be done. Cinc Wysocki had been right. Brainard's center screen showed that the Seatigers had at least a pair of heavily-armed hydrofoil gunboats in the archipelago, five miles away and closing on the Herd patrol at 42° off the port bow.

Brainard heard the *boonk!* over the wind roar, but he didn't recognize the sound until the high-altitude *pop* followed three seconds later and the heavens turned lambent white in the glare of a star shell. The gunboats opened fire.

K44's gun tub fired back.

Brainard was lost in the virtual environment of his console. Nothing was real, not even the coxswain and Lieutenant Tonello beside him in the narrow cockpit. K44's signature brightened by ten orders of magnitude near the center of the situation display.

"Don't shoot!" Brainard screamed in horror. "For God's sake, *don't!*"

Outside the cockpit, the Seatiger gunboats disappeared behind the dazzle of their tracers and muzzle flashes. Each hydrofoil mounted a 3-inch gun in the bow and 1-inch Gatlings in tubs abaft the cockpit to either side. On the gunboats' present closing course, all their weapons could fire.

K44's tracers mounted in a high arc as the gunner attempted to achieve an impossible range. The scarlet marker compound burned out before the bullets started their vain downward tumble.

"Tonello to crew," rasped the CO's voice, distorted by static on the interphone's masking circuit. "Do not fire.

Yee, I've locked the gun tub. Do not attempt to fire. Break. Blue Leader to—"

Brainard screamed silently as a pip glowed on the signature display. It was all right, tight-beam laser directed at K44 as Tonello gave orders to their consort, but *nothing* was all right.

"—Blue Two, cease fire and—"

K67 staggered. There was a bang and a puff of hot gas at the port bow on Brainard's thermal schematic. The CO had fired a decoy from the spigot mortar there.

"—conform to my movements. Out."

The sky ripped and roared. White streaks quivered like heat lightning in Brainard's peripheral vision. A sheet of spray lifted just ahead of the hovercraft, better shielding than anything the console provided, but the *whack/whack* from low in the hull added noise drumming through a double hole in the plenum chamber.

The decoy bloomed into a satisfying blob on Brainard's situation display, but centrifugal force shoved him to the left and the ghost image he had created on the audio schematic vanished in the modified airstream. Watkin's elbow blurred the navigation display for a moment as the coxswain fought to hold K67 in a tight starboard turn.

Brainard braced himself and began reworking their sonic signature. The CO was headed for the strait separating a pair of islands like pearls on a necklace. The hovercraft of the Herd patrol had thirty knots on their hydrofoil opponents, but Tonello was determined to hunt the narrow confines of the archipelago rather than return to Cinc Wysocki with word of a pair of screening vessels.

A triple crackling noise vibrated K67. Brainard's left-hand display vanished, then resumed before the curse reached his lips and his finger could stab the back-up control.

The islands would blur the hovercraft's horrifying racket. Maneuvering in tight waters was the CO's concern, not Brainard's.

Brainard had to concentrate on eliminating the torpedocraft's signatures.

Or he would die.

The night to the left exploded in hard white flashes. A gunboat had slammed its six-round burst into a skerry as K67 roared past. Fragments of rock, shell-casing, and barnacles three feet in diameter sprang into the air. They rained down on the hovercraft's deck. Shreds of barnacle flesh gave the air a fishy tinge and brought shoals of toothed creatures to the surface.

The firing was behind them. A series of low islands concealed the gunboats from K67's sensors. K44 had managed to join her leader, but hot spots on Brainard's situation display indicated the other hovercraft had battle damage.

"Tonello to crew!" the CO crackled over the interphone. "The Seatigers may think this is a great place to hide, but we'll see how well they dodge torpedoes in narrow waters!"

Something touched Brainard's shoulder. He turned around in shock. Tonello had loosened his harness in order to lean over to the countermeasures console.

The CO raised his visor and shouted over the wind rush, "Brainard, I've never known a man to stay so cool in his first action. I'm proud to have you aboard!"

Tonello swung back into his own seat.

Brainard stared at him. The CO's words had been distinct, but they didn't make any sense.

Wind buffeted Brainard at chest height. He shut down the signature display for a moment. There was a circular one-inch hole in the plastic behind the holographic panel.

Brainard wondered dully how the Gatling bullet had managed to miss him on the continuation of its course.

7

MAY 17, 382 AS. 1634 HOURS.

Wilding offered Brainard a hand. Brainard stared as if he were unable to comprehend the gesture.

The enlisted members of the crew ran back to their officers. Leaf picked up Brainard's rifle by the sling and demanded, "What was that? What the *hell* was that?"

"Goddam if I know," the ensign said in an emotionless voice. He levered himself to his knees, then stood upright. His bandolier swayed, making the magazines clatter against one another.

Wilding rubbed his hand on his thigh to give it something to do. "It's an ice mat," he said, looking at the crystalline form. Pale, stunted shoots sprang from nodes over the spikes driven into the tree. "A seed pod of sorts. It's descended from a thistle—the parent plant is, I mean."

Brainard took his rifle from Leaf. He touched the barrel; winced as the hot metal burned him. "All right," he said. "Let's get moving."

Wilding had forgotten the weight of his pack during the moments of panic. Now the straps cut into his shoulders. He was suddenly sure that the forty-pound loads which he had set—conservatively, he thought—were too heavy, at least for him.

"Yes, sir," he said as he strode back into the jungle.

The edges of the cleared area were already a tangle of thorns and poison. Wilding reopened the path with the powered cutting bar he carried, one of the two in K67's equipment locker before the crash. Caffey fell in behind him with the machine-gun.

"But it was alive," Leaf insisted from midway back in the line. "It wasn't just falling, it was *coming* for us."

"It doesn't have a mind," Wilding said. He knew he should concentrate on the terrain in front of him, but a part of him insisted that he dwell on Ensign Brainard's cold courage. "It has a very discriminating infra-red sensor, though. It would have avoided an open flame, but the CO lured it into a charred stump that had cooled to just above blood heat."

That was the second part of what Brainard had done. First, while Wilding ran in terror thinking, *Let it take one of the others,* the CO had used the hot, expanding propellant gases of his rifle to draw the ice mat toward himself. Brainard's combination of nerve and diamond-hard calculation was almost beyond conception.

The interphone only worked through K67's computer, but the visor-display compasses in the helmets were self-powered. Wilding set his on a vector to the peak. He began to follow it.

Almost immediately, the terrain lurched up in an outcrop too steep for the thin soil to cling to its surface. Wilding gripped rock, lifted himself, and kicked for a foothold from which he could push up the rest of the way.

A gigantic fig overhung the outcrop. The lower twenty

feet of its folded bark bubbled with bright red spittle. A colony of scale insects hid within the frothy protection.

"Don't touch the red!" Wilding shouted. "Anything that showy is probably poisonous."

"Give me a hand," Caffey said peremptorily. "Sir." He lifted his machine-gun.

Wilding grasped it by the barrel. He almost overbalanced. The gun weighed nearly thirty pounds with its ammunition drum.

The torpedoman clambered up the rock and took the weapon back. He bent to offer Yee, the third man in line, a hand.

A stand of yellow-barked willows was in the direct path. Wilding skirted them. There was a broad corridor through the copse, but bones and the sections of insect exoskeleton there showed its danger.

Trees at the front and back of the corridor wove closed when a large creature stepped within. The boles in the middle of the track squeezed down slowly and crushed their victim into a nitrate supplement for the poor soil.

"Okay," said Caffey, "that's how." The torpedoman panted softly, like a dog, between phrases. "About the ice mat, I mean. But how *come?* Or does it just like to kill things?"

"Like you, do you mean?" Leaf gibed from behind them.

"Hell, like us, if you want to be that way," said Caffey. "Like anybody in a Free Company."

"Not me, Fish," Leaf replied. "I just—" the motorman paused to grunt his way over a steep patch "—keep the fans spinning."

Wilding's whole body hurt. He swung the cutting bar mechanically because it had become too much mental effort to decide when a sweep of the blade was necessary.

"The ice mat needs nutrients to grow," he said.

He spoke aloud, but he wasn't sure that his words were distinct enough for the torpedoman to understand. "Animals are the best source of complex nutriments," he continued. "Insects, reptiles, it doesn't matter. Any animal has to be able to modify its body temperature against the ambient to function, so that's what the seed, the ice mat, homes on."

The lecture took Wilding's mind off the pain of moving; but the pain was still there, waiting for him.

The moss hanging from branches a hundred feet in the air was so thick that its shade had cleared the ground beneath to sandy red clay. Wilding altered course slightly from the compass vector to take advantage of the open area.

Through interstices in the trunks of moss-hung trees, Wilding glimpsed a steep terrace covered with bamboo. That was going to be a problem. They would either have to go around the tough, jointed grass or cut through it. Given that the belt might encircle the peak—and might be hundreds of feet deep—neither alternative was a good one. Perhaps—

Caffey and Yee both shouted. Caffey's voice choked off in mid-bleat.

Wilding spun around. The weight of his pack threw him off-balance. A strand of moss had spooled down and wrapped around the torpedoman's neck. Other strands bobbed just beneath the main mass on the branch, preparing to follow.

The tendril trying to strangle Caffey had snagged the barrel of his machine-gun as well. The gun muzzle crushed painfully against the torpedoman's forehead, but the rigid steel had saved his larynx.

Yee fired two deafening shots, trying vainly to blast the gray streamer apart. The moss parted like tissue paper when Wilding swiped his cutting bar through it.

Released tension lifted the severed strand fifty feet in the air. The tip continued to contract around its victim. Wilding and Yee tugged against the moss with their free hands. The cutting bar was too clumsy to use near Caffey's throat.

The short blade of Leaf's multitool snicked through the loop of moss. Half came away in Wilding's hand. The remainder uncoiled and dropped to the ground.

"Fish!" Leaf shouted. "Fish! You okay?"

The torpedoman sat down heavily. His eyes were unfocused. There was a line of red spots across his throat.

Wilding looked down at his own hands. Miniature thorns in the moss had pricked him also. He hoped the points weren't poisonous, though the inevitable infection would be bad enough.

Overhead—

"Do you need help?" Brainard demanded from the end of the line.

"Come on!" Wilding snarled, grabbing Caffey by one shoulder. "Help him! Move!"

Yee took Caffey's other arm. They pounded through the deadly clearing together. The torpedoman was barely able to keep his legs moving in time with those of the men supporting him, but for the moment Wilding forgot about weight and pain. Leaf, the machine-gun's sling in one hand and his multitool in the other, was on their heels.

When he reached the bamboo, Wilding looked back over his shoulder. The whole crew followed at a staggering run. There were no further problems. The moss reacted too slowly to be a serious threat to men who were prepared for it.

Wilding gasped for breath. A clearing meant danger. It was his fault. He'd been too tired to realize the obvious, and it cost—

"Caffey, how do you feel?" Ensign Brainard demanded before Wilding could remember to ask.

The torpedoman massaged his throat. "I'm okay," he wheezed. "Just gimme a minute, okay?"

The bamboo shoots were thumb-thick. The stems were yellow, and the lower leaves were yellow-brown.

The undersurface of each leaf was a hooked mat. The foliage began to tremble outward as the plants sensed human warmth.

God alone knew how thick the belt was.

Wilding bent and swung his cutting bar. Contact triggered the 20-inch blade in a petulant whine. Stems toppled, but their leaves clutched at Wilding's arm as they fell.

"Right," Brainard said. His voice was as calm as that of an accounting adding figures. "We need to get moving. Yee, take the Number Two slot and Caffey will fall in just in front of me for a while."

"Ah . . . ?" Yee said. "How about the gun?"

"Fuck you," said Caffey. Instinct, not intellect snarled in his voice. The injured man hugged his heavy weapon to him with both arms.

Wilding resumed cutting. The bamboo rustled as it fell. Sometimes the stems remained upright, gripped by the mass of their neighbors. Wilding forced them aside. His uniform was in shreds, and a sheen of blood coated his arms.

The bamboo went on forever. Wilding cut, and stepped, and cut. He lost track of time and was conscious only of dull pain.

"Hey," a voice said.

Wilding swung. The bar cut on either stroke, but the rotator muscles of his shoulder screamed with strain after ten minutes of alternate backhands.

"Sir?" said the voice. "I hear something."

Wilding swung. He couldn't see for the sweat in his eyes and the burning red haze which overlaid his mind.

Yee grabbed him by the shoulder. The bar dropped from Wilding's nerveless fingers. "Sir!" the gunner said. "I *hear* something."

So did Wilding, now that his body had stopped moving. His mind re-engaged. A rhythmic crunching sound, amazingly loud. He couldn't tell what direction it came from because of the scattering effect of the dense stems.

Wilding looked over his shoulder. Leaf had paused six feet behind Yee; the next man in line was hidden by the walls of the ragged trail. Nobody wanted to bunch up here. . . .

"Pass the word back to Mr Brainard," Wilding whispered to the nervous gunner. "Tell him that—"

The wall of bamboo crashed forward. Wilding shouted and grabbed for his cutting bar. The net of interlaced stems sprang down and held him as immobile as an insect in amber.

A three-ton grasshopper smashed its way across the trail. Its legs were modified to graviportal stumps. One of its clawed feet came down squarely on the net of bamboo which held Wilding.

The stems took up some of the shock, but Wilding screamed as he felt tendons go in his right ankle.

November 24, 379 AS. 0211 hours.

A dozen of them sauntered down the Palm Walk together, giddy with drink and the odor of the tropical blooms among the trees. The clubs were still open, but establishments in this restricted area had no need for garish advertisement. The entrances were lighted in pastels which set off the broad corridor rather than illuminating it.

Wilding was at the front of the loose group. The woman on his arm was a short-haired blonde from a cadet branch of the McLain family. He thought her name was Glory, but he was too drunkenly cautious to risk a scene if he were wrong.

The blonde said, "I want to go—*ooh!*"

Wilding tried to fold her in his arms. "I want to go ooh with you too, darling," he said. "Let's—"

The blonde twisted away from him. Wilding goggled at her in amazement.

"Oh my god!" grumbled one of the men. "Is Tootles still around? He stayed in the Azure, didn't he?"

"Hal?" called a woman's half-familiar voice.

Wilding turned. The figure shambling toward him was only a blur against the arbor in which she had waited, but her eyes were well adapted to the Palm Walk. "Oh, Hal," she blurted, "thank God it's you! You've got to help me."

"Patrol!" the blonde shrieked. "Patrol! Where are you, you lazy bastards?"

There were discrete cameras and audio pick-ups every hundred yards down the corridor. As soon as the blonde screamed, a bright blue strobe light flashed a quarter-mile away at the guarded entrance which separated the Palm Walk from the public areas of Wyoming Keep.

"Now, you haven't any business here, madam," Wilding said, queasy with the shock of the unknown. It *couldn't* be anyone he knew. He still couldn't make out the woman's features, but her body odor and the stench of cheap perfume flared his nostrils. "If you don't cause any trouble, then I'm sure the Patrol will let you—"

"Hal, my God, it's *me,* Francine!" the figure cried. "You've got to help me see Tootles."

Good God, it *was* Francine.

"Tootles picked her up somewhere," a man explained to his companion. "Then she found him in bed with her maid and hit him with a bottle. She tried to *kill* him!"

A Patrol scooter, silent except for the hiss of its tires against the pavement, sped toward the disturbance. Its strobe pulsed across Francine's swollen features. She looked as though she had applied her make-up in the dark.

"Tootles isn't here, Francine," Wilding said. He wondered if she was armed.

Chauncey Callahan, Tootles, had started the evening with their party but he'd dropped away hours ago. Nobody else in the group knew Francine as well as Wilding himself did.

Francine snatched his wrist. Her trembling grip had no strength, but her false nails felt like the touch of broken glass. "Hal, you're my friend," she wheezed. "You've got to explain to Tootles that it was just a mistake, that I *love* him."

"Sent her back where she belonged, of course," said an ice-voiced woman in answer to a question Wilding hadn't heard. "Which was nowhere."

The Patrol scooter pulled up so hard that it squealed. Three men jumped out. One of them swept the group with a hand-held spotlight. The white glare steadied on Francine's raddled, desperate face. Her dilated eyes glowed red in the beam.

"Hal, *please,*" she begged as the other two Patrolmen seized her elbows. Her nails left scratches as she lost her grip on Wilding. "Hal, you remember me! You *remember* me!"

Francine's blouse was of a natural material from the planetary surface, a soft clinging fabric that fluoresced in white and blue-white light. The cloth blazed now in spotlit radiance, but that only emphasized the stains and tears which had made the garment too worthless to barter for drugs.

Francine pulled the blouse open. Her breasts sagged. "You remember!" she screeched.

"Get her out of here!" Wilding shouted as he turned his face.

One of the Patrolmen injected Francine with something. She sprawled limp and let the pair of them load her into the scooter.

The third Patrolmen switched off the spotlight. The strobe pulsed twice more, then cut off also.

"I'm very sorry for this problem, ladies and gentlemen," the senior Patrolman said. His tone was unctuous over an edge of real concern. This could mean his rank, his job, or—or he could fall into the bleak emptiness reserved for those who had basked in the favor of the powerful, and then lost that favor. Empty days filled with algal protein and holonews images of the glittering folk with whom he had once been in daily contact. A life sentence to a prison bounded by the pressure walls of the Keep.

A life like that of Francine, drooling in the back of the Patrol vehicle.

"Unfortunately, the man at the entrance recognized the

woman and didn't check her name against the updated admissions list," the Patrolman continued. The filament of his spotlight was a fading orange blur. "I trust that none of you were injured, or . . . ?"

"You useless bastards!" the blonde shrilled. "We could have been—"

Wilding grabbed the woman's shoulder. "Shut *up,*" he said very distinctly.

Glory, if her name was Glory, gasped and nestled against him.

Wilding waved at the scooter and its contents. "Get her out of here," he demanded. His voice rose. "Get her out of my life!"

"At once, Mr Wilding," said the Patrolman in relief. He leaped aboard the vehicle. The driver had already started it rolling.

The scooter sped back toward the entrance to the Palm Walk and oblivion. Its tires keened like a woman sobbing.

May 17, 382 AS. 1723 hours.

We been rammed by a fucking battleship! Leaf thought as the bamboo crashed down in a monstrous bow wave.

The grasshopper's headplate was smoothly curved and a yard across. The waxy chitinous surface gave no purchase to the hooked foliage, and six powerful legs drove the creature through stems that proved a nearly impassible barrier to humans.

OT Wilding vanished beneath a mat of vegetation that

muffled his screams. Yee tried to jump out of the way, but the disaster was too sudden. He got his torso clear, but the stems that cascaded over the trail pinned the gunner's hips and feet to the ground.

Yee lay on his back, yelling as he tried to aim at the behemoth which knocked him down. The muzzle of his rifle was tangled, and its light bullets weren't going to have much effect on the grasshopper anyway.

Leaf's pack held forty pounds of barakite. He had squeezed the doughy explosive into fist-sized balls after he cut it from the second warhead. He reached over his shoulder with his left hand and grabbed a wad; his right thumb poised on his multitool's welding trigger.

He didn't light the explosive. The huge insect was just trying to get away.

The grasshopper's body was much like that of its Earthborn ancestors, but its armored legs were straight and short to carry the mass of its Venus-adapted form. It moved in a succession of tripods: the center leg on the right balancing with the front and back legs on the left while the other three drove forward, then the opposite pattern.

Because the grasshopper was at a full run, the cases of its vestigial wings lifted to uncover the creature's external lungs: fungoid blotches of red, oxygen-absorbent tissue spaced along the midline on both sides of the grasshopper's body. Air diffused through spiracles would not sufficiently fuel the life-processes of so large a body.

The digestive system in the grasshopper's yellow-striped abdomen rumbled a farewell to K67's crew as the beast vanished again into the bamboo.

Leaf giggled with relief. Then he saw the scorpion.

Yee's heavy pack had prevented him from being thrown

flat. *"Somebody fucking help me!"* the gunner bellowed as he used his rifle butt to lever himself upright.

"Look out!" Leaf shouted.

Yee rotated his head from Leaf—

To the new track the grasshopper had smashed through the vegetation—

To what had driven the grasshopper off in panic.

The grasshopper had been chewing a path through the bamboo entanglement for days. Leaf and Yee looked down the corridor. New shoots grew from the close-cropped soil at increasing height, in a pattern of pale green/bright green/yellow green.

The scorpion carried its flat belly six feet above the ground. It strode toward the humans with saw-toothed pincers advanced.

Yee screamed and fired the whole magazine of his rifle in a burst that made the barrel glow. Bullets sparkled across the lustrous purple-black head, destroying several of the simple eyes. Jacket fragments clipped tiny holes in the nearest foliage.

"Run!" the gunner shrieked. Bamboo still gripped his legs to the knees. He twisted, then twisted back when he realized he was trapped.

"Geddown!" Leaf bawled. The motorman pressed the stud trigger of his multitool, snapping the arc alight. The scorpion pounced.

Yee dropped the fresh magazine he was trying to insert into the rifle. He thrust the weapon out crosswise as a shield. The scorpion's right pincer gripped the rifle's receiver; its left reached beneath the weapon and caught Yee around the waist. The paired claws were eighteen inches long.

Leaf knew there was no use in running, but he would

have run anyway except that the bamboo held him also. He touched the welding arc to his lump of barakite.

He wasn't left-handed. He flung the explosive in a clumsy overhand motion as soon as it started to sputter. Tiny globules flicked his hand and wrist. The intense heat raised blisters instantly.

The scorpion tore Yee out of the bamboo. The gunner was no longer screaming. Blood soaked the waist of his torn uniform and fanned broadly across his chest from nose and mouth.

The blob of barakite was softened by its own combustion. It splattered over the arachnid's head instead of flying into the open mouth as Leaf had intended.

The scorpion's pincers thrust the victim between its side-hinged jawplates while the flames roared with blue-white laughter. Sparks flew in all directions. Somebody fired his rifle past the motorman.

Gobbets of burning barakite ignited the load of explosive in Yee's pack.

The spark became the sun—

Became a volcanic pressure—

That shriveled the vegetation gripping Leaf and hurled him back away from its white heart.

September 24, 366 AS. 1050 hours.

"Wait for us!" Peanut Leaf squealed in a voice that hadn't broken by now, his twelfth birthday, and didn't look like it would be getting any longer to try. The oil-drum barricade spouted smoke and orange flame before *any* of the retreating 5th-Level war party reached it, and the Leaf brothers were at the end of the rout.

"Yee-hah!" shrilled a 3rd-Level warrior as he flung a spear made of plastic tubing with a metal head.

The point nicked Peanut Leaf's thigh; the thick shaft caught the boy a blow solid enough to stagger him. Peanut would have fallen, but Jacko, fourteen and strong for his age, seized his brother's arm and propelled him like a tractor drawing a cart.

"Don't you fall, you little bastard!" he shouted. "They'll kill you!"

Peanut wasn't in the least doubt about that.

Mongo and Race were already down—which meant dead, unless the 3rd-Level warriors had been in too much of a hurry to make sure by slitting their throats. It had been a ratfuck, an ambush sprung in the air shaft while the 5th-Level war party was just setting out on what was supposed to be a raid.

Now. . . .

Kacentas, War Dragon of the 5th Level, had planned for the possibility of retreat by sliding drums of waste oil across the home corridor. Three hard-faced girls of the Auxiliary were stationed there with torches to ignite the barricade if the raiders were driven back.

The disaster had been so abrupt that the girls lit the drums in the faces of their own warriors, rather than those of the enemy.

The leading warriors cursed and squealed, leaping the drums before the oil was properly alight. The pall of smoke rolled upward and down, following the convection patterns of Block 81's climate control.

An arrow took Kacentas in the air. He tumbled to what would have been the safe side of the barricade.

The Leaf brothers sprinted into the curtain of smoke.

Peanut gagged, but the air was clear immediately in front of the barricade. Fuel blasted upward in terrifying columns to mushroom against the corridor ceiling.

The Patrol would arrive within minutes, but within seconds it would be too late.

"Come on!" Jacko cried.

All the other 5th-Level warriors had vanished—except Hurst, who lay at the base of the drums with eyes staring upward from a pool of blood. Hurst had managed to run all the way from the air shaft with his jugular torn open by a spearthrust.

Peanut skidded to a halt. "I can't!" he wailed to the barricade. The heat was a concrete presence.

"Come *on!*" Jacko repeated shrilly.

He picked up his brother by the throat and the seat of his pants. As he turned to hurl the younger boy to safety, a thrown club rang off Jacko's skull and stunned him.

Peanut fell to the floor. He had lost his steel mace back in the air shaft. There were 3rd-Level warriors all around them. His eyes were open, but his mind refused to accept what he saw.

Jacko was still on his feet. Two of the enemy prodded him with their spears. They didn't drive the points home. Instead, they thrust Jacko backwards, into the oil fires.

Jacko screamed. His arms flailed as if he were trying to swim away from the agony, but there was no way out. For a moment, Jacko's torso forced down the flames, but then the orange-red blanket roared up to cover him again.

And he still screamed.

Sirens and strobe lights flooded the corridor. The 3rd-Level warriors were running away, but Jacko did not move. His black arms lifted from the ebbing flames in a hollow embrace, and his skull greeted the Patrolmen with a lipless grin.

Jacko's throat had shriveled shut. His brother screamed for both of them.

May 17, 382 AS. 1724 Hours.

Newton was reloading. Brainard shoved past him and aimed his rifle.

He didn't fire. When the scorpion reared high over the trail it had a face like the heart of the sun and he had to glance away.

The roaring brilliance was barakite burning, not a vision of Hell.

When Brainard looked up again, the scorpion was careening away in a series of spastic convulsions. When its jointed tail straightened, the creature was more than twenty feet long from jaws to stinger . . . but the jaws were gone, the whole head was a blazing ruin, and so long as the decorticated monster continued in its current direction, it was no further danger to K67's crew.

Volleys of shots crackled and whined through the foliage as the ammunition in the backpack went off in the barakite fire. Cartridges without a gun-barrel to direct them weren't particularly dangerous. On a bad day, a bullet or fragment of casing might put an eye out.

That was nothing to worry about, since OT Wilding was gone and they were all dead without his special knowledge.

Just before the scorpion crashed out of sight through a thicket of hundred-foot willows, a human leg fell from the shriveled chitin of its mouth.

Brainard blinked at the purple afterimages of the flame. His ears rang, and his nostrils were numb with the smell of barakite and burning flesh. The suggestion of fried prawns was probably from the scorpion.

He didn't know what to do. He doubted there was anything they *could* do, now.

Leaf lay face down, moaning. Brainard reached out with his left hand and lifted the motorman. The bamboo had withered in the intense heat. It no longer clung to flesh and clothing.

"Good thinking," Brainard said. "With the barakite."

Must have been Leaf who ignited it, though it wasn't his pack because he was still carrying that. Caffey . . . no, Yee had been Number Two. Yee and Wilding were gone, just ahead of the rest of them.

The mat of flame-shrunken stems quivered, then moaned. OT Wilding's slim, aristocratic hand reached out of it.

"God help us!" blurted Caffey.

There was a swollen line across the torpedoman's neck, but he was enough himself again to push his way to the head of the column. He shifted the machinegun to his left hand and snatched the cutting bar from where Wilding must have dropped it.

"Not that," snapped Brainard. "D'ye want to take his leg off?"

He knelt and began to pry the bamboo upward with one hand and the muzzle of his rifle. The laser communicator flopped awkwardly against his knees. *With Wilding alive, they had a chance.*

The desiccated stems splintered without resistance. *Wilding could save them. . . .*

Wilding was able to sit up by himself when they cleared the bamboo from his chest. Fresh growth, protected like the officer-trainee by the insulating mat, left nasty sores where it had begun to suck at his back.

"Is he okay?" Bozman called from the back of the line.

Leaf and the cautiously used blade of his multitool worked Wilding's boots free.

"He's all right," Brainard said. A prayer of exultation danced in his mind as he heard his own flat statement.

"No," said Wilding. "I've sprained my ankle. You're going to have to leave me."

Brainard raised his eyes to the terrain ahead of them. It seemed to be a plateau, but they would have more climbing to do shortly.

"Who's got the first-aid kit?" he demanded. "Get a pressure bandage on the XO's ankle."

"You can't carry a cripple along with you," Wilding sneered. "Take what you need from my pack and get moving before something worse comes along."

Awareness that the officer-trainee might be right froze Brainard's heart. "Shut up," he snarled.

Wilding's face went blank. Leaf and Caffey, at the edge of Brainard's focused vision, stiffened.

Wheelwright said, "I got the kit," breaking the pulsing silence. "Lemme up to the front."

Men shifted. There was plenty of room in the broader pathway that the grasshopper had chewed through the jointed tangle. Caffey looked at the cutting bar in his hand and said, "Ah, I'll cut him a crutch, okay?"

Yee's rifle lay a few feet away. Brainard picked it up.

Shreds of bamboo fiber were stuck to the plastic stock where the barakite had softened it.

"No," said Wilding. He looked at Caffey, purposefully avoiding eye contact with the ensign. "That won't work. The bamboo—any surface vegetation. It'll keep growing after it's cut, and. . . ."

He made a negligent gesture toward the sores on his back. Wheelwright coated them with a clear antiseptic, but the edges were already puckering upward.

The scorpion's pincers had cut the rifle's beryllium receiver almost in half. There were bright gouges through the barrel's weatherproofing and into the steel beneath.

"Right," said Brainard. "We'll use this for a crutch. It's not good for much else." He handed the rifle to Wilding.

Wilding's tongue touched his lips. He looked at the ensign. "Sir?" he said. "I still can't march—"

"I'll help him, sir," said Leaf.

"The junior personnel will assist Mr Wilding in rotation," Brainard said as his mind clicked through the minuscule tasks that he could understand, could deal with. "Newton, Bozman, Wheelwright. Thirty-minute watches."

He'd almost assigned Yee a place in the watch list.

"Leaf, I want you at the end of the column," he continued. He held out his rifle to the motorman. "Take this. Caffey, give me the cutting bar. I'll lead, and I want you and the big gun right behind me."

Leaf turned his head as though he had not seen the proffered weapon. "I don't *want* a fucking gun," he snarled. "Why'n't you let me help the XO? I can do it."

"Newton's carrying the other bar, sir," Wilding said quietly. "You'd better use it. The charge on this one is almost flat."

Brainard slung his rifle. "All right," he said. "Newton, give me the other bar. Wheelwright, take the end slot. *Watch* yourself. Leaf, help Mr Wilding. Stay close. There's a lot of this place that I don't know anything about."

There was damn-all about this place that he *did* know anything about.

"Sir," offered Caffey. "Ah, d'ye want me to carry the communicator? It'll get in the way if there's much cutting to do."

Brainard looked at the torpedoman with a flat expression which he hoped hid the sudden terror in his mind. "We'll be following the grasshopper's path," he said coldly. "I'll keep the communicator."

The laser communicator was Brainard's lifeline. Its hard outlines were all that kept him sane. If he was still sane. . . .

JULY 23, 381 AS. 0301 HOURS.

The twenty-seven islands on Brainard's navigation display ranged from mere fangs of rock to a ridged mass rising to a thousand feet, worthy of a name.

Even the narrower perspective of the console's central situation display was splotched with islands. But the natural surroundings didn't matter, because a Seatiger warship was edging through a channel between two of the swampy blobs at a charted distance of 5721 yards.

"Ready torpedoes," Lieutenant Tonello rasped over the interphone. He stood to look over K67's cockpit coaming, while OT Brainard hid within his holographic environment. "Flank spee—"

A starshell popped. Tracers snarled overhead measurable seconds before Brainard heard the howl of the Gatlings that fired them.

"Torpedoes ready," Tech 2 Caffey reported. The interphone turned his voice into that of a soloist accompanied by the orchestra of Hell.

"Coxs'n, three degrees starboard."

K67 accelerated like a kicked can. Water slammed upward so near the port side that water drenched Brainard's console. The spout was luminous with the orange flames at its heart. The second shell was dead astern, the third astern to starboard.

Tonello had kept the fans on high, spilling air through the waste slots in the plenum chamber, as the torpedo craft nosed through the archipelago to find the targets he knew were present. OT Brainard had cursed the CO in silent terror because that technique made K67 a sonic beacon. Brainard hadn't been able to help matters at the countermeasures board, though the scattering effect of the islands themselves had turned the two-vessel patrol into a flotilla.

It would have taken the fans 90 seconds to spin up from low-signature mode to full power. It took a half-second to slam the waste slots closed and lurch toward the enemy. That was many times the difference between a waterspout astern—and a fireball which scattered indistinguishable bits of crew and vessel after a 5.5-inch shell detonated K67's own torpedoes.

Brainard punched up an identification sidebar on his situation display. When his mind and fingers did *something,* the roar and flashes couldn't drown him in their terror.

The sea was orange with waterspouts; muzzle flashes boiled the whole horizon red and white. K44 vanished from the display. Even the islands blurred and shrank as the shell-storm degraded the data reaching K67's sensors.

Brainard's console told him their opponent was a destroyer-leader with a full-load displacement of 2700 tons and a main armament of six 5.5-inch guns in triple turrets.

He didn't believe it. He was sure from the volume of fire that they'd jumped a dreadnought. He reached under the panel and switched to the back-up system. The holographic display vanished for a hideous fraction of a second, forcing Brainard to see the carnage around him. Light trembling from flares twisted sea creatures on the surface into shapes still more monstrous than those of nature. Horrors fought and feasted at the banquet laid by bursting shells.

Then the back-up circuits took over. The new display told Brainard the same thing the old one had, that K67 faced a minor fleet element, not a dreadnought. Only a destroyer-leader, only a hundred times the hovercraft's size—

"Launch one!" said Lieutenant Tonello in a voice as clear as glass breaking. K67 shuddered as studs blew open and dropped one of the torpedoes into the sea beneath her plenum chamber.

"Launch two!"

"Tracking!" Caffey reported as he hunched over his guidance controls. The torpedo's own sensors gave the operator a multispectral view of the target. If the enemy tried to dodge, Caffey could send steering commands along the cable of optical fiber which connected the weapon to the hovercraft.

The release thump of the second torpedo was lost in the burst of explosive bullets that buzz-sawed across K67.

Lieutenant Tonello's head vanished in a yellow flash. His body hurtled against the back bulkhead. The shatterproof windscreen disintegrated into a dazzle of microscopic beads, and all the cockpit displays went dead. The coxswain screamed and rolled out of his seat. K67 wallowed broadside, still at full power.

Each side-console had an emergency helm and throttle under the middle display. Brainard rotated his unit up and locked it into position. Wind blast through the missing screen hammered him. The destroyer-leader was a Roman candle of muzzle flashes.

A starshell had drifted almost to the surface astern of K67. By its flickering light, Brainard saw another blacked-out hovercraft race across the wave tops toward the target. He hadn't had time to think about K44 since the shooting started.

Brainard spun his miniature helm hard to starboard. The hovercraft did not respond.

A salvo of 5.5-inch shells straddled K67 with a roar louder than Doomsday. Waterspouts lifted the hovercraft and spilled the air out of her plenum chamber. She slammed the surface again with a bone-jarring crash.

The main circuit breakers had tripped. A battery-powered LED marked the breaker box, but Brainard's retinas still flickered with afterimages of the explosive bullets that raked the cockpit. He groped for the box, barked his knuckles on the edge of it, and finally got it open while several rounds of automatic fire slapped K67's skirts.

Brainard snapped the main switch into place. The console displays remained dark, but the hovercraft answered her helm.

The coxswain lay moaning on the deck. "Medic!" Brainard shouted. "Medic!" The interphone wasn't working either.

The circuit breaker overloaded again with a blue flash.

K67's fans continued to drive her, but the shell-frothed waves wrenched the vessel into a curve that would end on a rocky islet unless the Seatigers destroyed her first.

Brainard grabbed the circuit breaker with his left hand. He snapped the switch home and held it there. Sparks trembled and his forearm went numb. An overloaded component blew in the coxswain's station, but Brainard had control again.

He overcorrected. K67 reversed her curve as though Brainard intended a figure-8. A three-shell salvo ignited the sea along the hovercraft's previous course.

"Medic!" Brainard cried. He had no feeling on the left side of his body. His left foot thrashed a crazy jig against the cockpit bulkheads.

The sky behind them turned orange.

Brainard looked over his shoulder. Where the destroyer-leader had been, a bubble of light with sharp edges lifted five hundred feet above the horizon. Stark shadows ripped across the neighboring islands as a doughnut-shaped shock-wave pushed trees away from the light.

It must have been the target's own munitions, because no torpedo warhead could wreak such destruction.

The destroyer-leader was almost two miles away. The blast made K67 skip like a flung pebble.

Leaf crawled into the cockpit, carrying the first-aid kit. He wore gloves.

"Forget that!" Brainard squealed as the motorman crouched over the writhing coxswain. "Hold this breaker closed!"

K67 spewed air through dozens of holes in her skirts, but she would survive until a tender could take her aboard. K67's torpedoes had lost guidance when the system power failed, but her consort had driven in and nailed the Seatiger vessel.

Because of K44, Officer-Trainee Brainard was going to survive this night after all.

MAY 17, 382 AS. 2148 HOURS.

Leaf heard OT Wilding say, "That's rock, we stop here," as they struggled past a tangle of thorny, interlacing vines.

The words didn't matter to Leaf. Wilding'd been muttering nonsense for . . . a long time, a lot of stumbling steps whatever the clock time might have been. The last time Wheelwright had dressed the bamboo sores on the officer's back, they'd had scarlet edges and centers of yellow pus.

But they weren't any of them in shape for a dress parade. Leaf saw only blurs because of the sweat in his eyes. He didn't have the energy to wipe his face with his right cuff. The multitool filled Leaf's right hand, and his left arm helped support Wilding . . .

Who was handsome, and rich, and not a pussy after all. During bouts of fever, the officer-trainee couldn't control his tongue—but he kept his feet moving forward. Their route was mostly uphill and the rifle made a bad crutch, but Wilding didn't flop down and die the way Leaf had maybe expected.

Wilding shook himself out of the motorman's grasp. Swaying like a top about to fall over, Wilding said, "We *stop* here," in a voice well accustomed to giving orders.

Leaf realized he was ready to fall down himself. *Fuckin' A.* He rubbed his right eyesocket a little clearer on the point of his shoulder. "Fish!" he shouted to the torpedo-man's back. "Get the CO. Mr Wilding wants a word."

And a hell of a bad place to stop for one, but you didn't argue with officers.

They were in a belt of thirty-foot-tall grass which defended its territory against encroaching woody plants by sawing off their stems with glassy nodules along the edges of the narrow grassblades. The competition was as dynamic as that of surf and the shoreline.

Even now in the momentary pause, glitteringly serrated blades twisted close to treat the humans with the same mindless ferocity that would greet an oak or mahogany. All that could be said in favor of going through the grass was that it was possible to cut the stuff. The tangle of thorns to the side was impassable.

Ensign Brainard stepped back from the head of the path he had cleared. His face and hands were smeared with a slick of his own sweat-diluted blood. "What is it?" he asked calmly.

Wilding opened his mouth. He swayed. Leaf reached over to catch him, but the officer-trainee crossed both palms firmly on the butt of his crutch to steady himself.

"That's rock," Wilding said. "Where the berry bush is growing." He flicked his eyes sideways because he was afraid that he would topple if he so much as nodded his head. "We could rest there. A real rest."

Leaf looked at the tangle. The brambles were woven like a fishnet. Hundreds of small white flowers bloomed among the black stems and foliage, but nothing bigger than a man's arm could penetrate the mass.

A large insect might trust to its armor while browsing

on the vines and later berries, but Leaf already had enough experience with surface life to imagine the results. The brambles gave only until the animal was fully within their mass. Then—

Just like a fishnet. A thorn-studded fishnet.

The CO looked at the tangle without expression. "We'll go on," he said flatly. "I can't cut that."

"Hey!" said Caffey. "We can blow it clear! With the barakite."

"No," said Wilding. "We'll use the barakite to burn it. We don't want to pulverize the rock."

Brainard looked from Wilding to Leaf. "All right," he said. "Leaf, you'll lay the charges. All right?"

Leaf nodded. "Yessir."

He shrugged to slide the pack straps off his shoulders. At first his muscles wouldn't respond; then the load slipped abruptly. The straps scraped his arms, and the pack itself bruised the backs of his thighs.

"We'll use portions of the barakite from everybody's pack," the ensign continued. "And *don't* let any ignite that you don't mean to burn."

"Yessir," Leaf muttered. He knelt to begin work.

Brainard turned and cut at the grass rustling lethally closer to the human interlopers. Leaf saw that the CO had difficulty raising the cutting bar enough to use it.

Leaf rolled a ball of explosive between his palms, forming it into a coarse thread. The barakite was tacky in the moist heat, but the plasticizing additive retained its tensile strength so that Leaf could create a creamy white strand as thin as his little finger before the material broke under its own weight.

Caffey began forming a thread of his own when he saw what the motorman was doing. At Brainard's order, the other enlisted men passed blobs of barakite to the chiefs. They were probably glad to be rid of a few pounds of their burdens. . . .

When he had six strands of explosive, each a yard and a half long, the motorman paused. "Okay, that'll do," he muttered to his hands.

Caffey held out a canteen. "Have some water first," he said.

Leaf was too exhausted to argue with any suggestion. "Yeah, sure," he said. He reached for his own canteen.

Water was no problem. The condensing jacket on each crewman's canteen would fill the quart flask within ten minutes in this saturated atmosphere.

"Naw," said the torpedoman. "Use mine."

Leaf took the canteen and drank deeply. His eyes flashed open.

For the first time he noticed that the torpedoman carried two canteens. This one was full of rum.

Caffey grinned. "Essential to life," he said.

"You bet," said Leaf. "Now, everybody keep the hell back."

The brambles trembled softly toward him. He thought for a moment, then said, "Sir, lemme borrow the rifle, okay?"

Brainard handed the weapon over without comment. Leaf set one end of a barakite thread over the flash hider at the rifle's muzzle and used the weapon to feed the explosive through the thorns.

A black twig two feet into the mass suddenly flared its "bark" into a pincushion of spines tipped with brilliant blue. Leaf shouted and jumped backward.

Two black eyes winked at him; a forked tongue dabbed

at the air. The tiny lizard folded its scales as suddenly as it had erected them and scurried back into the tangle.

Caffey had his machine-gun leveled.

"What?" Ensign Brainard demanded. "What?"

Leaf took a deep breath. "Nothing," he said. "Stay clear."

He checked around him. Wheelwright supported OT Wilding, and Brainard had dragged Leaf's own pack a safe three yards away. The barakite strands lying on the ground were as good a compromise as Leaf could judge between being out of the way and being ready to use. . . .

He tucked the first thread another inch into the brambles which were already closing on it, withdrew the rifle and tossed it to Brainard, and lit the barakite with his multitool.

Leaf instinctively covered his ears as he ducked away, but the sound was a vicious snarl rather than an explosion. A wave of heat slapped his back.

When the motorman looked around, the half-consumed strand had already fallen through the gap its radiance cleared to land on rock. For several feet to either side, the brambles themselves burned with sullen orange flames, dim by contrast with the blue-white dazzle which had ignited them. Even beyond that range, vines drew back as heat seared away their moisture.

A haze of barakite residues oozed through the tangle. Leaf grabbed a second strand of explosive. He sucked in another deep breath and plunged into the sudden clearing while blobs of barakite still sputtered, cracking rock with the last of their energy.

There was no time for finesse now, but there was less need for it also. The initial blast of heat had stunned the brambles and robbed them of much of their thorn-clawed speed. Leaf tossed his thread of barakite over a slope of vines whose outer surface was already baked brown.

"Here!" shouted Caffey and handed the motorman more barakite.

Leaf laid that strand at an angle to the first, so the near ends were close together. "G' back!" he ordered, but Fish had already skipped to safety. Leaf lighted the explosive.

The barakite hissed forward with teeth of flame. Brambles ignited, roaring in green agony. Rock, calcined and broken, glinted beneath from the drifting ash. The three remaining strands would be enough to clear the outcrop's entire surface.

K67's whole crew was cheering Leaf.

The motorman reached for more barakite by reflex. Screams filled his ears, and his eyes stared at a curtain of rolling oil flames.

JULY 1, 379 AS. 2355 HOURS.

Tech 3 Leaf unsealed the front of his clown suit and removed the two-pound strand of barakite which he had wound around his waist. Sweat gave the surface of the explosive a greasy feel. More barakite appeared from beneath the carnival clothing of the other three members of the gang.

Silent fireworks flared above the Commons of Wyoming Keep. Light flickered from the zenith of the impervium dome and reflected even here, to the narrow back alleys of the warehouse district against the dome's outer curve. The air sighed as tens of thousands of throats cheered simultaneously.

"Oh, my god, they're gonna hear this sure," moaned

Epling, a hydrofoil gunner now dressed as a cherub. "The Patrol'll be down on us before we even get a drink!"

The buildings were thick ceramic castings. The material was hard as glass and so strong that a warehouse had remained undamaged when an out-of-control truck demolished itself against the structure. Originally the ceramic had had a pink tinge, but the grime of centuries had turned everything in the district gray.

"Just button your lip, Epling," Tech 3 Caffey said. "Leaf knows what he's doing. Don't you, Leafie?"

"Who's got the adhesive?" Leaf asked.

Caffey tossed him a finger-sized spray can. Caffey wore a pirate costume, with a broad-brimmed hat over his domino mask.

Leaf spritzed the warehouse wall five feet above the ground and pressed his strand of barakite against it. The adhesive held, despite sweat and the filthy ceramic. Leaf ran the spray down the wall, squeezing the explosive firmly against the surface.

More fireworks went off in sheets of flame. Braudel, dressed as a skeleton, held a tiny infrared lamp. The goggles beneath Leaf's clown mask filtered out the multicolored splendor of the display.

Leaf began attaching the second strip of barakite parallel to the ground, with one end in contact with the upper end of the first strand. He was outlining a square doorway on the warehouse's featureless back wall.

"My god," Epling muttered, "they'll lock us up 'n throw away the key. They'll give us life sentences to the netters and we'll just cruise up 'n down till something eats us."

Braudel chuckled. "That's better 'n what Cinc Hafner's gonna do if he learns we scooped this shit outa one a' Caffey's torpedoes, hey?"

"Look, cut it out," Caffey growled. "You'll see. It'll go slicker 'n snot. All the Patrol that isn't keeping the lid on parties is off partying themself. And there won't be a sound. Leaf knows what he's doing."

The third strip of barakite formed the other vertical. Leaf's body trembled. Present reality, his hands forming the explosive against the sheer wall, was a thin overlay to the quivering surface of memory.

In his mind, the distant cheers of the crowd became screams.

"Anyhow," Caffey added defensively, "d'ye think its going to matter if a warhead weighs a ton or just a ton less spit? And that's only if the fish hits, which they mostly don't."

Leaf set the last strand of barakite where the warehouse wall joined the alley floor in a smooth curve. Pavement and building had been cast as a single unit only a few decades after the dome of Wyoming Keep had been completed.

"Boy, I can taste the booze already!" Braudel said lovingly. "You know, this won't be cheap-ass shit. You 'n' me, we couldn't buy stuff this good if we had all the fuckin' money on Venus! This is Twelve Families booze!"

"Okay," Leaf heard his voice say. "It's ready."

He took out his multitool. The lanyard pulled open the blouse of his clown suit.

Braudel and Epling stepped, then scurried toward opposite ends of the alley.

"No, it's all right!" Caffey growled after them. "I tell you, there won't be a bang!"

"Maybe from the wall, Fish," Leaf said in a distant voice. "Pieces may fly off it."

"Christ!" snarled the torpedoman. "We come this far. Just do it!"

Leaf triggered the multitool's welder. He knelt, then touched the arc to one of the bottom corners of the barakite frame. Coiling fumes as white and solid as bones lifted from the explosive.

Caffey grabbed Leaf's shoulder and dragged him back a few steps. "Not *that* goddam close, for chrissake!" the torpedoman grunted.

The barakite caught with an echoing hiss which gave the lie to Caffey's promise of silence. Blue-white brilliance flowed up and across the refractory surface. The flames shivered through curtains of their own smoke.

The ribbons of light joined at the far corner so that for a moment fire outlined the square of wall. The hiss built into a snarl like that of a chainsaw, bouncing between the warehouse and the dome. Epling and Braudel drew closer again. Their postures indicated the nervousness which their masks attempted to conceal.

"Christ," Caffey murmured. "Is it going to—"

The outlined square of ceramic shattered.

Intense heat torqued the cast wall. The internal stresses finally overwhelmed the structure's ability to withstand them. Twenty-five cubic feet of ceramic disintegrated into a quivering pile of needles an inch long or shorter.

Globs of barakite, flung aside by the structure's shrug of release, vented their last energy up and down the alley. A dozen speckles of fire smoldered on Leaf's costume.

"Perfect, Leafie!" Caffey cried as he clapped the assistant motorman on the back. "Perfect!"

"Right, let's get it!" Braudel said. He stepped through the opening, ducking to clear the knife-edged transom.

The pile of needles shifted like sand beneath the mercenary's boots.

Fireworks shimmered above the column, and the carnival crowd cheered. Leaf's mind echoed with the screams of his burning brother.

MAY 18, 382 AS. 0035 HOURS.

Wilding lay on his back, reveling in the pain of his sores because that alone could cut through the veils of fever which otherwise isolated him from the universe. His right leg floated in air, and the jungle canopy wove a slow dance above him.

Venus took 257 Earth-days to rotate on its axis, a period useless for short-term human concerns. Colonists in domes beneath the Venerian seas had no interest in sidereal time anyway. They promptly adopted the Standard Day of Earth—and retained it for all purposes, even after nuclear holocaust had converted Earth into another star glowing in the unseen sky.

For the Free Companies, the conceit meant that four months of daylight followed four months of darkness. Wars continued, driven by imperatives which ignored the calendar as wars commonly ignore all other things.

Bozman, Leaf's striker, moaned beside Wilding in his sleep. The second watch was on duty now.

Everyone was exhausted. Brainard had put half the crew on watch at all times, not so much because that many pairs of eyes were constantly necessary . . . but because that way there were enough waking guards to shake alert each of their number when he inevitably dropped off.

Wilding was exempt from the watch list, but he was too feverish to sleep. Wheelwright had sprayed Wilding's ankle with a long-term analgesic before fitting the pressure bandage, so the injury did not hurt.

Wilding's subconscious *knew* that the ankle had swelled to the size of a balloon ascender. It was tugging his whole body upward. The bandaged ankle appeared to be normal size. The back of Wilding's mind told him that was an illusion.

The swollen balloon pulled. Wilding's back twisted queasily against the rock, trying to anchor him.

He stared at the ragged white patch of sky above him. The saw-grass hewed its surroundings clear at ground level, but branches encroached in the third canopy nonetheless. The slight interstices among the high leaves were barely enough to energize the grass for its murderous exertions.

On the other side of Bozman, Ensign Brainard muttered in his sleep. The CO's duties on point had been the most exhausting of all. Despite that, he insisted on adding the weight of the laser communicator to the normal load of pack and rifle.

Flying rays cut arcs through the air 300 feet up, dancing among the knobby branches of a monkey puzzle tree. Each ray was between one and two feet wide across the tips of its wings. The creatures were about as long as they were wide if the length of their slim, ruddering tails were added to that of their bodies.

Though the rays were descended from a purely aquatic species, they carried on an amphibious existence. Their nests were pools in the hollow hearts of mighty trees. Every ten minutes or so, the rays ducked back to wet their gills, but between dips they sailed among the branches and cleared swathes in the flying microlife. Their wings were so diaphanously thin at the edges that the sky glimmered through them.

Wilding watched the rays wheel without slowing. He thought of K67's commanding officer. Brainard went on no matter what, with stolid heroism of a sort that Wilding had thought was only myth.

Nothing fazed Brainard. If he had to carry them all on his shoulders, he would at least try. But the ensign wasn't an inspiration to lesser men like Hal Wilding, because Brainard was too obviously of a different species.

A ray suddenly folded its wings and plummeted toward the ground. Fever sharpened Wilding's sight or else gave him a hallucination of perfect clarity; in his present state, he neither knew nor cared which was the case. A large purple orchid had extended in a sluggish fashion from a monkey puzzle branch. It hung within the circuits the rays were cutting.

The flower's bulbous outline went flaccid when the orchid expelled the bubble of lethal gas which formed within its petals. The stem began to withdraw. The flower's work was done for the time being.

The ray's nervous system was paralyzed. The little creature was dead before it struck the ground. Its body would rot in the damp heat. Some of its matter would be eaten by scavengers. The rest would become a decaying soup, adding its substance to the thin soil at the roots of the monkey puzzle from which the orchid hung.

And the orchid in turn tapped the veins of the tree for part of its sustenance. Life was a chain, and mutual support created the strongest links. Even in a jungle.

Bozman moaned softly. Leaf, Caffey, and Newton were

on watch. Good men in their own way, but nothing without Brainard.

Officer-Trainee Hal Wilding was nothing at all, only a burden on the rest of the crew. His leg tried to float him upward, and the stone under his shoulders trembled like a wave trying to lull him to slee—

The rock *was* moving.

Wilding screamed. He lunged into a sitting position. His leg was a pillar of flame without substance.

Bozman cried out beside him. Wilding grabbed the assistant motorman by the shoulders and shouted, "Help! Help! You've got to get me up!"

Everybody was shouting. Brainard lurched to his feet and threatened the jungle with his rifle. A creature in the high canopy hooted in surprise, then hooted again at a greater distance from the commotion.

Wilding lifted himself with hysterical strength. Bozman came with him, but Bozman was a dead weight. The hot barakite flames had broken the outcrop as well as clearing it. In the hours that the men had rested, roots had crept through the fractures in quest of nutrients.

They had found Bozman.

Blood sprayed from the young technician's mouth, throat, and the dozen wounds in his chest. One thin tendril had broken off. It waggled a grisly come-on from Bozman's left nostril.

Other roots quivered in circles a hand's breadth out of the rock surface, sensing nearby sustenance. Their tips were scarlet for the depth they had burrowed into their victim.

Caffey pointed his machine-gun at the outcrop and fired. Bullets and rock fragments ricocheted in all directions.

A stone snatched at Wilding's left leg. It missed his flesh, but the tug was all the officer-trainee needed to overbalance him.

"Cease fire!" Ensign Brainard roared. "*Cease* fire!"

Bullets had blown flat, pale craters into the rock. The roots still waved in terrible eagerness. Wilding started to fall forward onto them.

Leaf grabbed the officer-trainee from behind. Bozman weighed down Wilding's arms.

"Let him go, for god's sake!" the motorman growled. "We can't help *him.*"

Wilding thought the weight had slipped away, but he was no longer conscious of his body. All he could see was the face of Ensign Brainard, surveying the situation with a look of calm control.

June 4, 381 AS. 1147 hours.

Recruit (Officer) Wilding braced in a push-up position as Chief Instructor Calfredi boomed, "Right! Everybody keeps doing push-ups until fatboy gives me twenty more!"

Calfredi's boot probed the ribs of Recruit (Enlisted) Groves, a pudgy youth of sixteen at the oldest. Groves lay blubbering on the ground, unable to rise.

"I want all you guys to know," the instructor continued to the dozen recruit, "that the reason you're still doing push-ups is Groves here is a *pussy.*"

Recruit (Officer) was not a rank, it was a statement of intent; but the scion of the Wilding Family did not need formal rank to act as anger dictated.

"No," Wilding said sharply. He would have liked to spring up with only a thrust of his arms, but fifty push-ups in the sun had cramped his muscles too. He rose to his knees, then lifted himself to his feet.

"No," he repeated, noticing that when he was angry his voice sounded thin and supercilious. "We're doing push-ups because you are a sadistic moron, Mr Calfredi. Except that I'm *not* doing push-ups any more. I'm going to take a shower."

The exercise yard was crushed coral that blazed brighter than the cloud-shrouded sun. Waves of dizziness quivered across Wilding's vision, making the chief instructor shrink and swell.

Calfredi stood motionless beneath his broad-brimmed hat. If there was an expression on his face, Wilding could not read it.

Wilding turned on his heel and strode toward the barracks. He expected an order—*he imagined a plea*—from Calfredi, but there was nothing.

Not a sound from the chief instructor. Gigantic pumps whined from the harbor, refilling a drydock now that repairs to the dreadnought *Mammoth* were complete. A mile away, railguns crashed and snarled at some creature trying to burst through the electrified perimeter of Hafner Base. A public address system croaked information which distance distorted into gibberish.

Just as he opened the door to the recruit barracks, Wilding heard Chief Instructor Calfredi's voice say, "*Down* and up and *down*. . . ."

Wilding slammed the door behind him, shutting out the hot, muggy atmosphere and the sounds of another portion of the universe which had decided it didn't need Hal Wilding.

He'd said he would shower, so he showered. The hot water massaged his aching muscles, and the dull pressure soothed what it could not wash away: the knowledge that he'd failed again. He had walked away from his commitment to Wysocki's Herd, and nobody had even bothered to call him back.

Joining a Free Company had seemed the only way Wilding could express his utter disdain to the Callahan and the whole Twelve Families: disdain for them and for their entire way of life. But the Twelve Families didn't care, and now it was evident that Wysocki's Herd didn't care either.

Wilding supposed he could try to join another mercenary company now that he'd washed out on his first attempt, but that would be pointless. He hadn't wanted to *be* a Free Companion, he'd wanted to make a statement.

Besides, he might fail ignominiously in training with a second company, just as he had with the first.

It didn't bother Wilding that he wasn't suited to be a mercenary. The problem was that he wasn't suited to be *anything* except a drone . . . and if it came to that, none of the humans surviving on Venus was really more useful than Wilding was himself. There were ranks and places, but those were merely means of marking time until the holders died or the sun grew cold.

Wilding shut off the shower. He would pack his gear and report to Cinc Wysocki. With luck, the cinc would send him off immediately to Wyoming Keep. It would be embarrassing to wait a day or more for a scheduled run to the keep, sleeping in the recruit barracks with the men he had turned his back on.

The barracks door opened. It had been about time for the training cycle to end anyway. If Wilding had managed to restrain his arrogance for another ten minutes—twenty push-ups—he might not have expelled himself from what he had begun to imagine might be a brotherhood of equals.

The lights went off.

"Hello?" said Wilding.

Boots scuffled on the polished floor. There were several of them. He could hear their nervous breathing.

Calfredi hadn't been ignoring Wilding after all. He'd just waited to gather a couple of his fellow instructors.

Now they were going to give the smart-ass recruit a going-away present, off the record.

Wilding ran to the side of the bunk room. His bare feet made only a slight squeal on the floor.

The barracks had a single door. If he could avoid the instructors in the dark, he might be able to duck outside. They wouldn't dare attack him in the open. There couldn't be more than three of them, so they might not have left a guard at the—

Wilding's foot slipped. He hit the floor with a thump. Two pairs of hands grabbed him before he could rise. He kicked with his bare feet, stubbing his toe on a booted shin.

More hands seized him. Many more hands. He tried to swing, but his wrists were pinioned.

"What do you bastards think you're doing?" Wilding demanded in a high, clear voice. He would have screamed if he'd thought there was any chance he could be heard outside the concrete walls of the barracks.

"I got the soap!" rasped an eager whisper. A moment after the words, something hard slammed Wilding in the ribs.

The whispering voice had been Groves.

There was a thump and a curse. "Well, back off!" another voice growled through a muffling towel. Panting, sweating bodies shuffled back, but the hands continued to grip Wilding's arms and legs as firmly as if they were preparing to crucify him.

A bar of soap in a sock whistled through the air and cracked against Wilding's right ear. A similar bludgeon caught him on the left side of the jaw as his mouth opened to scream with pain.

"Now listen, you jumped-up pissant," said the voice through the towel. It sounded like Hadion, the tall, intelligent-seeming recruit who bunked next to Wilding. "Some day we'll have to take orders from you—"

Hadion wasn't wielding one of the socks, because his voice didn't break as two more blows crunched into Wilding's ribs. The soap would deform instead of breaking bones, but the men swinging the bludgeons were putting all their strength into the project.

"—so we're gonna give you a lesson now, before you get somebody killed because you're pissed off."

"Stop, for god's—" Wilding wheezed.

But his fellow recruits didn't stop. Not until they had beaten him senseless.

12

May 18, 382 AS. 0156 hours.

Brainard looked at the body of the man he'd killed by incompetence. Bozman's corpse writhed, animated by the roots which resumed their meal as soon as Wilding let the dead flesh fall.

Something knocked loudly in the forest: a warning, or

perhaps merely an insect driving its sucking mouthparts into the veins of a tree.

Wheelwright knelt on the ground. He put his hands over his face and began to blubber. It must have been a general reaction. He and Bozman had barely been on speaking terms after trouble with a prostitute while they were on leave.

"S-stop . . . ," mumbled OT Wilding.

Leaf held Wilding upright, though the motorman himself was glassy-eyed. Fluids oozing from Wilding's back glued his shirt to the flesh. Rings of fungus—black at the edge, purple closer in, and bright scarlet at the center—were converting the pus-smeared fabric to food.

Brainard understood what Wilding was trying to mumble: *We can't stop now.*

"Right," the ensign said aloud. "Is everybody all right?"

Bozman twitched. Brainard's guts roiled. He gestured toward the corpse with his chin and added, "Everybody else."

Caffey wore a stunned expression. He put an hand on his striker's shoulder and said in a gentle voice, "S'okay, Wheelwright, it's all okay. Just put a sock in it, huh, buddy?"

Brainard looked up along his compass line, then back to the men he commanded. He should have known not to stay in one place for more than an hour. No place on Venus was safe if you gave the planet long enough to sight in on you.

"Right," he said aloud. "Fish, break up Bozman's pack and distribute the contents. We've had our rest. It's time to be moving on."

Wilding had saved them. Wilding, so tortured by pain that he could scarcely speak, had noticed the infiltrating roots. Wilding sounded the warning and, despite his injured leg, had tried to drag Bozman to safety.

A born leader. If Brainard were half the man his XO was, they'd have a real chance of survival.

Brainard hefted his pack. The effort made him dizzy. The other men weren't moving.

He would be left alone to die. . . .

"Technician Caffey, what the hell are you waiting for?" Brainard snarled. "An engraved invitation? Wait a few more minutes and I'm sure the jungle'll send you one. Just the way it did to Bozman."

The torpedoman blinked. He looked around for the dead man's pack. His limbs moved as if he were heavily drugged.

"Now!" Brainard said.

Leaf shook himself like a swimmer emerging from a pool. He bent over, still keeping one hand in contact with the officer-trainee. He groped for Wilding's makeshift crutch with the other.

Wheelwright helped Caffey rummage through Bozman's pack. They threw out the food packets and passed rifle magazines and chunks of barakite to the living personnel. Newton shrugged into his load with the stolid willingness of an ox.

"It's not far to the top, now," Brainard said.

True enough in terms of feet and inches, but the words sounded as flat in Brainard's own ears as they must in those of his subordinates. The peak was very possibly a lifetime away.

"*Stop . . .*" OT Wilding moaned.

Brainard helped Leaf fit the rifle butt into Wilding's hand. They had to wrap the injured man's fingers around the plastic for a moment until he could grip of his own accord.

"Don't worry, Hal," Brainard said. "We're not going to stop."

AUGUST 1, 381 AS. 1747 HOURS.

Officer-Trainee Brainard stared impassively toward the wall behind the table where the members of the Board of Review sat.

The Board was held in a lecture room with full holographic capability. The President of the Board, Captain Glenn, was the Officer in Charge of Screening Forces. He had set the rear-wall projectors to run a reconstruction of the previous week's battle, in which his units had wiped out the Seatiger ambush and set up the Herd's lopsided victory over the Seatiger main body.

Brainard's left arm was bandaged to the shoulder. He wasn't taking in the computer-generated images of heroic battle on the wall toward which his eyes were turned. His mind was too full of remembered terror.

"Though there's no further evidence—" Captain Glenn said.

Lieutenant Cabot Holman started to rise. He sat in the front row—but at the edge of the hall, as far as he could get from OT Brainard's seat in the center.

"Though as I say, there's no further *evidence,*" Glenn continued heavily, "the Board has agreed to recognize Lieutenant Holman for a few remarks. Lieutenant?"

Captain Glenn was bandaged also. Behind the Board, a hologram of the cruiser *Mouflon,* Glenn's flagship, ripped the night with bottle-shaped yellow flashes from her 8-inch guns. The *Mouflon*'s superstructure glittered: first with the white sparks of a Seatiger salvo hitting home, then burps of red flame as shells went off within the cruiser's armor.

Glenn was boastful, and he was rumored to have unpleasant sexual tastes; but he had paid his dues.

Cabot Holman saluted the Board, then turned to eye the audience. There were only thirty or thirty-five men within a hall that could have held ten times the number, but thousands of others watched the proceedings in hologram from their quarters.

"You all know what I'm here to say," Holman said. He stared at OT Brainard. Brainard did not turn his head—toward the glare or away from it, though he felt the pressure of Holman's eyes. "You all know what I'm saying is *true.*"

Glenn grimaced. The other Board members were Lieutenant Dabney, from the hydrofoil squadron, and Commander Peewhit, captain of the dreadnought *Buffalo.* Dabney looked at Peewhit. Peewhit, nodding, said, "The Board will be obliged if you just say your piece, then, Lieutenant."

Holman jerked his chin and faced the Board. "Yes sir," he said, clipping the syllables. "The critical incident of last week's victory occurred when Air-Cushion Torpedo boat K44 blew up a Seatiger destroyer-leader, the *Wiesel.* That proved the Seatigers had divided their fleet to stage an ambush, and so permitted our forces to defeat the enemy in detail."

Either a director or unlikely chance set the holographic display to the portion of the battle which Holman described. A close-up of the *Wiesel* filled the back wall. The patrolling hovercraft had caught its target at the most inauspicious time possible. The destroyer-leader was entering the archipelago's main channel from a shallow cross-channel barely twice the vessel's own width. The *Wiesel* could not turn to comb the torpedo tracks.

But she could shoot. The hologram erupted with salvoes from both triple turrets and from the dozens of multi-barreled automatic weapons on the destroyer-leader's port side.

Brainard found the image eerily unreal. There had been nothing so crisply visible on the morning of July 24; only smoke and glare and the stench of feces oozing from Lieutenant Tonello's bullet-ripped environmental suit.

"K44 drove in to close range to be sure of her kill," Holman said forcefully. "But she had to go it alone!"

The computer-generated hologram illustrated his words. Hovercraft K44, occasionally masked by crisp, ideally cylindrical waterspouts, drove through the maelstrom from the left foreground.

K44 cut away to the right, pursued by flashing lines of explosive bullets. The computer drew glowing tracks to indicate the hovercraft's torpedoes jinking to negate the *Wiesel*'s attempt to maneuver. There was no attempt to follow K44 trying vainly to escape.

Nothing was known of K44's end. The computer could have supplied the single bright flash of a shell, killing the hovercraft's crew instantly at the moment of victory. But—

All the small-craft men in the audience knew that something more lingering was also the more probable: a bullet-shattered hull sinking slowly in black water, while wounded men screamed and their blood drew the sea's fanged harvesters.

Better to show nothing. . . .

"If K67 had supported Ted—" Holman continued.

He caught himself, swallowed, and resumed, "If K67

had supported K44, the pair of targets might have confused the *Wiesel*'s gunners so that they both escaped."

He pointed at Brainard. "Instead, this *trainee*—" Holman's voice made the word a curse "—turned tail and ran, leaving m—k-K44 to take all the fire herself. This *coward* left my brother to die!"

The holographic destroyer-leader expanded into an orange fireball. The glare mounted until its reflection from the cloud layer lighted the night for ten miles in every direction. It was the perfect beacon to summon the Herd's strength against an ambushing squadron that was to have struck from the flank unawares.

But again, the image was too perfect to mesh with Brainard's memory. In his mind's eye:

Objects were outlined against the yellow-orange mushroom. A gun tub. Twenty square yards of decking which fluttered like a bat's wings. A spread-eagled man who burst into flame at the top of his arc and tumbled toward the sea as a human torch. . . .

"Lieutenant Holman," said Captain Glenn, "I promised you an opportunity to speak your mind. I appreciate your personal loss, but—"

Glenn's voice thinned. After the battle, the medics had taken a shell-splinter three inches long from Glenn's shoulder. Its jagged tip had been deep in the bone. His temper, never mild, had stretched as far as it was going to go with the need to show understanding for a junior lieutenant.

"—the Board *will* confer now and determine its findings."

Holman sat down abruptly. He flushed with anger.

"I don't think we need to adjourn, do we?" said Commander Peewhit. "I have an O-Group scheduled aboard the *Buffalo* at nineteen hundred that I'd like to get to."

Captain Glenn glared at the hall. Holman bit his lips but said nothing.

"No," said Glenn. "We'll just talk here for a moment."

The members of the Board of Review slid their chairs into a trefoil. A privacy screen sprang up around them to distort the passage of light and sound waves. Their figures were ghost images on the other side of a gray discontinuity.

The audience began to whisper among itself. Most of those present in the hall had some connection with the proceedings. The other surviving members of K67's crew formed a tight group two rows behind Brainard.

Cabot Holman stared at the officer-trainee with the fixity of a weasel for a rabbit. Brainard looked toward the computer panorama. His mind sorted through disconnected images, all of them terrifying.

The privacy screen dissolved. The Board members faced around. Dabney stifled a yawn. Glenn tried to scratch his bandaged shoulderblade with his good hand, but he couldn't stretch far enough.

"Right," said Glenn, glaring at the audience again.

The wall behind Glenn showed an overhead view of the Gehenna Archipelago as Herd vessels concentrated their fire against the hopelessly outnumbered ambush squadron. Glenn's screening forces were supported by a squadron of dreadnoughts. Every time a Seatiger ship was spotted or revealed itself by firing, salvoes of 18-inch shells blew the victim to scrap.

The holographic screen went gray.

"The Board has reviewed the actions of the officers and men of torpedo boat K67, patrolling against the Seatigers the morning of July 23," said Captain Glenn. "We find the salient points to be as follows."

The face of Tech 2 Leaf appeared on the back wall. The

motorman looked even more pugnacious when his features were expanded to the size of monumental sculpture. Leaf had given his evidence with a brutal directness that suggested he was willing to beat the hell out of anybody who doubted him.

"The crew of K67 believed their vessel was making its torpedo run alone," said Captain Glenn.

Leaf's holographic image said, "The target's automatics opened up—that's before the main guns fired. Right then I seen K44 pop all four of her decoys and sheer to port. I had a good place to see 'cause I was checkin' Fan Three and Holman, his boat was on our port quarter."

Leaf's image looked aside. Brainard had expected the motorman to spit, even here in front of the Board of Review. It had probably been a near thing.

Not quite. Leaf stared at the hologram pick-up and said, "I figured they'd cut 'n' run back up the channel we just came out of. I still figure that."

Glenn or a separate director blanked the holographic screen again. The captain resumed, "At the point Officer-Trainee Brainard broke off the action, K67 had received heavy damage."

This time the holographic screen was split. The face of Tech 2 Caffey gave evidence on the left side, while a damage assessment record made after K67 limped back aboard her tender showed to the right.

"I'd got my fish," Caffey said. The torpedoman was a slicker operator than Leaf, but recent memories gave his testimony a punchy credibility Caffey did not always command. "I was tracking. Then *bam!* The console was gone, just gone. Three explosive shells hit it."

The damage-assessment camera tracked over the torpedo station. Wires dangled from the dual-tracking console. What was left of the faceplate lay on the deck, distorted by electrical fires which followed the shell bursts. Blood spattered the deck and bulkheads.

"Wheelwright was hit," said Caffey's image. The torpedoman was trying very hard to sound calm. "He's my striker. Shrapnel in his legs, but he'd fallen down and I thought it was pretty bad. The interphone was out, and my suit lost its air. Turned out the hose was cut. I didn't know."

The other camera shifted aft from the torpedo station. There was a gap on the stern rail so empty that Brainard had to think to remember what should have been in that place.

"A salvo came in, then," the torpedoman continued. "Main gun. I swear I thought they was firing eighteens."

He forced a smile, but the magnified image showed sweat beading at the line of Caffey's close-cropped hair. "Right overhead. There's a flash, just a flash, and the balloon rig's gone. A shell hit it, but it didn't go off till it hit the sea. That's why we're any of us here. They was using armor-piercing shells with time-delay fuzes, so the one that hit us didn't go off till it was in the sea."

The damage-assessment picture switched to a general port-side view of K67. There were more than thirty thumb-sized dimples in the hovercraft's skirts. Each of the explosive bullets had further gashed the flexible fabric with stars of shrapnel around the black central hole.

"I shouted to the cockpit then," Caffey said. "I said, 'Get us the fuck out of here.' I don't know if they could hear me with the interphone shot away. Anyhow, I thought they was all dead."

He took a deep breath. The other camera steadied on the cockpit. Seventeen holes showed in the port-side bulkhead. Only a glittering memory of the shatterproof windscreen clung to its frame.

How did they miss me? Brainard thought. Then he thought, *Why?*

"I felt her take the helm," said the torpedoman's sweating image. "And I prayed to God, because I didn't think anybody else could bring us outa that one. But I was wrong. Mr Brainard could. Mr Brainard brought us out."

The holograms froze, but whoever was directing the display let them hang in the air for several seconds after Caffey ended his testimony.

Captain Glenn cleared his throat. The images vanished into a gray backdrop.

"The findings of the Board are as follows," Glenn said. He glared at the room. "The crew of torpedo craft K67 reasonably believed themselves to be in action alone. The only evidence that their consort did *not* withdraw when the patrol came under heavy fire—"

The captain nodded appreciatively to Lieutenant Cabot Holman.

"—is that the *Wiesel* was destroyed after K67's own torpedo-guidance apparatus had been put out of action. All honor to Ensign Edward Holman and his crew, who attacked from an unexpected angle while the target concentrated its fire on K67."

The change in Captain Glenn's voice as he continued was as slight as the click of a pistol's hammer rising to the half-cock notch. "The first duty of the patrolling hovercraft after they had released their weapons was to report the existence of the Seatiger ambush. Indeed—"

The screen commander's face hardened still further.

"—one might say the duty to report was *more* important than any potential effect four torpedoes could have on the enemy—"

Glenn's visage cleared. "But in any case, Lieutenant Tonello lived and died by his decision, and we do not choose to second-guess him now. When Officer-Trainee Brainard took command, he extricated his vessel from a difficult situation and withdrew at the best possible speed to give his report—in person, since K67's laser communicator had been rendered inoperative by battle damage."

The two junior members of the Board of Review watched Brainard with alert, open faces. Brainard stared past them, toward a wall as gray as his soul.

"Mr Brainard, will you stand?" said Glenn.

Brainard wasn't sure his legs would obey, but they did.

"Our recommendation, therefore, is as follows," the captain said: "That Officer-Trainee Brainard be commended for his actions on the night of July 22–23. That Officer-Trainee Brainard be granted a meritorious promotion to the rank of ensign."

Glenn surveyed the hall. "Lastly, that Ensign Brainard be confirmed in command of Air-Cushion Torpedo boat K67 as soon as he has recovered from the injuries he received in action against the enemy."

The audience unexpectedly dissolved into cheers.

Brainard blinked. His skin crawled with hot needles. Men pounded him on the back. The three members of the Board were coming around their table with arms out to shake Brainard's hand.

Across the bobbing faces Brainard saw the glaring eyes of Lieutenant Cabot Holman—the only other man in the hall who knew, as Brainard knew, that Brainard was a coward who had fled from battle with no thought in his mind but of escape.

13

May 18, 382 AS. 0615 hours.

Caffey crushed a three-inch ant against the bark of the cypress with the muzzle of his machine-gun. The insect's needle-sharp mandibles clicked against the muzzle brake, but chitin could not scar the corrosion-proofed steel.

When Caffey lifted the gun, the ant—still thrashing and alive—dropped almost onto Leaf as he squatted.

"You bastard!" the motorman shouted.

He jerked backward, trying to free his hands so that he could grab his multitool. He'd been kneading a lump of barakite into a ribbon, since K67 didn't carry det cord and they needed something to connect nodes of explosive.

The ant twisted toward the motion. Dying or healthy, the insect's only imperative was to attack whatever threatened the colony's tree. Leaf wasn't a member of the colony: that was all that the ant's instincts required in the way of threat definition.

"Are you all right there?" Ensign Brainard called. "Leaf?"

Leaf slapped the wad of barakite over the squirming insect and squeezed the stiff explosive into a trough in the cypress's bark.

"No problem," Caffey shouted back. "We're fine."

"Just watch what you're fucking doing!" Leaf growled in a low voice.

The two senior enlisted men worked while the remainder of K67's crew guarded them and one another from attack. Leaf squatted among the cypress's gnarled roots. He couldn't see any of the others except the torpedoman.

Like working in a fan nacelle during combat. The job required all your attention, but you knew your life depended on decisions made by people hidden from you. . . .

Another ant jogged swiftly down the trunk toward him. Leaf pulled his multitool down and locked the take-up spool so that the lanyard hung in the extended position.

The island's peak was dominated by a cypress tree over three hundred feet in girth. OT Wilding had mumbled that the monster probably combined the trunks of up to a dozen individual trees which had grown together. The gigantic result had crushed all lesser vegetation in the neighborhood. Its mighty bole added several hundred feet to the island's thousand-foot elevation.

Leaf's present job was to knock the cypress down.

The ant trotted closer, drawn by scent and movement. Leaf held his multitool out. The ant slashed at it. Leaf pressed the stud. The welding arc popped the insect with a stench of formic acid.

"Goddam!" Caffey shouted. "What're you trying to do, kill us both? What if the barakite had lighted, huh?"

"Shut up and gimme some more of it," Leaf said.

The motorman was dizzy with muscle strain and lack of sleep. There was a rash around the collar of his tunic; the others said it was bright red. The rash itched spasmodically, burning like a ring of fire at the random times something set it off. Leaf's limbs were crisscrossed by grass cuts, some of them poisoned and all of them festering.

He had to keep going with the explosive, because if he stopped for more than a moment, he was going to tear Caffey's throat out.

The torpedoman handed Leaf a wad of barakite, then looked into the knapsack from which it had come. "Not much left," he said.

Leaf grunted. He began to form the explosive into a rope. His hands, particularly the muscles at the base of his thumbs, ached with the effort.

Brainard had led the survivors as high as the ridge would take them. In order to send a laser message, they either had to climb the tree to the top of the canopy—or create a gap where it stood.

"Hang on," the torpedoman muttered. "I'm going to shoot 'em."

"Huh?" said Leaf.

WHAM!

"You fuckin' idiot!" the motorman screamed. He grabbed for Caffey with his left hand. The cutting blade winked from the multitool in his right.

His legs cramped. He fell back as the torpedoman skipped away.

"What is it?" Brainard demanded. His disembodied voice was as harshly emotionless as life in this surface wilderness.

"We're okay," Caffey shouted back. In a lower voice, he snarled, "Look, I *said* what I was gonna do. Fuck off, will you?"

Leaf looked up at the tree trunk. The gun's muzzle blast had driven fragments of three ants into the soft bark. The bullet scar was a white-cored russet dimple in the striated gray surface.

It had been a fucking stupid thing to do.

Leaf opened his mouth to snarl at the torpedoman. Light streaming through the cypress leaves illuminated Caffey.

The torpedoman's bare skin was blotched with sores. He was allergic to insect bites, and the first-aid cream did him no more good than it did Leaf's own rash. The hard weight of the machine-gun had broken the skin over Caffey's shoulder blades on both sides. The wounds oozed in an atmosphere purulent with fungus spores. His staring eyes were red with pain and fear.

Leaf shivered.

"Don't do it again, huh?" he said. He worked one end of the strand of barakite into the glob of explosive containing the ant. That was the present terminus of the daisy chain he was weaving as far around the tree's circumference as possible.

Climbing a tree was suicide. This particular monster was guarded by the ants which ate fleshy berries the cypress grew for the insects' sustenance. The ants in turn patrolled the vast expanse of bark and foliage, slaughtering interlopers with a catholic abandon.

No life form on the planet could survive the attack of up to ten thousand acid-tipped mandibles. Leaf and Caffey were at risk even on the ground, where they could move easily. Fifty feet up the trunk, with hands and feet constrained and gravity ready to strike the finishing blow, risk became the certainty of death.

The other option was to blow the tree down. That was emotionally satisfying as well as practical.

Leaf waddled two yards further around the trunk, pulling his thin strand of barakite with him. Though the bark had a smooth, glossy tinge, the explosive clung in an adequate fashion to fibrous irregularities in the surface.

"More," the motorman ordered, holding out his left hand. Undergrowth brushed his shoulder, then the back of his neck. Tiny hooks bit in; Leaf's rash flared incandescently. He turned and slashed in fury with the short blade of his multitool.

Caffey waited for the spasm to pass before he dropped a wad of barakite into the motorman's palm. "Just two besides this," he said. "And the one you've got in your pack."

Leaf pressed the barakite against the trunk in contact with the ribbon he had just laid there. "More," he said, and another doughy wad dropped into his hand.

The torpedoman crushed an ant to the bark with his gun muzzle. While the metal held the insect's head, Caffey reached over with his left hand and gripped one of its flailing legs. He moved with care worthy of a man handling white phosphorous.

When Caffey was sure he had the leg, he lifted the gun barrel and flicked the ant over his shoulder. It pattered into the undergrowth.

"Jeez!" Newton shouted from the direction in which the ant had flown.

Leaf and Caffey giggled hysterically.

There was a deep cleft in the cypress's roots. The motorman had to stretch in order to step across it. He continued to feed out the ribbon of barakite.

K67's crew carried about a hundred pounds of barakite among them. They couldn't blow the gigantic cypress *up* with that amount of explosive, but with luck they could knock it down. Leaf and Caffey spaced the charges along one arc of the circumference. When the barakite detonated, it would shatter the tree's root structure and push the trunk toward the steep drop-off on the north side of the ridge.

If the explosive push was hard enough, the toppling cypress would clear a line of sight to the navigational beacon-transponder in the center of Adonis Deep. If the blast didn't topple the tree—

"More," said Leaf, holding out his hand.

—the officers would figure something else out.

Caffey fired a three-second burst from his machine-gun, emptying the ammunition drum.

"You fucking—"

And then the motorman saw the land crab which had rushed from the cleft in the roots, kicked half-way back by the stream of bullets. Its armor was a deep blue-green. The claw which Caffey shot off was the length of Leaf's forearm. It would have severed the motorman's leg had the pincers closed as they had started to do.

"Technician Caffey, report!" Brainard ordered in a voice made tinny by the ringing in Leaf's ears.

"S'okay, sir, we're golden," Caffey shouted.

His face was white. His fingers fumbled as they replaced the empty magazine with a loaded drum.

"Sorry, Fish," Leaf muttered.

The torpedoman had dropped his knapsack. Leaf reached into it and removed the last wad of barakite. He pressed the explosive into the portion already in place instead of stretching it over another yard or two of circumference.

"Now," said the motorman, "let's get the fuck outa this place."

November 12, 378 AS. 1027 hours.

Seaman Mooker sat cross-legged on the upper bunk of the two-man room, wrapped in a sheet like a barbaric chieftain. His glittering eyes did not quiver when the two junior noncoms entered the room.

A tribal chant thundered from the recorder lying on top of one of the lockers. The volume was so high that the barracks' massive walls had become a sounding board. The noise was noticeable in the courtyard and deafening in the corridor; in the room itself, you couldn't hear yourself think.

Several one-shot drug injectors lay on floor. They were empty.

Tech 3 Leaf stepped quickly to the locker and switched the recorder off. The silence was a blow.

"You bastard," Tech 3 Caffey growled. " 'Come help me get one of my watch up for fatigue duty,' you say. You didn't tell me he was stoned!"

"Hey, Mookie," Leaf offered cautiously. "We come to help you."

The seaman sat like a statue. Leaf looked at Caffey and muttered, "C'mon, you know Mooker as well as I do. You figured he overslept?"

Caffey grimaced and toed one of the injectors. It was unmarked, so there was no way to guess what Mooker had been using.

"Suppose that's all he's got?" Caffey asked. Leaf shrugged.

The noncoms moved in silent coordination to either end of the bunk. Its height was a problem. "Hey, Mookie," Leaf wheedled. "How you feelin', man?"

Mooker turned his head toward Leaf slowly, as though he were learning a complex skill. His eyes did not focus.

Caffey's hand slid out with the speed and grace of a cat killing.

"*Got*cha!" he said with satisfaction. He flashed Leaf a peek at the trio of unused drug injectors he'd just palmed from the mattress. He slipped them into a side pocket of his tunic.

"Okay," said Leaf, "but how do we sober him up? If an officer sees him, he's fucked."

"*We're* fucked if we don't report this," Caffey grumbled. "Look, Koslowski's running the clinic this morning, and he owes me one. If we—"

"*No!*" Seaman Mooker screamed. "*No!*"

Mooker tried to stand up. His head slammed the ceiling hard enough to stun a shark. He flopped back onto the mattress.

"Now!" said Leaf as he grabbed the seaman's right ankle.

Caffey had Mooker's left wrist. Mooker's right hand came out of the tangled bedding with a powered cutting bar.

The noncoms sprang in opposite directions. Mooker swung the bar at Leaf, but the assistant motorman was already clear. The saw-edged blade struck the bed post and whined as it whacked through the tough plastic without slowing.

A few drops of blood speckled the wall. Mooker had managed to clip the end of his own big toe.

The seaman giggled. He leaped from the bed, spinning and cutting at the air. He had left the bedding behind. Contractions ran across his nude body, sharply defining alternate groups of muscles.

Mooker's skin shone with sweat although the room's environmental system was working normally. Leaf and Caffey backed as far away as they could get in the small room.

The seaman stood against the door, drawing disjointed patterns with the cutting bar. One swipe struck the corner of a locker. The blade caught momentarily. Leaf tensed, but Mooker dragged the weapon clear with a convulsive effort. He waggled it toward the noncom.

Caffey fumbled in his tunic pocket.

The seaman stared fixedly at him. The cutting bar nodded. Its blunt tip was less than a yard from the torpedoman's face.

Mooker slashed behind himself without looking around.

Leaf dodged back, barely in time. He was sweating also.

"Hey, Leaf," said Caffey. He was balancing a drug injector on his thumb. "You want one a these?"

The seaman froze. Behind Mooker's back, Leaf reached to his own collar and ripped off one of the rank insignia studs.

Caffey flipped the drug injector. The cone of gray plastic wobbled over Mooker's head. Leaf caught and palmed it as the seaman turned.

"Give me . . . ," Mooker demanded in a voice that would have sounded unexpectedly bestial even coming from a wolverine. He raised the cutting bar. Blood from his severed toe pooled on the floor around him.

"Sure, Mookie," Leaf said. He flicked his rank insignia onto the upper bunk.

Mooker trembled like a drive motor lugging. Caffey's mouth opened to scream, but at the last instant the seaman leaped for the bed.

Leaf snatched the door open. Both noncoms slipped into the corridor and slammed the door behind them.

The thunderous music resumed almost at once.

"My God," Leaf groaned. His eyes were closed. "My God, I didn't think. . . ."

"Shit," said Caffey. "No choice but the Shore Police now—omigod!"

Lieutenant-Commander Congreve strode down the corridor to them. He wore a dress uniform; his saucer hat was adjusted perfectly to the required tilt.

"What in the *hell* is going on here?" Congreve demanded. He did not so much shout as raise his cold voice to be heard over the chant booming from Mooker's billet.

Leaf and Caffey snapped to attention. Leaf hoped the other noncom could think of a way to explain—

But Congreve didn't want explanations, he wanted victims. There were a lot of officers like that. . . .

"You! Leaf!" Congreve said. "Open your hands."

"Sir, it's not—" Leaf said as he obeyed. The unused injector dropped to the floor.

Congreve glared at him. "The first thing you can do is take off the *other* rank stud, Seaman Leaf," he said. "You won't be needing it for a long time—if ever. Now, just what is going on here?"

Leaf swallowed. He was braced so stiffly that he was becoming dizzy, as though being rigid would protect him from what was happening.

"Ah, sir," said Caffey. "It's just, you know, a little party."

The lieutenant-commander's face went red, then white. He stared at the name tape on Caffey's tunic. "Well," he said in a voice of dangerous calm, "we'll just see about that."

Congreve pushed open the door of the billet and said, "All right, stand at—"

The scream and the whine of the cutting bar played a descant to the rumbling bass line from the recorder.

Leaf pulled the door closed. "Let's get the fuck outa here," he said.

May 18, 382 AS. 0622 hours.

Filters of cyan, magenta, and yellow shifted across Wilding's vision with every beat of his heart. After hundreds of repetitions, the colors locked suddenly into a polychrome whole. The officer-trainee watched Ensign Brainard take a grenade out of his tunic pocket.

A pair of grenades had turned up when Wilding searched K67's ammunition locker. Nobody'd remembered why they were aboard. Maybe to discourage sea life, maybe because somebody had had the notion they'd be useful if the hovercraft's crew had to board another vessel—a vanishingly improbable event.

But the survivors needed them now.

Brainard grimaced, tossing the grenade an inch or two on his palm to judge its heft. He stepped toward the giant cedar. Caffey and Leaf fell in beside him. They were trying to look in all directions at once.

"I said, 'Get to cover,' " the ensign ordered harshly.

The torpedoman opened his mouth to protest.

"I'll have five seconds after I pull this," Brainard said.

His finger tapped the grenade's safety pin. "I don't intend to spend it tripping over you two. *Get* to cover."

"Yessir," said Leaf. He touched the back of Caffey's hand on the machine-gun grip. Both noncoms shuffled past the roots of the fallen log in whose shelter the remainder of the crew waited.

Brainard disappeared into the sucking undergrowth.

K67's commanding officer was the only reason most of the hovercraft's crew was still alive. Brainard's absolute courage—and his coldly reasoned certainty when anyone else would have been in a blind panic—kept them all going.

"Jeez, I hope this works," Wheelwright muttered.

His hands squeezed the grip and fore-end of his rifle so fiercely that his knuckles were blotched. A grub poked its three-inch head through the bark of the fallen tree and rotated toward the young sailor. "I want to get outa here so bad."

Barakite was extremely stable under most conditions. A bullet impact would only splash a crater in the doughy explosive. Flame would ignite it; but a fire, although intense, would not topple the giant cypress.

To do that, they needed to detonate the barakite—and K67 hadn't carried blasting caps. A grenade placed directly against the explosive *might* provide the necessary combination of heat and shock to set off the daisy-chain.

The part of Wilding's mind which was not dissociated by pain and fever prayed that it would.

Caffey crushed the grub with the butt of his machine-gun as he slid in beside his striker. "Hell, we got this far, didn't we?" he said. "Now we just sit for an hour or two and let somebody else do all the work."

The log had been the trunk of an ebony ten feet in

diameter—a large tree by any standards short of those which included the dominant cypress. Branches of the ebony and cypress had battled for sunlight. Slowly but inexorably, the cypress had levered its rival sideways. Finally, aided by a squall, the giant had ripped the ebony's roots from the soil and toppled it in splendid ruin.

The dense log was fresh enough to cover the humans as they avenged the ebony's murder.

"Fire in the hole!" Brainard shouted. Foliage muffled his voice and the crashing progress of his run for cover.

Wilding drifted again through pallid filters. Images of Brainard with the grenade merged with his memories of the Board of Review. Then Brainard was an officer-trainee like Wilding, younger by a few years and with only a few more months of service in the Herd.

Wilding watched in awe. Brainard never boasted, never grew defensive. He answered questions with such simple precision that it was only in the words of his crewmen that Brainard's icy heroism became apparent.

Wilding had never met a man like that in twenty-five years of living as a prince in Wyoming Keep. As clearly as an epiphany, Wilding knew that he must beg or bribe his way into the executive officer slot aboard Brainard's vessel. That way even Prince Hal might be able to learn the traits of manhood. . . .

A flatworm, mottled and a yard long, rose from the leaf mold as Brainard dodged past the ebony's root ball. The worm fastened momentarily to the laser communicator strapped to the ensign's chest.

Leaf shouted in fury. Brainard crushed the creature against him with a swipe of his rifle butt. It fell writhing. Brainard flung himself down beside the others.

White light flashed across the underside of the leaves.

An instant later, the sharp crash of the explosion shocked the jungle to silence.

"Thank God . . ." Caffey murmured.

The blast was over in the split second of a lightning bolt. The following roar seemed to take forever. Over a hundred thousand tons of wood toppled down the island's north slope, carrying all before it.

"Yippee!" cried Newton. He jumped to his feet. Brainard grabbed the coxswain's belt. Newton was too strong for one man to bring down, but Brainard clung for a moment until Leaf and Caffey added their weight.

Newton slammed to the ground with a curse. Dirt, rocks, and chunks of vegetation kicked skyward by the explosion broke like a storm over the humans.

The sudden destruction drove the jungle berserk. Images printed across Wilding's fever in a surreal montage:

A phalanx of three-yard-long katydids crashed through the undergrowth. The flightless insects ran on four legs and scraped the middle pair deafeningly against their modified wing cases.

Caustic green liquid slurped from the hollow core of a cottonwood, then siphoned back into its hiding place. It left smoldering scars across the bark as it withdrew.

A thirty-foot serpent with eyes like fire opals plunged from high in the canopy. As the snake fell, it twisted to strike repeatedly at its own red-banded body.

A hundred other tragedies glimpsed simultaneously. Thousands more hidden in the massive chaos.

The rain of debris pattered to a halt. The noise of the falling tree continued. Ensign Brainard got to his feet and shambled forward. The able-bodied members of the crew followed . . . and Officer-Trainee Wilding rose as well.

The pain in his ankle no longer registered. Wilding

drifted on a cloud as pink as sunset. When he rounded the roots of the fallen ebony, the air was thick with the odors of barakite and pulverized dirt.

The explosion had not been enough to destroy the gigantic cypress, but it had caused the tree to destroy itself. Despite its thick trunk, the cypress was as carefully poised as a skyscraper. The blast shattered the support structures on one side while giving the enormous mass a violent shove in the opposite direction.

Gravity did the rest. When the cypress overbalanced, it ripped out the remainder of its roots and slid two thousand feet down an angle-of-repose slope into the bay beneath. The air above the track was gray with dust, pulverized life, and creatures leaping and swooping to gain advantage in the sudden no-man's-land.

The water boiled where cypress branches thrust into the shallows. Sea life was quick to accept the bounty which chance had thrust into its jaws.

"Move," Wilding whispered. "Move. . . ."

Every time Wilding's right foot touched the ground, the world became sepia-toned. Full color returned when he took his weight on his left leg and the makeshift crutch. Still he felt no pain.

The cypress, like most trees growing in thin jungle soils, had wrapped its roots across the surface instead of driving them deep into rock that was bare of nourishment. Even so, the giant took a great bite of ridge line along when it fell. Boulders shook free of the roots which gripped them and bounded in separate arcs through the jungle. The crew of K67 skirted the left side of the crater.

"Hey!" somebody cried. Wilding heard the crewmen's voices shifted up several octaves, by fever or by the ear-punishing blast. "There's a boat down there!"

At first glance, Wilding's heart leaped with hope that gilded what he saw. He shifted the magnifying function of his helmet visor to x20 and looked again.

It was still a boat, a hovercraft. But there was no hope at all.

The vessel was beached—almost beached—several hundred feet west of the seething ruin which the cypress had torn to the bay. It rode very low. Its skirts had grounded where the water off the shelving beach was still three feet deep, and the crew had been unable or unwilling to bring their craft ashore.

Instead, the shore had come to them.

Honeysuckle ruled the low ground behind the belt of salt-drenched sand on this side of the island. The foliage moved softly, turning toward the opportunity provided by the cypress's clearing operation. A bridge of vines was arched across the sand to the hovercraft.

The vessel appeared undamaged to the naked eye. Magnification showed that honeysuckle covered all the plastic surfaces in a thin mat. The leaves were brown and shrunken. The colonizing vine had become dormant while it awaited further sustenance.

"Sir, did they come for us?" squealed a foolish, hopeful voice. "Are they going to pick us up?"

Dust settled along the track of the cypress. The flailing roots had dragged torn-up material along, depositing it in a series of clumps and valleys like an oscilloscope pattern. Because the slope still vibrated with the tree's impact, the mounds continued to settle.

Something moved near the bottom of the track. It was big enough to be a shifting mass of vegetation, but it was coming uphill.

"Caffey, set up a tight perimeter," squeaked Ensign

Brainard. "We're in the open here, and that's not entirely good. Leaf—"

Wilding stepped closer to the edge. His helmet enhanced as well as magnifying the image. Mimosa fronds waved in the middle of the slope, but Wilding could not see what was beyond them.

No herbivore was likely to be racing to inspect the site of an explosion.

The ridge dropped sharply for a hundred feet, then splayed outward in a marshy knob where water seeped through a fold in rock layers. The cypress had hung there for a moment. When it continued its long slide to the sea, the tree had scraped the knob to mud.

Two hundred feet below the smear of flattened marsh, a pile of broken alders shuddered. A forked, black-and-yellow tongue, as long as a man was high, flicked over the wrack to sample the air.

"Get back!" Wilding screamed. His own voice was only the upper sideband of human speech. "Run! Something's coming!"

The head of a monitor lizard, the dominant land predator of the planet, twisted over the alders. The pile of debris scattered beneath the monster's eight-ton weight. Its tongue continued to slip in and out like light quivering over a swordblade.

Wilding stared into the lizard's magnified jaws. The cone-shaped teeth were six inches long, and the yellow gullet was large enough to swallow a man whole.

"Get back!" he screamed, but this time he was speaking to himself. The soil gave way beneath his left foot; his right held for a moment. When his right ankle buckled, the officer-trainee began to float effortlessly, through the air—

Down toward the fifty-foot lizard.

JULY 23, 381 AS. 0344 HOURS.

Officer-Trainee Wilding heard the shells howl.

The sound was more penetrating than the crash of the *Mouflon*'s main batteries or even the drumming bass note of 1-inch Gatlings trying to claw the incoming out of the air before it hit the cruiser.

He looked up from his console, trying instinctively to see through the armored ceiling. His mouth was open.

Two Seatiger shells burst in the storm of fire from the automatic weapons. The other four slammed into the *Mouflon*'s bridge and forward hull.

There was a green flash. All the lights went out. Wilding felt his buttocks lift from his chair. He had no sense of direction. The air smelled burned, and the shock waves of the blast were so severe that he felt them as pressure, not as noise.

Wilding hit his chair again. The emergency lights went on, yellow strips set into the deck and ceiling moldings. Wilding's console hummed and flickered as it re-created the display after the power interrupt.

Blue tungsten-sulphide letters on the margin of the display switched from BACK-UP to PRIMARY.

The regular gunnery officer, a senior lieutenant, sprawled at the console beside Wilding's. His face wore a surprised expression. One of the shell impacts had flexed the armored ceiling enough to spall fragments across the bridge. A saucer-sized disk had whacked through the lieutenant's neck, then sawed his workstation into sparkling ruin.

Wilding was now gunnery officer for the *Mouflon*'s starboard automatic weapons, though computers would fire the weapons unless Wilding chose to override their electronic decisions.

The *Mouflon* rippled off a salvo from her twelve 8-inch guns. Her hull twisted like a snake from the recoil stresses.

Captain Glenn got to his feet. His left shoulder was bleeding. His good hand pawed aimlessly.

Glenn's eyes focused. He looked down at the deck, picked up his commo helmet, and slapped it back in place over his short-cropped hair. "Damage report," he ordered harshly.

"Hull nominal," said Collor, the *Mouflon*'s executive officer. "Main battery nominal. Fires in three forward compartments, controllable at present." Collor looked up from his holographic display. In the same dry voice as before, he concluded, "Thirty percent damage to bridge command-and-control installations, but back-up systems are in place."

Shock had unbonded a ten-foot swath of sound-deadening foam from the ceiling. Damage-control personnel sawed at the fallen blanket to get it out of the way.

The foam was dense and twelve inches thick. It was supposed to be able to trap spalled fragments. It hadn't done its job well enough for Wilding's immediate superior. . . .

The *Mouflon* writhed with another outgoing salvo. Burning propellant expanded the gun breeches; they rang like huge bells.

Wilding's console indicated that no further Seatiger shells were in the air. The Gatlings were silent for want of targets.

Wilding's mouth was dry. He made an effort of will to close it. For a moment, he couldn't remember why he sat so rigidly in his chair. He was afraid that if he tried to move, his head would slip from his shoulders and bounce to the console, the way the lieutenant's had done. . . .

"Sir," said the lieutenant-commander in charge of communications. He reached over with the sheet of hard copy which his console had just run off.

Captain Glenn bent to take the flimsy. "Wait!" chirped the medic cutting away the back of Glenn's jacket. Glenn shouted a curse, reacting to the pain of the forgotten wound rather than the medic's order.

"First bloody time I wore this uniform," Glenn muttered as he snatched the print-out with his right hand. "*First* bloody time."

The eight-inch guns salvoed again. Each tube fired a half-second behind its predecessor. The firing sequence spaced the shockwaves and avoided a simultaneous recoil which would do more damage to the *Mouflon* than an enemy shell.

Wilding's mind rang with the scream the lieutenant had died too quickly to utter.

"Right," said Glenn. He keyed his commo helmet with his right hand, still holding the scrap of hard copy. "Cease fire," he ordered. His voice boomed from the bridge tannoy and echoed through every compartment of the cruiser.

"All Root elements," the captain continued. "Change course to one-one-two degrees and proceed at flank speed."

Wilding was fifteen feet away from the communications console. The red tinge of the characters flickering there indicated the *Mouflon* was now broadcasting to all the screening vessels—code-name Root.

Glenn stood at his console. His broad face wore a cat's grin. He seemed oblivious of the medic working behind him with scissors and a spray can of artificial skin.

"We've finished our job here," Glenn said. "Now we'll

join Trunk and finish the rest of it. We can expect to contact—" his voice boomed in exultation "—the Seatiger main body within twenty-five minutes unless they run . . . and they can't run fast enough!"

The *Mouflon* started to answer her helm, but for Wilding the sensation was almost lost in the vessel's pitch and yaw through the wave. A 15,000-ton cruiser requires a great deal of time to change heading by 120°.

"Sir?" said the *Mouflon*'s flag captain. "Should we, ah . . . detach some light craft to tend the vessels that have been disabled?"

"Negative," Captain Glenn snapped. "We have a job to do. We'll rescue survivors as soon as the Seatigers surrender. Until then, they'll have to fend for themself."

"I'm done, sir," muttered the medic.

Glenn flexed his shoulders and winced. By chance, he was glaring straight at Officer-Trainee as he concluded, "We're not running a nursery. It's the law of the jungle!"

15

MAY 18, 382 AS. 0626 HOURS.

Ensign Brainard looked downslope as the warning rang in his ears. With its keen sense of smell, the reptile would track them as inexorably as the tide came in.

OT Wilding leaped down the steep slope, sacrificing himself to the lizard's jaws in order to save the rest of them. Wilding repeated, "Get back!" even while he slid and tumbled along the track the cypress had bulldozed.

It would work. The gift of one life would conceal the existence of five more from the short-sighted reptile.

Brainard opened his mouth to shout, "Back from the edge!" to his remaining crew.

Off the beach far below, the vine-covered torpedo craft sat like a flaw against the beautiful water surface, which quivered with the thousand colors of a fire opal.

Ted Holman had sacrificed his life to torpedo the Wiesel*—and save K67 as it fled under Brainard's command. Brainard wasn't going to abandon Hal Wilding as well.*

The monitor lizard lifted onto its clawed toes to scramble over the debris. Its great head swung from side to side, bringing one black eye, then the other, to bear on the officer-trainee. It was the tongue, quivering like a fork-tailed serpent, which would guide the beast to its kill.

"Get back!" Brainard shouted to his crew. He leaped down from the crest to rescue his executive officer.

Brainard stayed upright for half the distance. He was running out of control, but his legs pumped swiftly enough that his boots crashed down each time just ahead of his center of mass.

Wilding lay spread-eagled in the muddy saddle. He rose to his hands and knees, then tried to force himself upright with the chewed rifle which he had somehow managed to grip during this fall. Wilding's back was toward the oncoming monster.

A sprig of running cedar, bruised but not destroyed by the avalanche of timber, lifted a feathery frond at motion and the chance of a meal. The tiny suckers on the underside of its leaves slipped from the ensign's heel, but the touch was enough to cost Brainard his balance. Instinct flung his arms and legs out in a grotesque cartwheel which could do nothing to save him.

Brainard hit on his shoulders. He somersaulted, chance rather than skill, until the roots of a tree demolished by the avalanche flung him into the air. He sailed twenty feet, scraped down on his left hip and arm, and rolled sideways into the man he had come to rescue.

"Come on," Brainard said.

Brainard's voice was a whisper because all the breath had been knocked out of his lungs. He stood up, trying to center himself as the universe spun around him. He had to concentrate on the job. Nothing but the job.

The sun seemed brighter. He'd lost his helmet. His rifle and the pack with his extra ammo had gone too, flung off in his chaotic dance downslope.

The laser communicator was still strapped to his chest. It clacked against Wilding's crutch as Brainard tried to grip the officer-trainee for a packstrap carry. Brainard slapped the quick-release buckle and dropped the communicator to which he had clung in hysterical determination from the time they abandoned K67.

"We can't . . . ," Wilding wheezed.

Brainard took a step. His boot slipped. He had to steady himself with his free hand. A curtain of tears and terror turned the torn slope into a gray-green blur.

Another step. Piled timber crashed nearby. A clod of mud jolted Brainard's back.

The stench of death drove aside every other sensory impression. Wilding twisted out of Brainard's grasp. The ensign turned to seize Wilding again and saw the monitor lizard.

The beast's forelegs and belly glistened with mud, but its hooked claws were clean. The beast's scales were knobby and thick enough, even on the wrinkled skin of its long throat, to shatter a rifle bullet.

Not that either man had a working rifle.

The monitor's open mouth stank with the rotting effluvium of its previous meals. Its tongue flicked out once more and sucked back as the beast struck at Wilding.

Wilding thrust the rifle he used for a crutch into the lizard's mouth, wedging it upright between the palate and lower jaws. He clung to the prop. The beast hissed like a boiler venting and reached out with its claws.

Brainard shouted. The laser communicator was at his feet. He picked it up by the strap and swung at the monitor's head.

The heavy mace crunched when it hit. The lizard's right foreleg twisted up and back to probe the point of impact. Wilding lost his grip on the rifle and fell down.

Brainard tottered as he tried to lift the communicator for another blow. "Geddown!" screamed Caffey from behind him. Brainard lost his footing as he looked back in surprise.

Caffey's machine-gun roared out a fifty-round burst that emptied the drum magazine and heated the barrel white. Blue-gray smoke from the flash suppressant in the gunpowder spurted around the scene in a bitter cloud.

Blood speckled the monitor's yellow maw and the bullet-drilled dimples in its scales. Several rounds sparked as they punched through the alloy receiver of the rifle in the lizard's mouth. The prop folded as the jaws began to close.

Newton and Wheelwright knelt/sprawled beside Caffey. They were firing also, but their shots were lost in the storm of heavier bullets from the machine-gun.

The injuries might be fatal . . . but a lizard this size would take days to die, even if some of the shots had been lucky enough to penetrate the bone-armored brain. Before that happened—

Leaf stepped forward. He thrust, rather than threw, a blob of burning barakite left-handed into the reptile's mouth just as the jaws closed. The long, yellow-gray neck spasmed. The lizard's autonomic nervous system caused the throat muscles to squeeze and carry the lethal cargo toward the belly.

Brainard rose into a crouch. He'd lost his pistol, but the butt of Wilding's sidearm still protruded from his holster. Brainard would take that and—

A muffled blast knocked all the humans down.

The monitor lizard's writhing body hurtled downslope in a series of convulsions. The monster's head had vanished. A cloud of liquified blood, bone, and flesh covered everything in a fifty-yard circle with pink slime.

The men roused themselves to sitting positions. Everybody seemed to be all right, even Wilding. *Hell, even Brainard, except for the ringing in his ears.*

Nobody spoke or tried to stand. Below them, the monitor lizard thrashed through the jungle beside the track the cypress had cleared. The beast rolled onto its back repeatedly. The motion flashed its mud-smeared belly scales against the less reflective green-brown mottling of its back and sides.

"I always heard," said Leaf finally, "that if you stepped on barakite while it was burning, it'd blow your goddam foot off. Guess it's not a good idea t' swallow it, neither."

Brainard swallowed. His conscious mind was totally disconnected from his body, but instinct braced him upright and started to bring his feet under him. "I thought I told you to use all the explosive on the cypress," he heard himself say. "So we were sure it went over."

"Sorry sir," the motorman said. "I guess I was in a hurry."

"That's okay," said Brainard.

He stood up and looked toward the top of the ridge. He couldn't imagine how they'd avoided breaking their necks on the steep, muddy slope. There was no way in hell that they could climb it again; nor was there any reason to do so now.

"Right," Brainard said. "We'll head for the other hovercraft now. If we move fast, we ought to be safe enough following where the tree slid."

He eyed a fig that stepped slowly toward them across the cleared swath. The plant tottered forward by extending one slanting root after another, like the legs of a man walking.

"But we better be fast," he added.

"Sir?" asked Wheelwright as he locked a loaded magazine into his rifle. "Is there going to be crew on the boat?"

"No," said Brainard flatly. "There isn't. The vines got them. There may be a working laser communicator, though."

He toed the unit he had carried from K67. The monitor lizard's claws had punched three finger-deep holes through the unit's tough outer casing.

"The other hovercraft . . . ," the ensign added softly, ". . . is K44."

August 2, 381 AS. 0212 hours.

He was dreaming:

The wand of honeysuckle wavered vertically against the opalescent dawn. A seaman fired at it. Three bullets slapped the tough vines and blew away scraps of foliage.

The bolt locked open. The seaman ejected the spent

magazine and reached for a fresh one. His ammunition pouches were empty. He began to cry.

The honeysuckle toppled forward. Its upper end scrunched over the hovercraft's bow, forming a bridge to the great mass of the plant trembling across the narrow stretches of sand and surf.

Leaves uncurled from the tip of the bridge. The speed at which the plant moved when driven by the rising sun was as unexpected as it was horrible.

The coxswain stepped close and slashed with a cutting bar. The multistranded vines resisted, but the shrill whine of the bar laid a swatch of the questing tendrils on the deck.

The bridge hunched as though it had nerves rather than tropisms. The coxswain shouted in triumph and took another cut. A tendril he had missed on the first pass wrapped around his ankle.

The man screamed. He chopped downward. His bar hit the deck short of the vine and howled vainly for a moment. Before he managed to free his ankle, three other tendrils had gripped his waist, left leg, and the wrist of the hand holding the cutting bar. His environmental suit was no protection. Hollow, inch-long thorns sprouted from the base of every leaf.

The coxswain screamed as though he would never stop. The burgeoning vines crept over him like a blanket drawn up to cover a sleeping infant.

A seaman with a knife lurched forward to help. A tendril lifted toward him. The seaman turned and ran.

The screaming did, of course, stop.

Giant crabs crawled in the surf foaming about the hovercraft. Their claws thumped against the skirts, trying to get a purchase on the tough fabric. Occasionally a crab drew itself halfway out of the water. The crustacean always lost its grip because of the plenum chamber's outward batter.

Honeysuckle fanned in a thin sheet across the deck. There was very little waste motion. Tendrils climbed the gun tub and explored its interior. They quickly realized that the warmth which drew them was that of hot metal rather than a source of nutrients.

The twin seventy-fives had twice blasted off the wand of honeysuckle rising on the shore. The big bullets cratered the beach and jungle beyond. Scavengers, drawn to the commotion, now battled on the torn sand.

But the gunner had fired all his ammunition. Minutes later, the crewmen emptied their personal weapons in a volley at the honeysuckle's third attempt to raise a boarding bridge.

Rifle bullets nibbled at but could not sever the thick strands of the vine's core. . . .

The tendrils which wrapped the breeches of the twin seventy-fives, and other vines that reached a dead end, immediately went dormant as the plant withdrew scarce resources. Leaves withered; the stems themselves went brown and brittle-looking.

Other vines humped and curved themselves more quickly, driven by light and drawn by the surviving crewmen huddled together in the stern. The sun was a ball of white heat shimmering through the clouds of the eastern horizon.

There was a slowly sinking mound of leaves where the coxswain had been. The epithelial cells carrying nutriment back to the core from that writhing pile had a red tinge.

Tendrils washed toward the hovercraft's stern in a sudden wave. The XO batted at a vine with his empty pistol. Foliage curved around his hand and gun like a green glove. He screamed and threw himself over the rail.

A crab sprang up from the surf. It caught the XO's thigh in pincers eighteen inches long. The honeysuckle did not relinquish its hold.

The young officer hung in the air. Vines wrapped his head and shoulders, muffling and finally choking off his screams. The sea beneath him was a froth of crabs struggling in the blood which poured from his severed femoral artery.

More men cried out. It had the whole crew, all but him. The stern rail pressed the small of his back. He drew himself up on it, raising his feet from the deck across which tendrils swept.

A column of honeysuckle rose from the twitching corpse of his motorman. The tip was as tall as his head. It quivered delicately, absorbing the data from sensors which measured temperature, sound waves, and the moisture content of air exhaled from an animal's lungs.

The vine toppled forward. He screamed as the hollow fangs drove into his face and chest. . . .

The door banged open. "Are you all right? Brainard! Are you all right?"

There was a light on in the hallway of the Junior Officer's Barracks. Brainard didn't at first recognize the speaker silhouetted in the doorway, but the hard, familiar lines of his own room brought him around like a douche of cold water.

He sat up. His sheet tangled him. He flung it off. Despite the room's climate control, his body was clammy with sweat.

"Are you all right?" the other man repeated. Lieutenant Dabney, who'd been on the Board of Review that afternoon. . . . He had the room across the hall. His voice was more calm now that he saw Brainard was under control.

"Oh, God," Brainard whispered. He covered his eyes with his hands, then realized that darkness was the last thing he wanted. He switched on the bed lamp.

There were more figures in the hallway. He must have let out one hell of a shout when the honeysuckle wrapped him. . . .

Lieutenant Dabney swung the door closed and knelt beside the bed. "Bad dream?" he asked mildly.

"Wasn't a dream," Brainard whispered. "I was aboard K44. I think I was Ted Holman. They all just died. The sun came up, and the honeysuckle got 'em all."

"Hey," said Dabney, "it was a dream. We all have them." He patted Brainard's knee, but his grip grew momentarily fierce. "Believe me," Dabney rasped in a bleak voice. "We all have them."

"Oh, God," Brainard repeated.

The lieutenant twitched. "Look," he went on, his tone cheerful, reasonable, "don't worry about K44. They took a direct hit. Hell, they probably got caught in the secondary explosions when the *Wiesel* went up. Instantaneous. A lot better than what happens to civilians, dying by inches in a bed while the medics cluck."

He patted Brainard again and stood up.

"Thanks, sir," Brainard said. "I'm fine. But—" He shrugged. "But that isn't what happened to K44's crew," he went on. "They beached their ship. And when the sun came up, the vines got moving."

Brainard smiled. It would have been a friendly expression if his eyes had been focused.

Dabney licked his lips. "Yeah," he said. "Well, if you're okay. . . ."

He reached for the door handle. Before he touched it, he turned and said, "Look, Ensign . . . this isn't exactly my business, but I've been in the Herd longer than you have."

Brainard nodded.

Dabney looked up at the ceiling. He cleared his throat and went on, "Cabot Holman, he's a good officer, don't get me wrong. But he'd always taken care of his kid brother even though there wasn't but three years between them. Ah, nobody's going to think anything's wrong with you if you decided to transfer out of hovercraft. Or. . . ." Dabney met Brainard's eyes. He relaxed visibly to see that the ensign's expression was normal again. "Or look, you could just transfer to some four-boat element besides the one that Holman commands. Okay?"

Brainard stood up. "No, that's okay," he said. "I appreciate what you're saying, but I'll do the job in front of me. Understand?"

Nobody could misunderstand the sudden crispness of Brainard's voice.

"Sure," agreed Dabney with a false smile. He opened the door, stepped through it, and closed it behind him in the same fluid motion.

Brainard sighed. He turned and unpolarized his outside window.

The sky was opalescent. Hafner Base was to the west of the Gehenna Archipelago. Dawn would have broken over the myriad small islands there half an hour earlier.

16

MAY 18, 382 AS. 1103 HOURS.

"Beautiful," said Officer-Trainee Wilding. He balanced cautiously on his left foot so that he could gesture with his new crutch toward the creatures wheeling in the bright sky. "Aren't they the most beautiful things you've ever seen, Mr. Leaf? Technician Leaf."

Wilding felt the motorman force down his right arm; gently at first, but with increasing firmness as the officer-trainee resisted. "Come on, sir," Leaf muttered. "We don't wanna stop just yet."

Wilding giggled. "Nope, we can't afford to stop," he said. "We've *got* to keep the common people interested, but we *can't* give them anything real to be interested in. Isn't that right? We can't stop!"

A facet of Wilding's mind knew that he was raving, but that facet was in charge only during brief flashes. The last of the analgesics had worn off hours earlier, but Wilding still felt no pain; only pressure. Pressure that seemed to swell his skin to the bursting point.

"C'mon, sir," said Leaf. "Just a little farther, and it's all on the flat now."

Wilding let himself be guided by the motorman's arm.

They were on sand, so it was hard to walk. The muzzle of the rifle Wilding used as a crutch dug into the yielding surface, punching divots and threatening to let him overbalance.

Wheelwright had burned the interior of his rifle barrel smooth with the long bursts he poured into the monitor lizard. Wilding used that weapon as a crutch, and Wheelwright carried the spare that had been Bozman's rifle. . . .

The beach was about fifty feet in width at this stage of the solar tide. The remainder of K67's crew stood in the middle of the strip of sand, staring from a safe distance at the hovercraft and its tracery of honeysuckle.

"I say we just run across it," suggested Caffey. "The vines, they're dead, but they'll hold us till we get to the ship. Just like they was a bridge."

"No," said Ensign Brainard.

The cypress lay in the surf a hundred yards from the humans. A school of flying frogs swept back and forth over the tree's path down the slope.

There were never less than two of the vividly colored amphibians in the air at any one time. At least a dozen were involved, but after a few passes each frog sailed back to the shadows to wet itself in the pools at the heart of spiky bromeliads. Generally the frogs would not venture into sunlight filtered only by the atmosphere, but the disaster had put up enormous numbers of small insects on which the frogs fed.

"Beautiful . . . ," Wilding murmured again.

"The end shoots will regenerate as soon as we get within fifty feet of them," Brainard said. "Mr Wilding can tell you."

Wilding tittered. His mind did not think that his lips made any sound.

Brainard pointed toward the bridge of honeysuckle with the first and second fingers of his left hand. Fresh leaves gleamed green against the ropes of brown stems. They moved very slowly, as if only the wind animated them.

"Look what's happening already," he said. "We'd get aboard, but we'd never get back. Believe me. To grow, that plant can pump food through its veins at the speed of a firehose."

Leaf looked at the hard-faced ensign. "You seen it, then, sir?" the motorman asked in puzzlement.

Wilding watched the other humans; watched the hovercraft; and watched the frogs overhead. The three images were pallid except where one chanced to encompass part of another. Overlaid viewpoints had rich colors and sharp lines.

"Yeah," said Ensign Brainard. "I've seen it."

The sea's gentle, back-and-forth motion hardened with stalked eyes, then claws stained shades of blue and lavender. Crabs edged sideways onto the sand, skittering a yard forward and half that distance back.

Their spike-edged shells were three feet across. There were already dozens of them on shore. More eyes peeked out of the water.

"Bet it'll burn," suggested Caffey. "The vine, I mean, dry as it is now. The boat, it's fireproof t'anything up to a thousand degrees."

The frogs flew by rhythmic motions of the skin stretched from their wrists to their hind feet. They retained their fore-paddles as canard rudders which allowed them to turn and bank with astonishing quickness in pursuit of their prey.

"You wouldn't think an amphibian could fly without drying out, would you, Leaf?" Wilding heard his voice say.

"Even in an atmosphere as saturated as this is. Isn't nature wonderful?"

"If it burns," protested Leaf, "then how do we get aboard? Have *them* carry us?"

He gestured toward the crabs with his multitool.

One of the crustaceans scuttled ten feet closer to the humans, then raced back toward the sea in a spray of sand.

Newton raised his rifle. He fired at the crab. His bullets cracked the carapace and broke the lower jaw of one pincer so that the saw-toothed edge hung askew on its fibers of internal muscle.

"Dumb shit!" Caffey shouted. "How much ammo you think we got left?"

The injured crab reached the edge of the sea before the weight of her fellows brought her down. They flailed the water in their haste to rend the sudden victim. Successful crabs raised long strips of pale meat in their claws, then sidled away to shred their sister further in their swiftly moving mouth parts.

"Look," growled Newton. "I hate 'em. Okay? Just keep off my back!"

A facet of Wilding's mind giggled at the fire discipline which the trek had hammered into K67's crew; a facet watched the wheeling frogs; and the facet in control of his muscles for the moment said crisply, "No, that was right. They would have rushed us very soon. Newton provided something else to occupy them."

The coxswain looked at Wilding and grinned shyly. Newton's stolid strength was so great, even now, that he hadn't bothered to shrug off his pack while they paused for consideration. "Thanks, sir," he said. "Things with claws, I just. . . ."

"Fish is right," said Ensign Brainard, returning to the

problem at hand. "The core stems are still full of sap in case there's a chance to grow. They won't burn, so we'll have the bridge to cross on. But all the tendrils will go, and that should slow down the regrowth. A lot. I think enough."

"It's a jungle out there," Officer-Trainee Wilding said to the crabs furiously demolishing their fellow. "It's a jungle everywhere, did you know?"

This time the laugh was internal but he spoke aloud the words, "It's a jungle in the keeps, too. Especially in the keeps."

"Right," said Brainard, putting the cap on his thoughts in his usual, coldly decisive fashion. "To make sure it ignites, we'll need to get a flame into the really dry portion, but it'll blaze back very quickly. What we need is a wad of barakite we can throw. Leaf, do we have any more?"

A machine could act as decisively; but no machine intelligence could process the scraps of available data into the survival of six human beings under the present conditions. . . .

The motorman winced as though he had been struck. "Sir, I'm sorry," he said, "but I cleaned out ever'body else when we blew up the tree, and the last bit. . . ."

"Don't apologize for following my orders, Technician," Brainard snapped.

The sand quivered slowly down the beach toward the humans. If Wilding had been limited to a single viewpoint, he would not have noticed it. When two images merged like a stereo pair, the trembling line was evident.

Brainard ran his fingertip down the front seam of his tunic, unsealing it. "This fabric's processed from cellulose. It should burn well enough."

"Newton," Wilding ordered. "Give me a magazine for this rifle."

"Sir!" said Leaf in concern. "Don't try t'shoot that without we knock the dirt outa the muzzle."

The coxswain handed Wilding a loaded magazine without comment or apparent interest. Wilding locked it home in the receiver well without lifting his 'crutch'. The muzzle brake was completely buried.

Ensign Brainard took his tunic off. There were dozens of puckered sores on his arms and among the hairs of his chest. "Weighted with a little sand," he said aloud, "we'll be able to throw it aboard K44 from halfway along the honeysuckle bridge. That should do."

Wilding retracted the charging handle and let it clang forward, loading the rifle. "Help me walk," he ordered Leaf curtly.

"Sir . . . ?" pleaded the motorman. He sighed and took his share of Wilding's weight. The officer-trainee stumped toward an event no one else was aware of.

"Better let me handle that, sir," Caffey said to the ensign. "It's going to backfire pretty quick, and—"

"Thank you, Technician," Brainard said, "but it's my job."

Both the thanks and the assertion were as false as a politician's faith. The ensign straightened, knotting the sleeve of his tunic to hold the weight inside. Sand dribbled out through tears in the fabric.

Wilding slanted his rifle outward and drove the muzzle deep in the sand. His surroundings were a montage of images in which nothing was clear. "Is it ready to fire, Leaf?" he demanded. "Is it off safe?"

"Yeah," said the motorman, "but for chrissake, sir—"

"Leaf," Ensign Brainard ordered, "give me your multitool for a—Wilding! What the hell are you doing?"

The line in the beach steadied, then merged with the pimple raised from the sand around the rifle muzzle. The surface mounded as something rose through it, drawn by vibration and pressure which compacted a point of the beach.

Hard chitin clacked against the steel muzzle brake as a shock drove the weapon upward. Wilding pulled the trigger.

The sound of the shot was muffled, but the sand exploded as if a grenade had gone off. Recoil knocked Wilding backward despite the motorman's attempt to hold him.

The magazine flew out. The muzzle brake was gone. Excessive pressure sprayed the cartridge casing in fragments and vapor from the ejection port, but the breech did not rupture.

A hand-sized fragment of bloody chitin lay in the center of the disturbed area. Instead of surfacing, the creature drove down in a series of circles that widened, leaving ever-fainter traces on the beach above. A line shivering toward the humans from the other direction changed course to intercept its injured peer.

Everyone else stared at Wilding. "It's a jungle," he repeated in a high, cheerful voice. "But it's our jungle too."

Leaf bent to help Wilding rise. In the same tone, the officer-trainee added, "There's a hand flare in Newton's pack. I put it there. We'll use that, don't you think? So that we torch the honeysuckle. And not the hero." He chortled.

Brainard shook his head as if to clear cobwebs. "Do you have a flare, Newton?" he asked.

"Huh?" said the coxswain. "I dunno."

Caffey reached into Newton's pack. His hand came out

with a short plastic baton: a flare, marked White Star Cluster. "Jeez," the torpedoman said. "We're golden!"

Of course we're golden, said Officer-Trainee Wilding. *We're being led by a hero.*

But no words came out of his mouth, only laughter.

July 3, 379 AS. 0912 hours.

Prince Hal's coach, one of less than a hundred private vehicles in Wyoming Keep, bulked in the midst of the Patrol scooters like the termite queen in a crowd of her workers.

A score of emergency flashers pulsed nervously. Each light had a different rate and sequence. The combination would drive a saint to fury.

Wilding jumped from his vehicle without waiting for his chauffeur's hand. The warehouse's double doors were flung back. Kenran, the Wilding major domo, stood in the entrance wringing his hands as Patrol personnel walked in and out of the building.

It was a moment before Kenran's eyes registered the arrival of his master. His face wrenched itself into a combination of misery and relief. "Oh, *sir!*" he cried, "it's terrible! Terrible what they did!"

"What *who* did?" Wilding demanded as he strode into the family warehouse. "Just what in heaven's name is going on?"

"Excuse me, sir," said a stocky man with close-cropped gray hair. He stepped between Wilding and the major domo with a studied nonchalance. "I'm Captain Petersen. Would you be the Wilding?"

"My father's indisposed," Wilding snapped. "I'm the

family's representative, if that's what you mean. Now, get out of my—"

He put his hand on the stranger's chest to push him aside. The momentary contact shocked Wilding in two ways: Petersen didn't move; and although Petersen wore good-quality—though drab—civilian clothes, there was a pistol in a shoulder holster beneath his tunic.

"I'm in charge of the investigation, sir," said Petersen as he stepped aside so smoothly that he seemed never to have been in the way. "You're welcome to enter, of course; but you'll understand that we don't want a mob of civilians making a bad situation worse."

"Why was it my servants who noticed the damage?" Wilding demanded as he walked into the warehouse. "Isn't that what we pay the Patrol to—good God!"

"Oh, sir!" Kenran wailed. "It's *terrible!*"

"We check the doors of these warehouses every few hours, sir," said Petersen as he followed Wilding into the building. "We don't bother with the back as a general rule, except to run off vagrants. With Carnival, we've been pretty busy, so it was your people who found the trouble when they opened up this morning."

The Patrol had set up additional lights, supplementing those integral to the warehouse. The combined glare turned the interior into a harsh, shadowless pit. It looked like a bomb site. Uniformed personnel recorded the scene and sifted through the debris while Wilding Family servants stood by in shock.

"We didn't think you *could* get through these walls without blowing the whole building to bits," Petersen went on. "Of course, with what they did when they got inside, they might as well have blasted it to smithereens."

Desks of light metal and thermoplastic: hacked or sawn

apart, probably with cutting bars. Chairs of similar flimsy construction: smashed, every one of them. Crates with padded interiors: ripped open, and the fixtures they contained hurled onto the floor to be stepped upon.

There was a hole in the back wall of the warehouse, a square so regular that Wilding thought for a moment it was part of the building's design. The edges of cast ceramic were so sharp that they winked in the cruel light. The thieves, the *vandals,* had somehow cut a neat hole in a wall that should have been able to resist cannon fire. . . .

"How?" Wilding whispered. His soul felt empty. The universe had turned to face him, and her face was a skull.

"We're still not sure of that, sir," Petersen said. " 'Why' is a bit of a question also, but we think they were looking for valuables, didn't find any, and wrecked what was here out of anger. Are these the normal contents of this warehouse?"

"No!" said Wilding. His face clouded as he tried to think. "But I'm not sure what's usually here, that's not my. . . ."

"Liquor for the party was stored here until the night before last," Kenran said. His voice steadied as it was permitted to deal with normal business matters. "The Family gives a Carnival party in its home, open to everyone in the keep who wishes to come. The quantity of beverages that entails is too great to store on the premises until the event, of course."

Petersen nodded in satisfaction. "Bingo," he said. "They knew about the booze, broke in some damn way, and missed what they were looking for by twenty-four hours."

He surveyed the wreckage again before adding, "So there was nothing left here but this old furniture?"

Wilding went pale. He couldn't speak.

"You, you—" Kenran stammered, "—*idiot!* Don't you know what this was? It was Settlement Period furniture! It came from *Earth!*"

"Oh, my god," Petersen said in a reverent tone. For the first time, the Patrol captain's look of cold propriety gave way to genuine concern.

Wilding stared at the hole in the warehouse wall. "With thousands of common people in the house," he said numbly, "we couldn't have irreplaceable artifacts like these out where they might be broken. We always store them in the warehouse for safekeeping."

Petersen shook his head. "So they could have walked in your front door and drunk themselves silly," he said. "But instead they do this."

He reached down and picked up a shattered tumbler. The scrap was made of plastic derived from petroleum, formed in turn by the bodies of Terran animals hundreds of millions of years in the past.

"Just for kicks," Petersen said. "Just to keep themselves entertained."

17

MAY 18, 382 AS. 1109 HOURS.

"When we get onto the honeysuckle, sir," said Leaf, "I'm gonna be holding you from behind. Okay? Like this."

Wilding's rifle was three inches shorter without the muzzle brake. He leaned against the "crutch" with an insouciant grin nonetheless. He made no comment as the motorman stepped around him to grip his left wrist and the tunic over his right shoulder.

Leaf felt Wilding shiver. The officer's wrist was cold and clammy. That was okay, not great but okay. There'd been spells of chills before and Wilding still seemed to be—

Hell, within parameters. Like a drive motor. Nobody expected perfect; just functional, and they were all functional, more or less.

"Right," said Ensign Brainard. "I'll take the flare."

Caffey uncapped the short cylinder instead of handing it to Brainard immediately. He looked at a patch of sky beyond the ensign's right ear and said in a mild voice, "You've got a lot of experience with these, then, sir?"

Brainard chopped out a laugh. "Not as much as you do, Fish," he said. "Sorry."

He surveyed his crew. Leaf straightened instinctively as he met the CO's eyes. Brainard looked back at the torpedoman and said, "Whenever you're ready."

Caffey switched the cap to the back end of the flare, where its firing pin touched the recessed primer. He aimed the tube in his left hand, then rapped the cap sharply. The charge blew the three packets out in a flat arc toward where the bridge of honeysuckle touched the hovercraft's deck.

The magnesium filler ignited while the packets were still in the air. The wavering glare was bright even against the white shimmer of daylight on Venus.

"What do we do if it don't catch the first—" began Wheelwright.

Orange flame overwhelmed the flare's white intensity. The brown, twisted vines blazed up with a roar and a propagation rate just short of that of diesel fuel. The fire's violence threw bits of stem and leaves into the air. The miniature brands were consumed to black ash before they reached the top of their curves.

The hovercraft vanished beneath a curtain of fire. Leaf couldn't believe there'd be anything left when the flames died away. The bridge of honeysuckle became a tube of roaring light. Loud crashing sounds like gunshots blew fragments away when pockets of sap deep in the core vine were heated to steam at pressures beyond the strength of cell walls.

The mass of honeysuckle which controlled the shore across the strip of sand was green with nutrients sucked from the soil. The plant trembled and drew back under the stress of heat, but the line of conflagration halted as if the upper edge of the beach were a wall.

The hovercraft re-emerged. Its mottled gray finish was now overpatterned with the black/gray/white of ash. Orange hot-spots continued to dance on the deck, but the stunning roar had ceased.

The bridge still arched across sand and water. When the withered foliage was stripped away, it left a coarsely woven hawser of interlaced stems. The mass was almost a yard in diameter, but its surface was neither flat nor regular.

"Right," ordered Ensign Brainard. "Caffey, lead Mr Wilding while Leaf follows. Let's go."

When the crew shambled to the bridge at their best possible speed, Leaf realized how badly off they were. He and Caffey carried the officer-trainee by the elbows. Wilding twice had to brace them with his crutch and to keep them all from falling down.

Newton was pretty much okay—maybe having no brains was an advantage in this crap—but the CO wobbled when he reached the top of the core vines. He gave Newton a hand, then stumbled aboard the hovercraft as the coxswain hauled the others up.

A four-foot climb with hand and footholds should have been easy. It wasn't.

The stems had a coating of ash, but the heat-cracked surface kept them from being slippery. Wilding managed to stride across the twisted vines as though he had two good ankles. He was chuckling. Leaf figured that was the fever, but maybe the Founding Families really *were* supermen. . . .

The hovercraft's deck had rippled in the fire, but it was still firm and better 'n' pussy after a week at sea. Close up, the vessel's number was visible on the side of the cockpit. K44, but they'd known that. . . .

Caffey, his escort job done, let go of the officer-trainee. He clamped his machine-gun onto the railing where it covered the shore from which they had just escaped.

"The communicator's here but the ascender's gone!" Brainard shouted from the cockpit. "We've got fuel!"

Honeysuckle aboard the vessel had burned itself into a slime of ash. Leaf slipped and barely caught himself. Wilding sprawled onto the deck where he'd be fine, just fine, while the motorman did his real job.

They hadn't any of them said it. Maybe they hadn't even admitted it to themselves. But now that K67's crew was back aboard a hovercraft, they were going to sail *off* this fucking hellhole if they had to paddle with their feet!

Leaf slid into the motorman's scuttle. Ensign Brainard had lighted the auxiliary power unit, so the drive status panel was live. Number Three fan was flatlined.

A glance to the side showed the motorman why: an armor-piercing shell had sledged away the top half of the housing and everything within the nacelle. "Armor-piercing," because HE Common would've detonated on impact, leaving nothing of the hovercraft that you couldn't pack in a shoebox.

But the other three fans would lift a hovercraft with no sweat, so long as the skirts were—

"The skirts 're shot to shit," Caffey called. He was in the cockpit with the CO, using the portside console. Nobody needed a torpedoman right now, and OT Wilding was doing good just to sit up straight against a post. "Nothing we can't patch, though."

Caffey opened the repair locker which formed the cockpit's aft bulkhead. Newton and Wheelwright were forward, sawing at the bridge of honeysuckle. The coxswain's cutting bar was out of power, but he still made chips fly with powerful strokes of his arms.

"Caffey," Ensign Brainard ordered. "Shoot that vine apart with the machine-gun. Burned like this, you'll be able to do it."

Leaf got out of his scuttle. After a moment's relaxation, his arms cramped with agony as he forced them to raise part of his weight.

"Sir, we're short of ammo—" the torpedoman said doubtfully.

Leaf started forward to the plenum-chamber access port. Wilding gave the motorman a thumbs-up and chirped something. It sounded like, "Teamwork in the jungle! Keep it up!"

"We're shorter on time!" Brainard snapped. "I've seen what that vine can do when it gets its growth spurt."

Tendrils lifted across the beach. The mass of honeysuckle had begun to recover from its singeing. The blackened core stems showed no sign of life, but nobody was going to press an argument with *this* CO. Caffey stepped to his gun and aimed.

Leaf tugged the screw dog recessed in the center of the access port. The vine that bound it had burned away, but grit and ash clogged the threads. The double handles fought Leaf for a moment, then spun.

Caffey fired a short burst that sent spray back over the rail. The surface of the clear sea multiplied both the muzzle blasts and the *whack* of bullets parting the dry stems. A second burst—then three shots as the machine-gun expended the few rounds remaining in their last drum of ammunition.

Leaf turned the handle to its stop so that it withdrew the dogs in all four sides of the port. He lifted the panel against the friction of its hinges.

"That's got it, sir!" the torpedoman announced.

"Newton," Leaf called. "Cover me with your rifle in case there's something down here who—"

He'd raised the edge of the port about halfway. Because the hovercraft sat on the shelving bottom, not a bubble of air, the water level within was close to the underside of the vessel's deck. Sunlight through the opening showed shapes but not details because the motorman's eyes were adapted to the open sky.

The motion was inhumanly fast, but the storm of cavitation bubbles in the water gave Leaf just enough warning. He threw his weight onto the upper side of the panel before the creature slammed against it from below.

The shock lifted him, but the creature recoiled also. The access port closed. Leaf spun the dogging handle to keep it that way. "Jesus!" he cried. "There's a moray down there longer 'n the boat!"

"I'll take care of it!" said Wheelwright. He reached for his backpack on the deck. "I've got a grenade!"

"Are you crazy?" Leaf demanded. "You'll kill us all!"

The hovercraft shuddered as the eel's sinuous body brushed the skirts from the inside. The creature was agitated with the thought of prey.

Caffey looked at the motorman in surprise. "Hey, it's no sweat, Leafie," he said soothingly. "Concussion'll kill the moray, but the water down there'll stop the shrapnel before it gets to the skirts."

The torpedoman's toe tapped the deck. "Or us. It's no sweat."

"Naw," said Leaf. He'd forgotten that the others hadn't seen what *he* saw when the port was open. "That's not what I mean. The torpedoes are still on their hooks down there. If the grenade sets one of them off—"

Memory strangled his voice.

Leaf didn't have to finish. Caffey knew what a torpedo could do, even to vessel a thousand times the size of this little hovercraft.

"But that's impossible!" the CO blurted.

Leaf looked at him.

Ensign Brainard's face was suddenly gray. "This is K44, and they torpedoed the *Wiesel* to save our lives!"

AUGUST 1, 382 AS. 2215 HOURS.

Technician 2nd Class Leaf filled his glass from the pitcher and said, " 'Bout time you fetch us some more beer, kid," to K67's assistant motorman.

Bozman looked doubtfully at the pitcher, then over his shoulder toward the long, crowded bar of the Dirtside Saloon. "There's plenty left," he said, raising his voice slightly more than the saloon's ambient noise required. "And anyway, I got the last one."

Caffey filled his own glass, then poured the remainder of the pitcher into Bozman's half-full tumbler. He banged the empty pitcher back on the table among its four brethren.

Caffey grinned at Leaf's striker. "You were saying, kid?"

"I was saying," growled Bozman, "that I got the last *two.*"

Leaf belched. "That's the price newbies pay for being allowed to sit with vets like me and Fish," he said. "Pay gladly, if they're smart."

The motorman's voice was mellow—for Leaf. The beer had given him enough of a buzz to dull memories the afternoon's Board of Review had churned up. He basked in the glow of being alive.

The Herd, like all the Free Companies, granted its personnel liberal leave to browse the rich entertainments of the keeps. Despite that, men on base duty needed after-hours relaxation; base facilities gave credit against pay; and a certain percentage of mercenaries found they simply didn't like the company of civilians.

The Dirtside Saloon was one of scores of bars within Hafner Base's fortified perimeter. It was full of men, and so were all its sister clubs and saloons.

"Got through another, didn't we, Leafie?" Caffey said in a reflective tone. "Been a few of those."

The Dirtside was lighted by bands of muted green which drifted slowly across the ceiling. The illumination was adequate for the duty squad of Shore Police who kept watch through their image-intensification visors, but Leaf found it hard to be sure of the torpedoman's expression.

"There was a few of them back on Block Eighty-One," Leaf rasped. "Fuck it. Any one you walk away from."

"You two knew each other when you were growing up, didn't you?" Bozman said over the rim of his glass. He was careful not to look at either of the chiefs as he spoke.

"In a manner of speaking, kid," Caffey said.

Leaf laughed without humor. The lights in his mind brightened to billowing red flames for a moment before sinking back into the bar's cool green. "We wasn't friends, if that's what you mean."

"Hell, Leafie," the torpedoman said. "We didn't kill each other. That counts for something on Block Eighty-One." The liquid in Caffey's glass trembled as his fist tightened. His eyes were unfocused. "D'ye ever go back, Leafie?" he asked. All the joking, all the easy fellowship, had been flayed from his voice.

Leaf gulped his beer. "Hell, no," he said. "*Hell*, no."

Caffey looked at the assistant motorman. "Kid," he ordered, "get us another pitcher."

Bozman bobbed his head and scraped his chair back from the table. The noncoms stared at his back as he fought through the press to the bar, but their minds were on other things.

"You're smart," Caffey said. "I went back the once. Half the guys we knew was dead, and the rest of them was in jail. Or on the netters for life, if that counts as life. It's a jungle back there, Leafie. It's worse 'n what's out beyond the perimeter."

The automatic cannon which guarded the electrified frontier of Hafner Base crashed a regular accompaniment to Herd life. It was only by concentrating that the mercenaries noticed them. Leaf's experienced ears could differentiate muzzle blasts from the slightly sharper counterpoint of shells bursting at the jungle rim. Occasionally, a heavier gun would join in to deal with a particular threat.

"God," Leaf muttered.

Bozman was back with a pitcher so full that it sloshed when he set it on the table. The motorman blinked. Caffey looked surprised too. It hadn't seemed there'd been enough time. . . .

"Look," said Bozman as he sat down again, "I got a question. Not—"

Both noncoms jerked their heads around like gun turrets, ready to fire.

"—about any of that," the assistant motorman blurted quickly. "About the Board of Review this afternoon." He forced a smile.

Neither of the chiefs smiled back. "Go ahead," Leaf said.

Bozman licked his lips. "Look," he said. "It's about you guys testifying that K44 sheered off when the shooting started. I didn't say nothing to the Board—"

"Not as dumb as he looks," Caffey said to Leaf. His voice twinkled like light on broken glass.

"I didn't say nothing," Bozman continued, staring determinedly at the table, "but I *saw* K44 running in ahead of us all the way."

He swallowed and looked up again, attempting another smile. "I mean, y'know, I thought I did."

Caffey started to laugh. Bozman's expression became so gogglingly silly that the motorman laughed the harder. Leaf leaned over to slap his striker on the back.

"Oh, kid," the motorman chortled. "I forget what a goddam newbie you are!"

Bozman looked as stiff and angry as a whore with a broom stuffed up her backside. "But I *saw*—" he said.

"Our shadow," Leaf interrupted. "You saw our shadow. When the starshells dropped, they threw shadows over the waves ahead of us."

The assistant torpedoman opened his mouth in amazement.

"Don't feel bad," Leaf added. "It happens a lot."

Caffey belched and poured himself another beer. "It happens a lot to *newbies,*" he said.

Both noncoms were relaxed and buoyant again. The motorman slid his own glass over to be filled.

"You didn't know Ted Holman, kid," he said, "so I'll tell you: he didn't have any balls. His brother kept pushin' him t'be a hero, but Teddy just wasn't cut out fer that. There's less chance he ran K44 in ahead of us than there is this glass is gonna turn t' gold in my hand."

He raised it, then drank. "Nope, still beer."

Caffey laughed. "I'll tell you something else, kid," he said. "I don't believe K44 circled around and came back, neither."

"But they had to come back," Bozman exclaimed. "They torpedoed the *Wiesel.* I *know* that happened!"

"*We* did for the *Wiesel,*" Caffey said.

He raised his left hand to silence Bozman's certain protest. "I know, the console was shot away so our fish lost guidance—but that don't mean they stopped and rolled belly up. Tonello aimed the boat for a hand's-off run, and the *Wiesel* wasn't doing any maneuvering the way she was caught in the channel like that."

"Ted Holman's welcome to be a dead hero," the motorman said between swallows, "seeing as he's dead. But I figure K44 took a shell up the ass as she ran."

"You can't outrun a bullet, after all," Caffey agreed philosophically.

"I tell you," said Leaf, watching the patterns his blunt fingertip drew in the condensate on his glass. "I'd sooner have a skipper with the guts to still do the job when the shit hits the fan. It's safer. And sooner or later in this business, the shit always hits the fan."

"Hell, in life," the torpedoman muttered.

"Lieutenant Tonello was a goddam good skipper that way," Leaf said. He slid his empty glass to Caffey.

"And you know?" he continued. "I think this new kid Brainard may be even better."

May 18, 382 AS. 1118 hours.

K44 rested in a tidal pool, though the bar a quarter mile to the north was submerged at this stage of solar attraction. Brainard stared over the portside rail. The water was so clear between waves that when he spit, his subconscious expected to see the gobbet dimple the sandy bottom. Instead, there was a splash.

A dozen tiny fish, scarcely more than teeth with fins, converged on the spot. They continued to froth the surface for minutes after they must have been certain there was no prey to justify a battle.

Other iridescent fish prowled among the fragments of crab armor which littered the bottom in a wide fan to seaward. Occasionally a fish found a further scrap of meat to worry from the chitin. Others flashed in to attack their lucky fellow while his jaws were engaged with the scavenged tidbit.

Officer-Trainee Wilding stumped around the cockpit to join Brainard. The enlisted crewmen waited for orders with evident concern.

Brainard knew they were worried. He knew that he *had* to decide what to do . . . but his whole universe had overturned when he learned that the commander of K44 hadn't saved his life. Maybe Fate had done so, maybe there was a friendly God; and maybe the whole universe was a game of chance in which men were chips, not players.

Wilding leaned against the rail and took a deep breath. His face looked pale; cold sweat flecked his skin. He wedged the rifle into the corner where his body met the railing, then gestured at the bottom with his right index finger.

The officer-trainee was doing better since he'd gotten a solid plastic deck underneath him. Not physically better. Physically, he looked worse than the rest of them, and they all looked like yesterday's corpses.

The fever had stopped twisting Wilding's mind. Even when he'd dragged his thoughts through delirious pathways, he'd still managed to save all their lives, though. . . .

"At least having the moray here limits our problem to one," he said. "Otherwise there'd be hundreds of crabs trying to get at us. That'd be a lot worse."

"Rifle bullets aren't going to kill an eel that big," Brainard said. He turned around and nodded to the men. "Leaf's right, though. I won't chance using the grenade with two torpedoes down in the plenum chamber."

Those were the first words he'd spoken since he learned about the torpedoes. The relief on the faces of his crew was palpable.

"Maybe we could patch the holes from outside the skirts?" Wheelwright offered.

"Don't be a bigger fool 'n God made you, kid," the motorman snapped without real malice. "It's pressure that holds the patching film in place. Stick it on from the outside, and it'll just blow free when we fire up the fans."

"That wouldn't help anyway," said Wilding gently. "The eel lairs in the plenum chamber, but it hunts outside."

The officer-trainee leaned cautiously over the railing and pointed forward along the hovercraft's side. There was a flared tunnel in the sand where the skirts began to curve in toward the bow. Fragments of crab shell were particularly concentrated near that end of the vessel.

From the size of the opening, the moray was three feet in diameter. That was even bigger than Brainard had thought. A grenade could still do the job.

They couldn't just wait until fresh prey drew the eel away from the torpedoes, though. . . .

"Leaf," the ensign said. "I've seen the damage-control menu, I know what it says. But will K44 *really* float if we just patch her plenum chamber?"

The motorman frowned as he met Brainard's gaze. "Well, sir," he said, "the one fan's fucked, that's a dockyard job to replace. But three fans 're plenty if you don't need top speed—and if your skirts ain't shot to shit, so they won't hold pressure."

He shrugged. "The read-out says there's nothing so big we can't patch it. Eyeballing the skirts from up here on deck, it looks the same. Lotta little holes, one maybe from a six-inch—but just the hole, it didn't go off. Maybe we get down inside the chamber, there'll be a problem after all. But I don't see bloody why there oughta be."

Caffey, back in the cockpit studying the holographic display Brainard had called up, nodded. "Get rid of the eel, run patching film around the plenum chamber—and we're golden. We can sail the sucker home."

"Then why," said Brainard, "didn't K44's crew do that? They must've known that with their ascender gear shot off, nobody was going to pick up their distress calls more than a few miles away."

His eyes glazed with the vision of spike-thorned honeysuckle, toppling toward him to drain his blood. "Why did they stay here to d-d-die?"

Nobody spoke for a moment. Officer-Trainee Wilding put his hand on Brainard's arm.

"Sir," Wilding said, "I don't think you can understand, because you've never been afraid. But they were just normal men, Holman and his crew. Maybe there wasn't an eel in the plenum chamber, not at first. But something was—crabs, bloodworms. Or it might have been."

"Down there, it gets darker 'n a yard up a hog's ass," Leaf said soberly. "And nobody was gonna risk his life because a chickenshit like Ted Holman told him t' do it."

"Don't tell me about being afraid," Brainard whispered.

A column of spike-thorned honeysuckle toppling forward to drink. . . .

"Right," he said. "We need to bait the eel into the open."

He put his rifle on the deck and bent to unfasten his boots. *Boots and trousers would drag in the water, slowing him down.*

"Caffey and Wheelwright, you'll hold my left wrist and haul me back aboard when Mr Wilding gives the order," Brainard went on. "Leaf and Newton, you're on my right. Mr Wilding, you'll be in charge of the operation—"

The ensign kicked off one boot, then the other. He was afraid to order anybody else to do what had to be done.

Ulcers on Brainard's insteps had leaked blood and serum, gluing his socks to his feet.

"—and you'll throw the grenade. Are you up to that?"

"Look, sir," said the motorman, "I can—"

"Shut up," said Brainard. "Are you up to that duty, Mr Wilding?"

The officer-trainee licked his lips. "Yes sir," he said. "Ah, we'll want to—be—here at the stern, as far from the eel's tunnel as we can get."

"Yes," said Brainard. "Yes, of course."

He pulled off his trousers, moving stiffly because of fatigue and injuries . . . and fear.

"Then let's get on with it, shall we?" he said.

Before the jaws of the moray eel in his mind closed and crushed him into a trembling fetal ball.

December 14, 380 AS. 0655 hours.

Brainard and four other youths sat in a circle on the Commons of Iowa Keep, drinking and viewing air-projection holograms.

Commuters watched as they rode to work on the slidewalks surrounding the Commons. There wasn't much to notice in the gathering, but the youths at least showed some life. They were a relief from the backs of other workers going to empty jobs—or the pensioners hunched on benches beneath the elms, waiting for their empty lives to end.

"See, Brainard?" Rufus said. "It's past time already. They decided they didn't want you—so let's go home, huh?"

He swigged and offered Brainard the bottle. Its original

contents had been replaced with a sweet punch made from fruit juice and industrial alcohol.

Brainard waved the bottle away. He looked at the clock on a pole in the middle of the Commons.

"It's not time," he snapped. He was angry that Rufus's gibe took him in for a moment. "Anyway, a few minutes aren't a big deal. Since when did you ever get to your first class on time?"

"We're here now, Brainard, baby," Kohl said in a lugubrious voice. "Seeing our buddy off. Pallbearers at your funeral, that's what we are."

"If he doesn't come to his senses," said Price. "Hey Rufe? Pass me the bottle if soldier boy doesn't want it."

"Hey, look at this one," Lilly said as he switched the chip in his hologram projector.

The image of a tracked vehicle seared the jungle with a rod of flame. As soon as the flamethrower shut off, two armored bulldozers snarled in to clear the gap before it could regrow. Despite the bath of fire, vines lifted and slashed until the dozer blades and crushing treads managed to sever them.

One of the bulldozers broke through the vines into a fifty-foot circle of sand. The driver started to back away. The surface lurched. The bulldozer sank to the top of its treads.

An armored recovery vehicle roared to life. Its path was blocked by the self-propelled plows which tore through the surface layers behind the bulldozers and injected herbicides into the cuts.

The stricken bulldozer lurched again and tilted forward. The engine compartment sank completely beneath the surface. The treads still rotated in reverse, but they could not bite on the loose sand.

The hatch at the rear of the cab flew open. The driver climbed onto the mounting ladder and poised there. Firm ground was twenty feet away.

The bulldozer shuddered. It began to slide downward as swiftly as a submarine which has vented its ballast. Two jointed, hairy arms as thick as tree trunks reached up from the center of the clearing and pulled the vehicle deeper.

The driver leaped desperately. He landed on the agitated sand. As the bulldozer slipped beneath the surface, its turbulence dragged the man along with it.

The image went blank. Lilly put another chip into the projector. "And that's just land-clearing!" he said gleefully. "You're gonna have people shooting at you besides!"

He'd lifted the chips from the library of Iowa Technical School, where he was completing work in biology. In a year, Lilly would sit glassy-eyed in a chair while his computer plotted plankton patterns onto charts—

Which might be transmitted to the netters—

Which would ignore the charts in favor of continuing their plodding progress across the fishing grounds, stolid in the certainty that any slight gains would be offset by time lost in departing from the preset pattern.

All five of the youths were students . . . except for Rufus and for Brainard, who had just received their two-year degrees.

Brainard swallowed and looked across the sidewalk to the recruiting office. It was still closed, a massively armored portal as forbidding as a bank vault. Mercenary recruiters were frequent targets of mob violence, both because of what they were and because they were different from the normal round of life in the keeps.

For that matter, the mob didn't need much of a reason to riot.

"Here's one for you, Brainard," Lilly said as he loaded another chip. "Take a look at this!"

Some Free Companies maintained recruiting offices in one or two of the keeps by whom those companies were frequently hired. But Wysocki's Herd, the Seatigers, and the Battlestars shared choice locations on a rotating basis in more than a dozen of the undersea domes. This technique spread the three companies' recruiting base and advertised their wares to the upper levels of keep society: the men who made decisions on war, peace, and hiring.

Brainard thought the recruiter for Wysocki's Herd was on duty in Iowa Keep this week, but he wasn't sure.

And it didn't really matter.

"Back in the Settlement Period, they planned to colonize the surface," said Kline, the other biotechnician. "Nothing came of it."

"Earth came of it," Kohl snorted. "People blowing themselves all up. Hey Rufe—how about some more of that punch."

"Hey, you guys. *Look* at this. It's a neat one."

"Dead soldier," said Rufus, turning the bottle upside down. The drop that formed on the rim did not fall.

"We got beer left in the cooler," Kohl offered. He spun the lid open.

The hologram hanging above the middle of the circle was of a lifeboat, bright yellow and seemingly empty. It bobbed as the sea's glassy surface swelled slowly, then subsided. The boat's image enlarged as the camera closed in.

"That didn't really affect things," Kline said. "The Holocaust, I mean. The surface colonies were supposed to be sent from the keeps, not Earth. They just weren't. Too big an effort, I guess."

The lifeboat filled the holographic field. The camera was

positioned above the little vessel, looking straight down. It seemed to be empty until the cameraman increased magnification still further.

A few quarts of water sloshed in the lifeboat's bilges. Tiny toothed things flashed and quivered there. They were fighting over the disarticulated bones of a human hand.

"C'mon, Brainard," Kohl said. "Have a beer at least. Keep your strength up."

Rufus chuckled. "The condemned man drank a hearty meal," he said.

"Want to see what happens when stinging nettles get through a Free Company's perimeter?" Lilly said with enthusiasm as he changed chips.

A tall, fit-looking man in a blue-and-silver uniform stepped off the slidewalk in front of the recruiting office. His exposed skin had the mahogany tan of surface radiation. He reached toward the door with a chip-coded key in his hand.

Brainard stood up.

"Aw, c'mon, Brainard," said Rufus as he struggled to rise also. "You don't really wanna do this."

When the mercenary saw the group of young men, he shifted the key to his left hand and did not unlock the door. "Yes?" he called across the slidewalk.

His right hand hovered at waist level, almost innocently. His little finger carefully teased open the flap of the pistol holster which completed his uniform.

"I've come to enlist," Brainard said loudly as he strode toward the slidewalk.

"Aw, Brainard," Kohl muttered.

A professional smile brightened the recruiter's face. "Then you've come to the right place," he said as he reached toward the door again.

"And why spend the effort to die on the surface?" said Kline rhetorically as he sucked on the bottle he had already emptied. "Life in the keeps is just fine the way it is!"

The slidewalk carried Brainard sideways, though he crossed it in two quick strides. He walked back along the berm.

In the center of Iowa Keep and every other domed city beneath the seas of Venus was the Earth Memorial. An image of Mankind's home blazed, representing the white light of the self-sustaining silicon reaction in the rocks of the actual planet. A wreath of black crepe encircled the display.

The armored doors of the recruiting office spread before Brainard like the jaws of death.

May 18, 382 AS. 1125 hours.

Wilding hallucinated.

He sensed his environment as if every detail were engraved in crystal. He had infinite time to pore over his surroundings and rotate them through his viewpoint.

Pores on Brainard's cold face as the ensign knelt with his back to the water.

Pressure blotches where the enlisted men gripped Brainard, four scarred hands holding each of his.

Individual scales jeweling the sides of fish. Sunlight shone through clouds and clear water to turn fanged horrors into things of miniature beauty.

Wisps of sand drifting in vortices near the mouth of the

tunnel fifty feet away, marking movements of the monster within the plenum chamber.

"Right," said Brainard. "Is everybody ready?"

Yessir/Yeah/Uh-huh/Yessir

A wide variety of syllables, timbres, volume—and it all had the same meaning. *You are willing to die for us, so we will stand by you.* A computer would not understand, but men understood.

Hal Wilding understood for the first time how Nature ordered the jungle—and what it meant to be a man.

"Mr Wilding," said Brainard. His voice trembled minusculely with fear and anticipation. "Are you ready?"

Wilding nodded. "I'm ready," his voice said. His mind marveled at the precise normality of the words. "I understand."

Doubt flecked the corners of Brainard's eyes, briefly there—and gone. No use worrying, and no time for it either.

"All right," the ensign said. "I'm going in." He lurched backward into the glassy water.

Large fish swirled shadows at the limits of visibility. They were drawn by sound and movement aboard the hovercraft, but they sensed also the huge moray which laired beneath the vessel. They would not attack—unless enough blood scented the water to overwhelm their instinct for self-preservation with the desire to kill.

Crabs marched closer in the shallows. Their legs stirred the fine sand of the bottom into a smoky ambiance through which the flat, spike-armored carapaces drifted sideways. The crabs' outstretched fighting claws scissored open and closed, for the moment cutting only water.

The moray's tunnel was still and dark. The hovercraft shivered as a slimy body brushed its underside.

Ensign Brainard kicked, stirring the surface.

The four enlisted men looked more like corpses than they did able-bodied humans. The cuts, scrapes, and sores that covered their bodies were individually minor, but the cumulative effect would have sapped the will of the strongest of men. Their faces were stark. They knew that they would have to pull their commander out of the water more swiftly than the moray could strike; and all of them doubted their ability to succeed.

"Has the eel . . . ," Brainard asked, pausing to kick again. His exhausted muscles trembled with the effort of keeping his head out of water, but his eyes were indomitable. ". . . shown itself?"

"It's moving inside the plenum chamber," Wilding said. His tone was calm, soothing. He was a part of Nature. "It'll come soon."

All of their clothing was in rags. Leaf knelt beside the officer-trainee. His feet were turned outward. The soles of his seaboots were a synthetic which combined a gummy grip with the toughness of mild steel and stability at temperatures up to 880°.

A purple fungus had devoured half the thickness of the right sole and was sucking a dimple from the heel of the left boot as well.

"Do you know what we're fighting for?" Wilding asked softly.

A twenty-foot shark curled in toward the hovercraft. A rifle on the deck beside Wilding pointed out over the sea. He knew the weapon was unnecessary at the moment.

The shark banked and fled toward the safety of its distant fellows, showing its pale belly. Its pectoral fins were spread like wings.

"For our lives, you bloody fool!" Leaf gasped. "That's what we're fighting for!"

Sweat blinded the motorman. He was desperately afraid that the sweat sliming his palms would cause his hands to slip when Ensign Brainard's life depended on him.

"No," explained Wilding, "that isn't why we're still fighting, still here."

His fingertips knew the surface of the grenade. On the deck lay the safety pin. The grenade's spoon handle pressed upward against Wilding's palm, straining to ignite the fuze train. The safety pin could be reinserted if the moray refused the bait . . . but Wilding knew that the beast would come.

Soon.

"Any one of us would have given up long ago if he'd been alone," he said aloud. "Even you, sir. Even you."

It was a wonder the way his tongue shaped to the words.

"For God's sake, man!" Caffey snarled. "Are you watching for the fucking eel?"

"I'm ready," Wilding said. "I understand."

Brainard's face lifted toward the officer-trainee. The ensign's face showed no concern; no expectation, even. Only the physical strain of making his wracked muscles kick the water to bring the jaws of a multiton monster down on him. . . .

Miniature fish darted in and out, confused by the thrashing. One of them snatched at the pus-soaked fabric of Brainard's sock. The scavenger's jaws stayed clamped although a kick lifted it from the water. When the fish splashed down again, one of its fellows sheared through its body just behind the head.

The torpedoman muttered a curse or a prayer.

"We're fighting for each other," Wilding said. "That's

good, but it's not good enough. When we get back, we have to fight for all Mankind."

The crabs scurried away like a mob fleeing a madman with an axe when Brainard started to kick. They resumed their sidelong advance, each moving individually but marching in lock-step because identical imperatives ruled their rudimentary minds.

The crustaceans pulsed forward and dashed back; but a little closer with every cycle. Soon one of them would spring from the sea floor with its claws wide to seize the man in the water. . . .

"Otherwise we're part of the jungle," Wilding said. "And the jungle will win."

"Oh God!" Leaf cried in despair. "I can't hold—"

It was the moment.

"Now!" shouted the officer-trainee. As the word came from his mouth, electric motion slid out of the tunnel.

The moray was green. Its jaws were open. The ragged fangs were up to ten inches long.

The sharks and lesser fish at the edge of vision vanished. The ranked crabs exploded backward behind a curtain of sand, tumbling over one another in their haste to escape nemesis.

The moray struck through the sea more swiftly than gravity could have pulled a boulder in thin air. The undulant movement slapped water violently against the hovercraft.

The grenade left Wilding's fingers as if it were playing its part in a marionette show in which strings connected all existence.

"Hah!" shouted one of the enlisted men as the four straightened and lunged backward in unison. Ensign Brainard rose toward the shell-torn gap in K44's railing.

Brainard was still in the air. His head and shoulders were over the deck, but his legs flailed above the sea.

The moray's head slid out of the water. Its palate was a cottony white. Leaf threw himself forward to block the monster's spearpoint teeth with his body. Wilding *knew* what was about to happen. He held the motorman's shoulders with the strength of a madman.

The grenade went off in the moray's throat. The creature's head flew apart. The thick slime coating its body was bright yellow, and the scales beneath were blue. The tons of fresh carrion thrashed, enough meat to draw all lesser predators for the minutes the crew needed to repair K44's skirts.

The spray of the moray's blood in the air was red, and the spreading red blur in Wilding's mind overwhelmed his consciousness.

JULY 2, 379 AS. 0101 HOURS.

Wilding watched Francine's coiffure echo the fireworks with increased intensity. Charged strands woven among the hairs trapped and re-emitted the light a band higher on the spectrum.

When the fireworks flashed silver, Francine's hair sparkled with all the colors of the rainbow.

She turned to face him. Her body moved against the balcony rail like that of a cat rubbing itself, and the smile on her broad lips was feline as well.

"What are you thinking about, Prince Hal?" she asked in a purring chuckle which admitted she knew what *any* man was thinking about when he looked at her.

She was here with Tootles. Neither she nor Wilding

wanted to arouse the hostility of the Callahan Family; but she would flirt and he—

He had invited her out on the roof of his penthouse.

Members of the Twelve Families and their entourage partied two levels below. A drunken mob of common people spilled onto the street from the ground floor of Wilding House, keeping Carnival in their own way.

More fireworks burst against the dome. Sparks spun down in varicolored corkscrews, and the crowd howled.

Wilding grinned, cat-smooth himself. He pointed a languid finger toward the boulevard. "Oh," he said, "I was thinking about them, Francine. What is it that they really want?"

The woman's stance did not change, but all the softness went out of her features. "Why ask me?" she said in a brittle voice. "How would I know?"

They were no longer flirting.

"Because you should know," he said. "Because I *want* to know."

Since he was host, he had not drunk heavily. There was enough alcohol in his brain to free the sharp-edged knowledge that he usually hid under an urbane exterior: he was a Wilding. For all practical purposes, he was *the* Wilding.

While Francine was a tart whom Tootles, Chauncey Callahan, had lifted from the gutter.

Her dress was a metallic sheath. It fitted Francine's hard curves as a scabbard of hammered silver would fit a scimitar. The natural color of her hair was black, and she wore it black tonight. It formed a pair of shoulder-length curls to frame her face, heart-shaped and carefully expressionless at this moment.

A door opened onto the balcony below. Half a dozen slurred, cheerful voices prattled merrily. "And *then*,"

Glory McLain trilled, "he wanted her to lie in cold water, I mean *really* cold, before she came to bed, and—"

The McLain girl's voice lowered into the general babble. The balcony was thirty feet below the penthouse roof; the partiers were unaware that there was anyone above them.

Francine moved away from the railing with a sinuous motion. She did not glance down to betray her concern about being seen—by Tootles, by someone who would mention the fact to Tootles.

Wilding stepped to the side also. "Don't they ever want a better life, Francine?" he said softly.

Fireworks began to spell letters across the dome: W-Y-O. . . .

Common people cheered and drank, while aristocrats gossiped about necrophilia.

The penthouse roof was planted with grass and palmettoes. The seedstock had come to Venus in the colony ships rather than being packed into terraforming capsules. It had not been exposed to the actinic radiation and adaptive pressures which had turned the Earth-sprung surface life into a purulent hell.

Francine spread the fingers of one hand and held them out against a palmetto frond, as if to compare her delicacy with the green coarseness.

"They don't want anything better," she said. She turned to look at Wilding. "They don't deserve anything better," she added fiercely. "If they did, they'd have it, wouldn't they? *I* bettered myself!"

There was a pause in the fireworks and the sound of the crowd in the street. " . . . and I don't mean young *girls*, either . . ." drifted up from the balcony.

Wilding turned to look out over the railing. He stayed

back from the edge so that he could see the half the width of the boulevard while remaining hidden from the partiers on the balcony. In the boulevard women who might have been prostitutes danced a clog-step with partners of all ages, accompanied by a hand-held sound system.

"They've got energy," Wilding said. "They could do. . . . *something.* Instead, what they get is a constant round of shortages and carouses."

He felt the warmth of Francine's body. When he turned, she was standing next to him again.

"Artificial hatred of neighboring keeps," he went on, astounded at the harshness in his own voice. "Artificial wars, fought by mercenaries—"

Francine's dress had a high neck and covered her ankles. The fabric was opaque but so thin and tight that the shimmering fireworks displayed her nipples with nude clarity. She was breathing rapidly.

"—under artificial conditions," Wilding said, "so that war can be entertainment but not destroy the planet the way Earth was destroyed. But that's not the only way Mankind can die, is it?"

"Prince Hal," the woman said in whispered desperation. She took his hands in hers. Her palms were clammy.

He'd drunk too much, or—

But he must have drunk too much. "Those people down there could colonize the surface some day," Wilding said. He enfolded the woman's small hands in his own, trying instinctively to warm her. "They could colonize the stars. All they need are leaders."

"Prince Hal," Francine begged, "don't *talk* like this. Please? You're scaring me."

"You're afraid of change," Wilding said. "The mob's afraid of change, *everybody's* afraid of change. So Wyoming Keep has the Twelve Families, and all the other keeps have their equivalents. Comfortable oligarchies determined to preserve the status quo until the whole system runs down. And no leaders!"

Francine lifted Wilding's hand to her mouth. She pressed it with her teeth and lips, an action somewhere between a kiss and a nibble. He could feel her heart beating.

More fireworks went off to amuse the Carnival crowd.

"It's nothing but a jungle life," Wilding whispered.

The woman stepped back and raised her hands to her neckline. There was hard decision in her eyes. "All right, Prince Hal," she said. "You want a leader? Then I'll lead you!"

Francine touched a catch. Her garment slid away to become a pool at her feet. She was nude beneath it. Her body was hairless and perfect.

"And you'll like where I take you, honey," she added with practiced enthusiasm.

EPILOGUE

SEPTEMBER 5, 387 AS. 1751 HOURS.

"Here ye go, buddy," said the short, grinning thug with the scarred face. He tapped on the door marked CHIEF OF STAFF. "Mr Brainard'll fix you up just fine, I'll bet."

The Callahan kept his face impassive, though a vein stood out from his neck. He did not care to lose his temper in front of underlings.

The man who had brought him from the guarded entrance to *here,* when he had demanded to be taken directly to the Wilding, was named Leaf. The Callahan knew Leaf by reputation—rather better than he wished were the case.

The Chief of Staff's office was opened from the inside by another thug. This one was named Caffey, and the Callahan knew of him also.

"Gen'leman to see Mr Brainard, Fish," Leaf said with a broad smile.

He was play-acting; both of them were. This was nothing but a show, with the Callahan forming both the straight man and the audience.

Caffey raised an eyebrow. "Alone?" he said.

He was a marginally smoother character than Leaf. At any rate, the muted beige tunic and trousers affected by all the Association functionaries had a civilian appearance on Caffey, while the garments seemed to be a prison uniform when Leaf wore them.

Looks were immaterial. Leaf and Caffey had equal authority as the Association's Commissioners of Security. They were equally brutal, equally ruthless; and equally dedicated to their job.

"There's half a dozen more come with him," Leaf said, "but one at a time seemed safer. The rest 're cooling their heels in the guardroom. Unless they got smart with Newton, in which case they're just cooling."

Caffey chuckled. "Takes a real direct view, that boy. Too dumb to get tricky, I s'pose."

"The men you're talking about are the Council of the Twelve Families," said the Callahan, finally stung to a response. "*Not* a street gang! We're here to meet with the Wilding."

Leaf grinned. "Not a *street* gang, I guess," he said. The soft change of emphasis made his words a threat.

Caffey looked over his shoulder. His stocky body still blocked the doorway. "D'ye want to see Mr Callahan, sir?" he called, proving he had known perfectly well from the beginning who he was dealing with.

"Of course, Fish," answered the unseen within. "I'd be delighted."

Caffey stepped aside, gestured the Callahan mockingly forward, and closed the door behind himself.

Brainard sat at a desk which was large and expensively outfitted, but cluttered with hard copy. He had the tired, worn appearance of a man older than his chronological age. His face and hands were flecked with minute dimples. Plastic surgery had not quite restored the texture Brainard's skin had had before jungle sores ate into it.

The Wilding's chief of staff did not look hard or dangerous. The Callahan had reason to know that Brainard was both those things, and more.

"I didn't come to talk with you, Brainard," the Callahan said. "My business—*our* business—is with the Wilding."

Brainard shrugged. "Have a seat," he said, gesturing the Callahan to one of the comfortable chairs facing the desk. "Since you're going to talk to me anyway."

He smiled at his visitor. The expression was as precise as the click of a gunlock. "And as a suggestion, Mr Callahan . . . unless you refer to him as Director Wilding, I'm the only one you *are* going to talk to this afternoon."

The walls of the Chief of Staff's office were decorated with holographic views recorded on the surface of Venus. The images were not retouched for propaganda purposes.

To the Callahan's right, huge land-clearing equipment tore at the jungle. On the wall over the door, other machinery formed barracks blocks and small bungalows from stabilized earth. On the visitor's left, humans of both sexes inspected an experimental plot of vegetables growing beneath an ultraviolet screen.

The wall behind Brainard did not carry a hologram. An automatic rifle hung there in a horizontal rack. To even the Callahan's inexperienced eye, the weapon was in poor condition. The metal surfaces were scarred, and fungus had pitted the plastic stock and fore-end.

The Callahan grimaced, then sat down. Forcing himself to look Brainard in the eyes, he said, "All right. What is it that he really wants?"

Brainard smiled. This time the expression was almost gentle. "Just what he says he wants, Mr Callahan," he said.

The Council had—the Callahan had; he was the Council and they all knew it—offered Brainard a bribe early on in the process. Brainard had sent back a polite note with the money—enough money to have set him up for life in any keep on Venus.

The next night, a mob of thousands of Association supporters had sacked and burned Callahan House. A Patrol detachment stood by and watched. They were outnumbered fifty to one by the rioters.

Patrol Headquarters directed the detachment to open fire. The on-site Patrol commander countermanded the order immediately. He realized that the men on the mob's fringes had the deeply tanned skin of Free Companions—and that the objects outlined against their cloaks were surely automatic weapons.

"Listen, Brainard," the Callahan snarled, "the time for playing games is over! You're a practical man. *You* know that the notion is impossibly expensive."

"Expensive, of course," Brainard said. "And while we pay Free Companions to defend large surface settlements, neighboring keeps will raid our fishing grounds." He leaned forward. His tunic touched the papers on his desk and made them rustle. "But the fishing grounds are played out, and the settlements will be exporting protein in a few years." Brainard's eyes were hard and empty, like a pair of gun muzzles.

"It's not impossible, Mr Callahan," he said. "And it's not expensive at all, compared to the centuries of phony war that you and yours have kept going!"

The Council made approaches to Leaf and Caffey after the attempt to subvert Brainard failed. This time the money did not come back—but neither did the agents carrying it.

Three days later, one male member of each of the Twelve Families was kidnapped. The operations were simultaneous and went off flawlessly, though several guards were killed in vain attempts to interfere.

The victims were dumped in front of the Council Building the next morning. They were alive, but they had been shaved bald and their skin dyed a bright blue.

After that debacle, the Callahan shelved what he had thought of as his final contingency plan. He was afraid to think about what would happen if he attempted assassination—and failed.

"Phony wars, Brainard?" the Callahan sneered. "It's real lives your master's scheme will cost, and there'll be a lot of them. Has he thought of *that?*"

Brainard's fingers gently explored the dimples on his cheek. It was a habitual gesture, an unconscious one. "We've seen death before, Mr Callahan," he said tonelessly. "People die no matter what. This way—" His eyes had gone unfocused. Now they locked on the Callahan. "This way they have a chance to die for something. And they're willing to. By *God,* they're willing to!"

"Yes, because you've stirred them up!" the Callahan

shouted. He gripped the arms of his chair fiercely, as if to hold himself down.

Brainard chuckled unexpectedly. He slid his chair back and stood with an easy motion. "That's right, Mr Callahan," he said. "Because we stirred them up. Because we're leading them. But—" The relaxed voice and posture vanished as suddenly as it had appeared. Brainard pointed his index finger at his visitor and went on, "—the common people *are* willing to go. And they're going to go. The only choice the Twelve Families has now is to support the process." Brainard's features changed. For the first time, the Callahan saw the face of the man who directed the activities of killers like Leaf and Caffey. "Or be burned out of the way," Brainard said, voice husky. "Like so much honeysuckle."

The Callahan stared across the desk at Brainard. He had never before in his life hated a human being as much as he hated this man—and his master.

But he had not ruled Wyoming Keep for twenty years by being a fool.

The Callahan stood up. "All right," he said quietly. "Then I suppose we'd better support the process, hadn't we? May I see Director Wilding now?"

The two men walked down the hallway together, toward the office of the Director of the Surface Settlement Association.

AUTHOR'S NOTE

In 1947 (when Heinlein, Asimov, and DeCamp were in their prime) the Fifth World Science Fiction Convention was held in Philadelphia. Attendees voted on their favorite author.

Henry Kuttner came in first.

My initial contact with Henry Kuttner's work came in 1958—though I didn't know it at the time. My parents gave me a copy of *The Astounding Science Fiction Anthology* for my thirteenth birthday. Included—and the story that among so many classics really blew me away—was a novella titled *Clash by Night,* written by Lawrence O'Donnell.

A year or two later I read *Destination: Infinity,* a Henry Kuttner novel set in the same milieu as *Clash by Night.* (Calling the novel a sequel would overstate the case, since the action takes place a thousand years later and the focus is wholly different.) The front matter noted that the novel had originally been serialized under the (much better) title *Fury,* and that the author of the serialized version was listed as "Lawrence O'Donnell."

I'd been a Kuttner fan before I knew it. I'm still a Kuttner fan.

Henry Kuttner, often writing with his wife C. L. Moore (the solo author of *Shambleau,* a first story as remarkably good as those of Heinlein and Van Vogt), used many pseudonyms. Partly this was because Kuttner was very prolific, and the magazines of the day rarely published two or more stories under the same byline in an issue.

Partly it was because Kuttner had started out as a writer in the '30s, when he was still in his teens. Many of his early stories were imitative and marked more by enthusiasm and facility than skill. A friend at the time (probably Mort Weisinger) described Kuttner's work filling the two semi-porn issues of *Marvel Science Fiction* as "Kill a monster, grab a tit. Kill a monster, grab a tit."

By the time Kuttner had improved his craft to a degree which put him in the first rank of his profession, his own name was ruined. In the 1940s, his best work came out under a variety of pseudonyms, particularly Lewis Padgett and (not often, but always exceptional) Lawrence O'Donnell.

I should note that C. L. Moore certainly worked on *Fury* and probably on *Clash by Night* also. Her influence on her husband's work goes beyond such direct involvement: even before the couple met, Kuttner was obviously imitating Moore's style in his heroic fantasy writing.

Having said that, I add that when Ms Moore recopywrited *Fury* and *Clash by Night* after Kuttner's death, she did so under his name alone. I accept her assessment of Kuttner and Moore's individual involvement in the pieces.

Clash by Night is an adventure story, which is as important to me now as it was in 1958. It's considerably more than that, however. The aspect that makes the story remarkable even today is Kuttner's awareness that mercenary soldiers were in business.

"Condottiere," the title of the men who led the mercenary bands of the Italian Renaissance, is not a military term: it means quite simply Contractor, and that's what the leaders were. The condottieri provided armed men instead of grain or timber; and they expected to make a businessman's profit on their outlay.

If you think that's an obvious piece of economics, read other science fiction and fantasy works involving mercenaries—even many of those written long after Kuttner's death.

When Tor through Marty Greenberg offered me the chance to do a sequel to *Clash by Night,* I jumped at it. *The Jungle* is *not,* however, a Kuttner pastiche (I did that elsewhere). This time I set out to write a David Drake story set in the milieu of Kuttner's *Clash by Night,* which is a very different thing. *The Jungle* could not possibly have been published in *Astounding* in 1943.

But neither could I have written *The Jungle* had I not read and reread the stories by which Kuttner continued for as long as he lived to push the bounds of what was stylistically possible in science fiction. The man who wrote *Private Eye* and *Home Is the Hunter,* to take two not-quite-random examples, has a great deal to teach any writer who is willing to learn.

Kuttner's willingness to take risks, and his awareness that there's more to style than "fine writing," are the core of *The Jungle.* As I said above, this isn't a Kuttner pastiche.

But it *is* a homage to Henry Kuttner, and I hope he would have approved my use of his setting.

—David Drake
Chapel Hill, North Carolina

HENRY KUTTNER

CLASH BY NIGHT

Introduction

A half mile beneath the shallow Venusian Sea the black impervium dome that protects Montana Keep rests frowningly on the bottom. Within the Keep is carnival, for the Montanans celebrate the four-hundred-year anniversary of Earthman's landing on Venus. Under the great dome that houses the city all is light and color and gaiety. Masked men and women, bright in celoflex and silks, wander through the broad streets, laughing, drinking the strong native wines of Venus. The sea bottom has been combed, like the hydroponic tanks, for rare delicacies to grace the tables of the nobles.

Through the festival grim shadows stalk, men whose faces mark them unmistakably as members of a Free Company. Their finery cannot disguise that stamp, hard-won through years of battle. Under the domino masks their mouths are hard and harsh. Unlike the undersea dwellers, their skins are burned black with the ultraviolet rays that filter through the cloud layer of Venus. They are skeletons at the feast. They are respected but resented. They are Free Companions—

We are on Venus, nine hundred years ago, beneath the Sea of Shoals, not much north of the equator. But there is a wide range in time and space. All over the cloud planet the underwater Keeps are dotted, and life will not change for many centuries. Looking back, as we do now, from the civilized days of the Thirty-fourth Century, it is too easy to regard the men of the Keeps as savages, groping, stupid, and brutal. The Free Companies have long since vanished. The islands and continents of Venus have been tamed, and there is no war.

But in periods of transition, of desperate rivalry, there is always war. The Keeps fought among themselves, each striving to draw the fangs of the others by depriving them of their reserves of korium, the power source of the day. Students of that era find pleasure in sifting the legends and winnowing out the basic social and geopolitical truths. It is fairly well known that only one factor saved the Keeps from annihilating one another—the gentlemen's agreement that left war to the warriors, and allowed the undersea cities to develop their science and social cultures. That particular compromise was, perhaps, inevitable. And it caused the organization of the Free Companies, the roving bands of mercenaries, highly trained for their duties, who hired themselves out to fight for whatever Keeps were attacked or wished to attack.

Ap Towrn, in his monumental "Cycle of Venus," tells the saga through symbolic legends. Many historians have recorded the sober truth, which, unfortunately, seems often Mars-dry. But it is not generally realized that the Free Companions were almost directly responsible for our present high culture. War, because of them, was not permitted to usurp the place of peace-time social and scientific work. Fighting was highly specialized, and, because of technical advances, manpower was no longer important. Each band of Free Companions numbered a few thousand, seldom more.

It was a strange, lonely life they must have led, shut out from the normal life of the Keeps. They were vestigian but necessary, like the fangs of the marsupians who eventually evolved into Homo sapiens. But without those warriors, the

Keeps would have been plunged completely into total war, with fatally destructive results.

Harsh, gallant, indomitable, serving the god of battles so that it might be destroyed—working toward their own obliteration—the Free Companies roar down the pages of history, the banner of Mars streaming above them in the misty air of Venus. They were doomed as Tyrannosaur Rex was doomed, and they fought on as he did, serving, in their strange way, the shape of Minerva that stood behind Mars.

Now they are gone. We can learn much by studying the place they held in the Undersea Period. For, because of them, civilization rose again to the heights it had once reached on Earth, and far beyond.

"These lords shall light the mystery
Of mastery or victory,
And these ride high in history,
But these shall not return."

The Free Companions hold their place in interplanetary literature. They are a legend now, archaic and strange. For they were fighters, and war has gone with unification. But we can understand them a little more than could the people of the Keeps.

This story, built on legends and fact, is about a typical warrior of the period—Captain Brian Scott of Doone's Free Companions. He may never have existed—

I

O, IT'S TOMMY THIS, AN' TOMMY THAT, AN' "TOMMY, GO AWAY";
BUT IT'S "THANK YOU, MR. ATKINS," WHEN THE BAND BEGINS TO PLAY,
THE BAND BEGINS TO PLAY, MY BOYS, THE BAND BEGINS TO PLAY—
O, IT'S "THANK YOU, MR. ATKINS," WHEN THE BAND BEGINS TO PLAY.

—R. KIPLING, CIRCA 1900

Scott drank stinging uisqueplus and glowered across the smoky tavern. He was a hard, stocky man, with thick gray-shot brown hair and the scar of an old wound crinkling his chin. He was thirty-odd, looking like the veteran he was, and he had sense enough to wear a plain suit of blue celoflex, rather than the garish silks and rainbow fabrics that were all around him.

Outside, through the transparent walls, a laughing throng was carried to and fro along the movable ways. But in the tavern it was silent, except for the low voice of a harpman as he chanted some old ballad, accompanying himself on his complicated instrument. The song came to an end. There was scattered applause, and from the hot-box overhead the blaring music of an orchestra burst out. Instantly the restraint was gone. In the booths and at the bar men and women began to laugh and talk with casual unrestraint. Couples were dancing now.

The girl beside Scott, a slim, tan-skinned figure with glossy black ringlets cascading to her shoulders, turned inquiring eyes to him.

"Want to, Brian?"

Scott's mouth twisted in a wry grimace. "Suppose so, Jeana. Eh?" He rose, and she came gracefully into his arms. Brian did not dance too well, but what he lacked in practice he made up in integration. Jeana's heart-shaped face, with its high cheekbones and vividly crimson lips, lifted to him.

"Forget Bienne. He's just trying to ride you."

Scott glanced toward a distant booth, where two girls sat with a man–Commander Fredric Bienne of the Doones. He was a gaunt, tall, bitter-faced man, his regular features twisted into a perpetual sneer, his eyes somber under heavy dark brows. He was pointing, now, toward the couple on the floor.

"I know," Scott said. "He's doing it, too. Well, the hell with him. So I'm a captain now and he's still a commander. That's tough. Next time he'll obey orders and not send his ship out of the line, trying to ram."

"That was it, eh?" Jeana asked. "I wasn't sure. There's plenty of talk."

"There always is. Oh, Bienne's hated me for years. I reciprocate. We simply don't get on together. Never did. Every time I got a promotion, he chewed his nails. Figured he had a longer service record than I had, and deserved to move up faster. But he's too much of an individualist—at the wrong times."

"He's drinking a lot," Jeana said.

"Let him. Three months we've been in Montana Keep.

The boys get tired of inaction—being treated like this." Scott nodded toward the door, where a Free Companion was arguing with the keeper. "No noncoms allowed in here. Well, the devil with it."

They could not hear the conversation above the hubbub, but its importance was evident. Presently the soldier shrugged, his mouth forming a curse, and departed. A fat man in scarlet silks shouted encouragement.

"—want any . . . Companions here!"

Scott saw Commander Bienne, his eyes half closed, get up and walk toward the fat man's booth. His shoulder moved in an imperceptible shrug. The hell with civilians, anyhow. Serve the lug right if Bienne smashed his greasy face. And that seemed the probable outcome. For the fat man was accompanied by a girl, and obviously wasn't going to back down, though Bienne, standing too close to him, was saying something insulting, apparently.

The auxiliary hot-box snapped some quick syllables, lost in the general tumult. But Scott's trained ear caught the words. He nodded to Jeana, made a significant clicking noise with his tongue, and said, "This is it."

She, too, had heard. She let Scott go. He headed toward the fat man's booth just in time to see the beginning of a brawl. The civilian, red as a turkey cock, had struck out suddenly, landing purely by accident on Bienne's gaunt cheek. The commander, grinning tightly, stepped back a pace, his fist clenching. Scott caught the other's arm.

"Hold it, Commander."

Bienne swung around, glaring. "What business is it of yours? Let—"

The fat man, seeing his opponent's attention distracted, acquired more courage and came in swinging. Scott reached past Bienne, planted his open hand in the civilian's face, and pushed hard. The fat man almost fell backward on his table.

As he rebounded, he saw a gun in Scott's hand. The captain said curtly, "Tend to your knitting, mister."

The civilian licked his lips, hesitated, and sat down. Under his breath he muttered something about too-damn-cocky Free Companions.

Bienne was trying to break free, ready to swing on the captain. Scott holstered his gun. "Orders," he told the other, jerking his head toward the hot-box. "Get it?"

"—mobilization. Doonemen report to headquarters. Captain Scott to Administration. Immediate mobilization—"

"Oh," Bienne said, though he still scowled. "O.K. I'll take over. There was time for me to take a crack at that louse, though."

"You know what instant mobilization means," Scott grunted. "We may have to leave at an instant's notice. Orders, Commander."

Bienne saluted halfheartedly and turned away. Scott went back to his own booth. Jeana had already gathered her purse and gloves and was applying lip juice.

She met his eyes calmly enough.

"I'll be at the apartment, Brian. Luck."

He kissed her briefly, conscious of a surging excitement at the prospect of a new venture. Jeana understood his emotion. She gave him a quick, wry smile, touched his hair lightly, and rose. They went out into the gay tumult of the ways.

Perfumed wind blew into Scott's face. He wrinkled his nose disgustedly. During carnival seasons the Keeps were less pleasant to the Free Companions than otherwise; they felt more keenly the gulf that lay between them and the undersea dwellers. Scott pushed his way through the crowd and took Jeana across the ways to the center fast-speed strip. They found seats.

At a clover-leaf intersection Scott left the girl, heading toward Administration, the cluster of taller buildings in the city's center. The technical and political headquarters were centered here, except for the laboratories, which were in the suburbs near the base of the Dome. There were a few small test-domes a mile or so distant from the city, but these were used only for more precarious experiments. Glancing up, Scott was reminded of the catastrophe that had unified science into something like a free-masonry. Above him, hanging without gravity over a central plaza, was the globe of the Earth, half shrouded by the folds of a black plastic pall. In every Keep on Venus there was a similar ever-present reminder of the lost mother planet.

Scott's gaze went up farther, to the Dome, as though he could penetrate the impervium and the mile-deep layer of water and the clouded atmosphere to the white star that hung in space, one quarter as brilliant as the Sun. A star—all that remained of Earth, since atomic power had been unleashed there two centuries ago. The scourge had spread like flame, melting continents and leveling mountains. In the libraries there were wire-tape pictorial records of the Holocaust. A religious cult—Men of the New Judgment—had sprung up, and advocated the complete destruction of science; followers of that dogma still existed here and there. But the cult's teeth had been drawn when technicians unified, outlawing experiments with atomic power forever, making use of that force punishable by death, and permitting no one to join their society without taking the Minervan Oath.

"—to work for the ultimate good of mankind . . . taking all precaution against harming humanity and science . . . requiring permission from those in authority before undertaking any experiment involving peril to the race . . . remembering always the extent of the trust placed in us and remembering forever the death of the mother planet through misuse of knowledge—"

The Earth. A strange sort of world it must have been, Scott thought. Sunlight, for one thing, unfiltered by the cloud layer. In the old days, there had been few unexplored areas left on Earth. But here on Venus, where the continents had not yet been conquered—there was no need, of course, since everything necessary to life could be produced under the Domes—here on Venus, there was still a frontier. In the Keeps, a highly specialized social culture. Above the surface, a primeval world, where only the Free Companions had their fortresses and navies—the navies for fighting, the forts to house the technicians who provided the latter-day sinews of war, science instead of money. The Keeps tolerated visits from the Free Companions, but would not offer them headquarters, so violent the feeling, so sharp the schism, in the public mind, between war and cultural progress.

Under Scott's feet the sliding way turned into an escalator, carrying him into the Administration Building. He stepped to another way which took him to a lift, and, a moment or two later, was facing the door-curtain bearing the face of President Dane Crosby of Montana Keep.

Crosby's voice said, "Come in, captain," and Scott brushed through the curtain, finding himself in a medium-sized room with muraled walls and a great window overlooking the city. Crosby, a white-haired, thin figure in blue silks, was at his desk. He looked like a tired old clerk out of Dickens, Scott thought suddenly, entirely undistinguished and ordinary. Yet Crosby was one of the greatest socio-politicians on Venus.

Cinc Rhys, leader of Doone's Free Companions, was sitting in a relaxer, the apparent antithesis of Crosby. All the moisture in Rhys's body seemed to have been sucked out of him years ago by ultraviolet actinic, leaving a mummy of brown leather and whipcord sinew. There was no softness in the man. His smile was a grimace. Muscles lay like wire under the swarthy cheeks.

Scott saluted. Rhys waved him to a relaxer. The look of subdued eagerness in the cinc's eyes was significant—an eagle poising himself, smelling blood. Crosby sensed that, and a wry grin showed on his pale face.

"Every man to his trade," he remarked, semi-ironically. "I suppose I'd be bored stiff if I had too long a vacation. But you'll have quite a battle on your hands this time, Cinc Rhys."

Scott's stocky body tensed automatically. Rhys glanced at him.

"Virginia Keep is attacking, Captain. They've hired the Helldivers—Flynn's outfit."

There was a pause. Both Free Companions were anxious to discuss the angles, but unwilling to do so in the presence of a civilian, even the president of Montana Keep. Crosby rose.

"The money settlement's satisfactory, then?"

Rhys nodded. "Yes, that's all right. I expect the battle

will take place in a couple of days. In the neighborhood of Venus Deep, at a rough guess."

"Good. I've a favor to ask, so if you'll excuse me for a few minutes, I'll—" He left the sentence unfinished and went out through the door-curtain. Rhys offered Scott a cigarette.

"You get the implications, captain—the Helldivers?"

"Yes, sir. Thanks. We can't do it alone."

"Right. We're short on manpower and armament both. And the Helldivers recently merged with O'Brien's Legion, after O'Brien was killed in that polar scrap. They're a strong outfit, plenty strong. Then they've got their specialty—submarine attack. I'd say we'll have to use H-plan 7."

Scott closed his eyes, remembering the files. Each Free Company kept up-to-date plans of attack suited to the merits of every other Company of Venus. Frequently revised as new advances were made, as groups merged, and as the balance of power changed on each side, the plans were so detailed that they could be carried into action at literally a moment's notice. H-plan 7, Scott recalled, involved enlisting the aid of the Mob, a small but well-organized band of Free Companions led by Cinc Tom Mendez.

"Right," Scott said. "Can you get him?"

"I think so. We haven't agreed yet on the bonus. I've been telaudioing him on a tight beam, but he keeps putting me off—waiting till the last moment, when he can dictate his own terms."

"What's he asking, sir?"

"Fifty thousand cash and a fifty percent cut on the loot."

"I'd say thirty percent would be about right."

Rhys nodded. "I've offered him thirty-five. I may send you to his fort—carte blanche. We can get another Company, but Mendez has got beautiful subdetectors—which would come in handy against the Helldivers. Maybe I can settle things by audio. If not, you'll have to fly over to Mendez and buy his services, at less than fifty per if you can."

Scott rubbed the old scar on his chin with a calloused forefinger. "Meantime Commander Bienne's in charge of mobilization. When—"

"I telaudioed our fort. Air transports are on the way now."

"It'll be quite a scrap," Scott said, and the eyes of the two men met in perfect understanding. Rhys chuckled dryly.

"And good profits. Virginia Keep has a big supply of korium . . . dunno how much, but plenty."

"What started the fracas this time?"

"The usual thing, I suppose," Rhys said disinterestedly. "Imperialism. Somebody in Virginia Keep worked out a new plan for annexing the rest of the Keeps. Same as usual."

They stood up as the door-curtain swung back, admitting President Crosby, another man, and a girl. The man looked young, his boyish face not yet toughened under actinic burn. The girl was lovely in the manner of a plastic figurine, lit from within by vibrant life. Her blond hair was cropped in the prevalent mode, and her eyes, Scott saw, were an unusual shade of green. She was more than merely pretty—she was instantly exciting.

Crosby said, "My niece, Ilene Kane—and my nephew,

Norman Kane." He performed introductions, and they found seats.

"What about drinks?" Ilene suggested. "This is rather revoltingly formal. The fight hasn't started yet, after all."

"O.K.," Ilene murmured. "I can wait." She eyed Scott interestedly.

Norman Kane broke in. "I'd like to join Doone's Free Companions, sir. I've already applied, but now that there's a battle coming up, I hate to wait till my application's approved. So I thought—"

Crosby looked at Cinc Rhys. "A personal favor, but the decision's up to you. My nephew's a misfit—a romanticist. Never liked the life of a Keep. A year ago he went off and joined Starling's outfit."

Rhys raised an eyebrow. "That gang? It's not a recommendation, Kane. They're not even classed as Free Companions. More like a band of guerrillas, and entirely without ethics. There've even been rumors they're messing around with atomic power."

Crosby looked startled. "I hadn't heard that."

"It's no more than a rumor. If it's ever proved, the Free Companions—all of them—will get together and smash Starling in a hurry."

Norman Kane looked slightly uncomfortable. "I suppose I was rather a fool. But I wanted to get in the fighting game, and Starling's group appealed to me—"

The cinc made a sound in his throat. "They would. Swashbuckling romantics, with no idea of what war means. They've not more than a dozen technicians. And they've no discipline—it's like a pirate outfit. War today, Kane, isn't won by romantic animals dashing at forlorn hopes. The modern soldier is a tactician who knows how to think, integrate, and obey. If you join our Company, you'll have to forget what you learned with Starling."

"Will you take me, sir?"

"I think it would be unwise. You need the training course."

"I've had experience—"

Crosby said, "It would be a favor, Cinc Rhys, if you'd skip the red tape. I'd appreciate it. Since my nephew wants to be a soldier, I'd much prefer to see him with the Doones."

Rhys shrugged. "Very well. Captain Scott will give you your orders, Kane. Remember that discipline is vitally important with us."

The boy tried to force back a delighted grin. "Thank you, sir."

"Captain—"

Scott rose and nodded to Kane. They went out together. In the anteroom was a telaudio set, and Scott called the Doone's local headquarters in Montana Keep. An integrator answered, his face looking inquiringly from the screen.

"Captain Scott calling, subject induction."

"Yes, sir. Ready to record."

Scott drew Kane forward. "Photosnap this man. He'll report to headquarters immediately. Name, Norman Kane. Enlist him without training course—special orders from Cinc Rhys."

"Acknowledged sir."

Scott broke the connection. Kane couldn't quite repress his grin.

"All right," the captain grunted, a sympathetic gleam in

his eyes. "That fixes it. They'll put you in my command. What's your specialty."

"Flitterboats, sir."

"Good. One more thing. Don't forget what Cinc Rhys said, Kane. Discipline is damned important, and you may not have realized that yet. This isn't a cloak-and-sword war. There are no Charges of Light Brigades. No grandstand plays—that stuff went out with the Crusades. Just obey orders, and you'll have no trouble. Good luck."

"Thank you, sir." Kane saluted and strode out with a perceptible swagger. Scott grinned. The kid would have *that* knocked out of him pretty soon.

A voice at his side made him turn quickly. Ilene Kane was standing there, slim and lovely in her celoflex gown.

"You seem pretty human after all, captain," she said. "I heard what you told Norman."

Scott shrugged. "I did that for his own good—and the good of the Company. One man off the beam can cause plenty of trouble, Mistress Kane."

"I envy Norman," she said. "It must be a fascinating life you lead. I'd like it—for a while. Not for long. I'm one of the useless offshoots of this civilization, not much good for anything. So I've perfected one talent."

"What's that?"

"Oh, hedonism, I suppose you'd call it. I enjoy myself. It's not often too boring. But I'm a bit bored now. I'd like to talk to you, Captain."

"Well, I'm listening," Scott said.

Ilene Kane made a small grimace. "Wrong semantic term. I'd like to get inside of you psychologically. But painlessly. Dinner and dancing. Can do?"

"There's no time," Scott told her. "We may get our orders any moment." He wasn't sure he wanted to go out with this girl of the Keeps, though there was definitely a subtle fascination for him, an appeal he could not analyze. She typified the most pleasurable part of a world he did not know. The other facets of that world could not impinge on him; geopolitics or nonmilitary science held no appeal, were too alien. But all worlds touch at one point—pleasure. Scott could understand the relaxation of the undersea groups, as he could not understand or feel sympathy for their work or their social impulses.

Cinc Rhys came through the door-curtain, his eyes narrowed. "I've some telaudioing to do, captain," he said. Scott knew what implications the words held: the incipient bargain with Cinc Mendez. He nodded.

"Yes, sir. Shall I report to headquarters?"

Rhys's harsh face seemed to relax suddenly as he looked from Ilene to Scott. "You're free till dawn. I won't need you till then, but report to me at six a.m. No doubt you've a few details to clean up."

"Very well, sir." Scott watched Rhys go out. The cinc had meant Jeana, of course. But Ilene did not know that.

"So?" she asked. "Do I get a turn-down? You might buy me a drink, anyway."

There was plenty of time. Scott said, "It'll be a pleasure," and Ilene linked her arm with his. They took the dropper to ground-level.

As they came out on one of the ways, Ilene turned her head and caught Scott's glance. "I forgot something, captain. You may have a previous engagement. I didn't realize—"

"There's nothing," he said. "Nothing important."

It was true; he felt a mild gratitude toward Jeana at the realization. His relationship with her was the peculiar one rendered advisable by his career. Free-marriage was the word for it; Jeana was neither his wife nor his mistress, but something midway between. The Free Companions had no firmly grounded foundation for social life; in the Keeps they were visitors, and in their coastal forts they were—well, soldiers. One would no more bring a woman to a fort than aboard a ship of the line. So the women of the Free Companions lived in the Keeps, moving from one to another as their men did; and because of the ever-present shadow of death, ties were purposely left loose. Jeana and Scott had been free-married for five years now. Neither made demands on the other. No one expected fidelity of a Free Companion. Soldiers lived under such iron disciplines that when they were released, during the brief peacetimes, the pendulum often swung far in the opposite direction.

To Scott, Ilene Kane was a key that might unlock the doors of the Keep—doors that opened to a world of which he was not a part, and which he could not quite understand.

I, A STRANGER AND AFRAID
IN A WORLD I NEVER MADE.

—HOUSMAN

There were nuances, Scott found, which he had never known existed. A hedonist like Ilene devoted her life to such nuances; they were her career. Such minor matters as making the powerful, insipid Moonflower Cocktails more palatable by filtering them through lime-soaked sugar held between the teeth. Scott was a uisqueplus man, having the average soldier's contempt for what he termed hydroponic drinks, but the cocktails Ilene suggested were quite as effective as acrid, burning amber uisqueplus. She taught him, that night, such tricks as pausing between glasses to sniff lightly at happy-gas, to mingle sensual excitement with mental by trying the amusement rides designed to give one the violent physical intoxication of breathless speed. Nuances all, which only a girl with Ilene's background could know. She was not representative of Keep life. As she had said, she was an offshoot, a casual and useless flower on the great vine that struck up inexorably to the skies, its strength in its tough, reaching tendrils—scientists and technicians and socio-politicians. She was doomed in her own way, as Scott was in his. The undersea folk served Minerva; Scott served Mars; and Ilene served Aphrodite—not purely the sexual goddess, but the patron of arts and pleasure. Between Scott and Ilene was the difference between Wagner and Strauss; the difference between crashing chords and tinkling arpeggios. In both was a muted bittersweet sadness, seldom realized by either. But that undertone was brought out by their contact. The sense of dim hopelessness in each responded to the other.

It was carnival, but neither Ilene nor Scott wore masks. Their faces were masks enough, and both had been trained to reserve, though in different ways. Scott's hard mouth kept its tight grimness even when he smiled. And Ilene's smiles came so often that they were meaningless.

Through her, Scott was able to understand more of the undersea life than he had ever done before. She was for him a catalyst. A tacit understanding grew between them, not needing words. Both realized that, in the course of progress, they would eventually die out. Mankind tolerated them because that was necessary for a little time. Each responded differently. Scott served Mars; he served actively; and the girl, who was passive, was attracted by the antithesis.

Scott's drunkenness struck psychically deep. He did not show it. His stiff silver-brown hair was not disarranged, and his hard, burned face was impassive as ever. But when his brown eyes met Ilene's green ones a spark of—something—met between them.

Color and light and sound. They began to form a pattern now, were not quite meaningless to Scott. They were, long past midnight, sitting in an Olympus, which was a private cosmos. The walls of the room in which they were seemed nonexistent. The gusty tides of gray, faintly luminous clouds seemed to drive chaotically past them, and, dimly, they could hear the muffled screaming of an artificial wind. They had the isolation of the gods.

And the Earth was without form, and void; and darkness was upon the face of the deep—That was, of course, the theory of the Olympus room. No one existed, no world existed, outside of the chamber; values automatically shifted, and inhibitions seemed absurd.

Scott relaxed on a translucent cushion like a cloud. Beside him, Ilene lifted the bit of a happy-gas tube to his nostrils. He shook his head.

"Not now, Ilene."

She let the tube slide back into its reel. "Nor I. Too much of anything is unsatisfactory, Brian. There should always be something untasted, some anticipation left—You have that. I haven't."

"How?"

"Pleasures—well, there's a limit. There's a limit to human endurance. And eventually I build up a resistance psychically, as I do physically, to everything. With you, there's always the last adventure. You never know when death will come. You can't plan. Plans are dull; it's the unexpected that's important."

Scott shook his head slightly. "Death isn't important either. It's an automatic cancellation of values. Or, rather—" He hesitated, seeking words. "In this life you can plan, you can work out values, because they're all based on certain conditions. On—let's say—arithmetic. Death is a change to a different plane of conditions, quite unknown. Arithmetical rules don't apply as such to geometry."

"You think death has its rules?"

"It may be a lack of rules, Ilene. One lives realizing that life is subject to death; civilization is based on that. That's why civilization concentrates on the race instead of the individual. Social self-preservation."

She looked at him gravely. "I didn't think a Free Companion could theorize that way."

Scott closed his eyes, relaxing. "The Keeps know nothing about Free Companions. They don't want to. We're men. Intelligent men. Our technicians are as great as the scientists under the Domes."

"But they work for war."

"War's necessary," Scott said. "Now, anyway."

"How did you get into it? Should I ask?"

He laughed a little at that. "Oh, I've no dark secrets in my past. I'm not a runaway murderer. One—drifts. I was born in Australia Keep. My father was a tech, but my grandfather had been a soldier. I guess it was in my blood. I tried various trades and professions. Meaningless. I wanted something that . . . hell, I don't know. Something, maybe, that needs all of a man. Fighting does. It's like a religion. Those cultists—Men of the New Judgment—they're fanatics, but you can see that their religion is the only thing that matters to them."

"Bearded, dirty men with twisted minds, though."

"It happens to be a religion based on false premises. There are others, appealing to different types. But religion was too passive for me, in these days."

Ilene examined his harsh face. "You'd have preferred the church militant—the Knights of Malta, fighting Saracens."

"I suppose. I had no values. Anyhow, I'm a fighter."

"Just how important is it to you? The Free Companions?"

Scott opened his eyes and grinned at the girl. He looked unexpectedly boyish.

"Damn little, really. It has emotional appeal. Intellectually, I know that it's a huge fake. Always has been. As absurd as the Men of the New Judgment. Fighting's doomed. So we've no real purpose. I suppose most of us know there's no future for the Free Companions. In a few hundred years—well!"

"And still you go on. Why? It isn't money."

"No. There is a . . . a drunkenness to it. The ancient Norsemen had their berserker madness. We have something similar. To a Dooneman, his group is father, mother, child, and God Almighty. He fights the other Free Companions when he's paid to do so, but he doesn't hate the others. They serve the same toppling idol. And it *is* toppling, Ilene. Each battle we win or lose brings us closer to the end. We fight to protect the culture that eventually will wipe us out. The Keeps—when they finally unify, will they need a military arm? I can see the trend. If war was an essential part of civilization, each Keep would maintain its own military. But they shut us out—a necessary evil. If they would end war now!" Scott's fist unconsciously clenched. "So many men would find happier places in Venus—undersea. But as long as the Free Companions exist, there'll be new recruits."

Ilene sipped her cocktail, watching the gray chaos of clouds flow like a tide around them. In the dimly luminous light Scott's face seemed like dark stone, flecks of brightness showing in his eyes. She touched his hand gently.

"You're a soldier, Brian. You wouldn't change."

His laugh was intensely bitter. "Like hell I wouldn't, Mistress Ilene Kane! Do you think fighting's just pulling a trigger? I'm a military strategist. That took ten years. Harder cramming than I'd have had in a Keep Tech-Institute. I have to know everything about war from trajectories to mass psychology. This is the greatest science the System has ever known, and the most useless. Because war will die in a few centuries at most. Ilene—you've never seen a Free Company's fort. It's science, marvelous science, aimed at military ends only. We have our psych-specialists. We have our engineers, who plan everything from ordnance to the frictional quotient on flitterboats. We have the foundries and mills. Each fortress is a city made for war, as the Keeps are made for social progress."

"As complicated as that?"

"Beautifully complicated and beautifully useless. There are so many of us who realize that. Oh, we fight—it's a poison. We worship the Company—that is an emotional poison. But we live only during wartime. It's an incomplete life. Men in the Keeps have full lives; they have their work, and their relaxations are geared to fit them. We don't fit."

"Not all the undersea races," Ilene said. "There's always the fringe that doesn't fit. At least you have a *raison d'être.* You're a soldier. I can't make a lifework out of pleasure. But there's nothing else for me."

Scott's fingers tightened on hers. "You're the product of a civilization, at least. I'm left out."

"With you, Brian, it might be better. For a while. I don't think it would last for long."

"It might."

"You think so now. It's quite a horrible thing, feeling yourself a shadow."

"I know."

"I want you, Brian," Ilene said, turning to face him. "I want you to come to Montana Keep and stay here. Until our experiment fails. I think it'll fail presently. But, perhaps, not for some time. I need your strength. I can show you how to get the most out of this sort of life—how to enter into it. True hedonism. You can give me—companionship perhaps. For me the companionship of hedonists who know nothing else isn't enough."

Scott was silent. Ilene watched him for a while.

"Is war so important?" she asked at last.

"No," he said, "it isn't at all. It's a balloon. And it's empty, I know that. Honor of the regiment!" Scott laughed. "I'm not hesitating, really. I've been shut out for a long time. A social unit shouldn't be founded on an obviously doomed fallacy. Men and women are important, nothing else, I suppose."

"Men and women—or the race?"

"Not the race," he said with abrupt violence. "Damn the race! It's done nothing for me. I can fit myself into a new life. Not necessarily hedonism. I'm an expert in several lines; I have to be. I can find work in Montana Keep."

"If you like. I've never tried. I'm more of a fatalist, I suppose. But . . . what about it, Brian?"

Her eyes were almost luminous, like shining emerald, in the ghostly light.

"Yes," Scott said. "I'll come back. To stay."

Ilene said, "Come back? Why not stay now?"

"Because I'm a complete fool, I guess. I'm a key man, and Cinc Rhys needs me just now."

"Is it Rhys or the Company?"

Scott smiled crookedly. "Not the Company. It's just a job I have to do. When I think how many years I've been slaving, pretending absurdities were important, knowing that I was bowing to a straw dummy—*No!* I want your life—the sort of life I didn't know could exist in the Keeps. I'll be back, Ilene. It's something more important than love. Separately we're halves. Together we may be a complete whole."

She didn't answer. Her eyes were steady on Scott's. He kissed her.

Before morning bell he was back in the apartment. Jeana had already packed the necessary light equipment. She was asleep, her dark hair cascading over the pillow, and Scott did not waken her. Quietly he shaved, showered, and dressed. A heavy, waiting silence seemed to fill the city like a cup brimmed with stillness.

As he emerged from the bathroom, buttoning his tunic, he saw the table had been let down and two places set at it. Jeana came in, wearing a cool morning frock. She set cups down and poured coffee.

"Morning, soldier," she said. "You've time for this, haven't you?"

"Uh-huh." Scott kissed her, a bit hesitantly. Up till this moment, the breaking with Jeana had seemed easy enough. She would raise no objections. That was the chief reason for free-marriage. However—

She was sitting in the relaxer, sweeting the coffee, opening a fresh celo-pack of cigarettes. "Hung over?"

"No. I vitamized. Feel pretty good." Most bars had a vitamizing chamber to nullify the effects of too much stimulant. Scott was, in fact, feeling fresh and keenly alert. He was wondering how to broach the subject of Ilene to Jeana.

She saved him the trouble.

"If it's a girl, Brian, just take it easy. No use doing anything till this war's over. How long will it take?"

"Oh, not long. A week at most. One battle may settle it, you know. The girl—"

"She's not a Keep girl."

"Yes."

Jeana looked up, startled. "You're crazy."

"I started to tell you," Scott said impatiently. "It isn't just—her. I'm sick of the Doones. I'm going to quit."

"Hm-m-m. Like that?"

"Like that."

Jeana shook her head. "Keep women aren't tough."

"They don't need to be. Their men aren't soldiers."

"Have it your own way. I'll wait till you get back. Maybe I've got a hunch. You see, Brian, we've been together for five years. We fit. Not because of anything like philosophy or psychology—it's a lot more personal. It's just us. As man and woman, we get along comfortably. There's love, too. Those close emotional feelings are more important, really, than the long view. You can get excited about futures, but you can't live them."

Scott shrugged. "Could be I'm starting to forget about futures. Concentrating on Brian Scott."

"More coffee . . . there. Well, for five years now I've gone with you from Keep to Keep, waiting every time you went off to war, wondering if you'd come back, knowing that I was just a part of your life, but—I sometimes thought—the most important part. Soldiering's seventy-five percent. I'm the other quarter. I think you need that quarter—you need the whole thing, in that proportion, actually. You could find another woman, but she'd have to be willing to take twenty-five percent."

Scott didn't answer. Jeana blew smoke through her nostrils.

"O.K., Brian. I'll wait."

"It isn't the girl so much. She happens to fit into the pattern of what I want. You—"

"I'd never be able to fit that pattern," Jeana said softly. "The Free Companions need women who are willing to be soldiers' wives. Free-wives, if you like. Chiefly it's a matter of not being too demanding. But there are other things. No, Brian. Even if you wanted that, I couldn't make myself over into one of the Keep people. It wouldn't be me. I wouldn't respect myself, living a life that'd be false to me; and you wouldn't like me that way either. I couldn't and wouldn't change. I'll have to stay as I am. A soldier's wife. As long as you're a Dooneman, you'll need me. But if *you* change—" She didn't finish.

Scott lit a cigarette, scowling. "It's hard to know, exactly."

"I may not understand you, but I don't ask questions and I don't try to change you. As long as you want that, you can have it from me. I've nothing else to offer you. It's enough for a Free Companion. It's not enough—or too much—for a Keep-dweller."

"I'll miss you," he said.

"That'll depend, too. I'll miss you." Under the table her fingers writhed together, but her face did not change. "It's getting late. Here, let me check your chronometer." Jeana leaned across the table, lifted Scott's wrist, and compared his watch with the central-time clock on the wall. "O.K. On your way, soldier."

Scott stood up, tightening his belt. He bent to kiss Jeana, and, though she began to turn her face away, after a moment she raised her lips to his.

They didn't speak. Scott went out quickly, and the girl sat motionless, the cigarette smoldering out unheeded between her fingers. Somehow it did not matter so much now that Brian was leaving her for another woman and another life. As always, the one thing of real importance was that he was going into danger.

Guard him from harm, she thought, not knowing that she was praying. *Guard him from harm!*

And now there would be silence, and waiting. That, at least, had not changed. Her eyes turned to the clock.

Already the minutes were longer.

'E'S THE KIND OF A GIDDY HARUMFRODITE
—SOLDIER AN' SAILOR TOO!
—KIPLING

Commander Bienne was superintending the embarkation of the last Dooneman when Scott arrived at headquarters. He saluted the captain briskly, apparently untired by his night's work of handling the transportation routine.

"All checked, sir."

Scott nodded. "Good. Is Cinc Rhys here?"

"He just arrived." Bienne nodded toward a door-curtain. As Scott moved away, the other followed.

"What's up, commander?"

Bienne pitched his voice low. "Bronson's laid up with endemic fever." He forgot to say "sir." "He was to handle the left wing of the fleet. I'd appreciate that job."

"I'll see if I can do it."

Bienne's lips tightened, but he said nothing more. He turned back to his men, and Scott went on into the cinc's office. Rhys was at the telaudio. He looked up, his eyes narrowed.

"Morning, Captain. I've just heard from Mendez."

"Yes, sir?"

"He's still holding out for a fifty-percent cut on the korium ransom from Virginia Keep. You'll have to see him. Try and get the Mob for less than fifty if you can. Telaudio me from Mendez's fort."

"Check, sir."

"Another thing. Bronson's in sick bay."

"I heard that. If I may suggest Commander Bienne to take his place at left-wing command—"

But Cinc Rhys raised his hand. "Not this time. We can't afford individualism. The commander tried to play a lone hand in the last war. You know we can't risk it till he's back in line—thinking of the Doones instead of Fredric Bienne."

"He's a good man, sir. A fine strategist."

"But not yet a good integrating factor. Perhaps next time. Put Commander Geer on the left wing. Keep Bienne with you. He needs discipline. And—take a flitterboat to Mendez."

"Not a plane?"

"One of the technicians just finished a new tight-beam camouflager for communications. I'm having it installed immediately on all our planes and gliders. Use the boat; it isn't far to the Mob's fort—that long peninsula on the coast of Southern Hell."

Even on the charts that continent was named Hell—for obvious reasons. Heat was only one of them. And, even with the best equipment, a party exploring the jungle there would soon find itself suffering the tortures of the damned. On the land of Venus, flora and fauna combined diabolically to make the place uninhabitable to Earthmen. Many of the plants even exhaled poisonous gases. Only the protected coastal forts of the Free Companies could exist—and that was because they *were* forts.

Cinc Rhys frowned at Scott. "We'll use H-plan 7 if we can get the Mob. Otherwise we'll have to fall back on another outfit, and I don't want to do that. The Helldivers have too many subs, and we haven't enough detectors. So do your damnedest."

Scott saluted. "I'll do that, sir." Rhys waved him away, and he went out into the next room, finding Commander Bienne alone. The officer turned an inquiring look toward him.

"Sorry," Scott said. "Geer gets the left-wing command this time."

Bienne's sour face turned dark red. "I'm sorry I didn't take a crack at you before mobilization," he said. "You hate competition, don't you?"

Scott's nostrils flared. "If it had been up to me, you'd have got that command, Bienne."

"Sure. I'll bet. All right, Captain. Where's my bunk? A flitterboat?"

"You'll be on right wing, with me. Control ship *Flintlock.*"

"With you. Under you, you mean," Bienne said tightly. His eyes were blazing. "Yeah."

Scott's dark cheeks were flushed too. "Orders, commander," he snapped. "Get me a flitterboat pilot. I'm going topside."

Without a word Bienne turned to the telaudio. Scott, a tight, furious knot in his stomach, stamped out of headquarters, trying to fight down his anger. Bienne was a jackass. A lot he cared about the Doones—

Scott caught himself and grinned sheepishly. Well, he cared little about the Doones himself. But while he was in the Company, discipline was important—integration with the smoothly running fighting machine. No place for individualism. One thing he and Bienne had in common; neither had any sentiment about the Company.

He took a lift to the ceiling of the Dome. Beneath him Montana Keep dropped away, shrinking to doll size. Somewhere down there, he thought, was Ilene. He'd be back. Perhaps this war would be a short one—not that they were ever much longer than a week, except in unusual cases where a Company developed new strategies.

He was conducted through an air lock into a bubble, a tough, transparent sphere with a central vertical core through which the cable ran. Except for Scott, the bubble was empty. After a moment it started up with a slight jar. Gradually the water outside the curving walls changed from black to deep green, and thence to translucent chartreuse. Sea creatures were visible, but they were nothing new to Scott; he scarcely saw them.

The bubble broke surface. Since air pressure had been constant, there was no possibility of the bends, and Scott opened the panel and stepped out on one of the buoyant floats that dotted the water above Montana Keep. A few sightseers crowded into the chamber he had left, and presently it was drawn down, out of sight.

In the distance Free Companions were embarking from a larger float to an air ferry. Scott glanced up with a weather eye. No storm, he saw, though the low ceiling was, as usual, torn and twisted into boiling currents by the winds. He remembered, suddenly, that the battle would probably take place over Venus Deep. That would make it somewhat harder for the gliders—there would be few of the thermals found, for instance, above the Sea of Shallows here.

A flitterboat, low, fast, and beautifully maneuverable, shot in toward the quay. The pilot flipped back the overhead shell and saluted Scott. It was Norman Kane, looking shipshape in his tight-fitting gray uniform, and apparently ready to grin at the slightest provocation.

Scott jumped lightly down into the craft and seated himself beside the pilot. Kane drew the transparent shell back over them. He looked at Scott.

"Orders, Captain?"

"Know where the Mob's fort is? Good. Head there. Fast."

Kane shot the flitterboat out from the float with a curtain of V-shaped spray rising form the bow. Drawing little water, maneuverable, incredibly fast, these tiny craft were invaluable in naval battle. It was difficult to hit one, they moved so fast. They had no armor to slow them down. They carried high-explosive bullets fired from small-caliber guns, and were, as a rule, two-man craft. They complemented the heavier ordnance of the battlewagons and destroyers.

Scott handed Kane a cigarette. The boy hesitated.

"We're not under fire," the Captain chuckled. "Discipline clamps down during a battle, but it's O. K. for you to have a smoke with me. Here!" He lit the white tube for Kane.

"Thanks, sir. I guess I'm a bit—over-anxious?"

"Well, war has its rules. Not many, but they mustn't be broken." Both men were silent for a while, watching the blank gray surface of the ocean ahead. A transport plane passed them, flying low.

"Is Ilene Kane your sister?" Scott asked presently.

Kane nodded. "Yes, sir."

"Thought so. If she'd been a man, I imagine she'd have been a Free Companion."

The boy shrugged. "Oh, I don't know. She doesn't have the—I don't know. She'd consider it too much effort. She doesn't like discipline."

"Do you?"

"It's fighting that's important to me. Sir." That was an afterthought. "Winning, really."

"You can lose a battle even though you win it," Scott said rather somberly.

"Well, I'd rather be a Free Companion than do anything else I know of. Not that I've had much experience—"

"You've had experience of war with Starling's outfit, but you probably learned some dangerous stuff at the same time. War isn't swashbuckling piracy these days. If the Doones tried to win battles by that sort of thing, there'd be no more Doones in a week or so."

"But—" Kane hesitated. "Isn't that sort of thing rather necessary? Taking blind chances, I mean—"

"There are desperate chances," Scott told him, "but there are no blind chances in war—not to a good soldier. When I was green in the service, I ran a cruiser out of the line to ram. I was demoted, for a very good reason. The enemy ship I rammed wasn't as important to the enemy as our cruiser was to us. If I'd stayed on course, I'd have helped sink three or four ships instead of disabling one and putting my cruiser out of action. It's the great god integration we worship, Kane. It's much more important now than it ever was on Earth, because the military has consolidated. Army, navy, air, undersea—they're all part of one organization now. I suppose the only important change was in the air."

"Gliders, you mean? I knew powered planes couldn't be used in battle."

"Not in the atmosphere of Venus," Scott agreed. "Once powered planes get up in the cloud strata, they're fighting crosscurrents and pockets so much they've got no time to do accurate firing. If they're armored, they're slow. If they're light, detectors can spot them and antiaircraft can smash them. Unpowered gliders are valuable not for bombing but for directing attacks. They get into the clouds, stay hidden, and use infrared telecameras which are broadcast on a tight beam back to the control ships. They're the eyes of the fleet. They can tell us—*White water ahead, Kane! Swerve!*"

The pilot had already seen the ominous boiling froth foaming out in front of the bow. Instinctively he swung the flitterboat in a wrenching turn. The craft heeled sidewise, throwing its occupants almost out of their seats.

"Sea beast?" Scott asked, and answered his own question. "No, not with those spouts. It's volcanic. And it's spreading fast."

"I can circle it, sir," Kane suggested.

Scott shook his head. "Too dangerous. Backtrack."

Obediently the boy sent the flitterboat racing out of the area of danger. Scott had been right about the extent of the danger; the boiling turmoil was widening almost faster than the tiny ship could flee. Suddenly the line of white water caught up with them. The flitterboat jounced like a chip, the wheel being nearly torn from Kane's grip. Scott reached over and helped steady it. Even with two men handling the wheel, there was a possibility that it might wrench itself free. Steam rose in veils beyond the transparent shell. The water had turned a scummy brown under the froth.

Kane jammed on the power. The flitterboat sprang forward like a ricocheting bullet, dancing over the surface of the seething waves. Once they plunged head-on into a swell, and a screaming of outraged metal vibrated through the craft. Kane, tight-lipped, instantly slammed in the auxiliary, cutting out the smashed motor unit. Then, unexpectedly, they were in clear water, cutting back toward Montana Keep.

Scott grinned. "Nice handling. Lucky you didn't try to circle. We'd never have made it."

"Yes, sir." Kane took a deep breath. His eyes were bright with excitement.

"Circle now. Here." He thrust a lighted cigarette between the boy's lips. "You'll be a good Dooneman, Kane. Your reactions are good and fast."

"Thanks, sir."

Scott smoked silently for a while. He glanced toward the north, but, with the poor visibility, he could not make out the towering range of volcanic peaks that were the backbone of Southern Hell. Venus was a comparatively young planet, the internal fires still bursting forth unexpectedly. Which was why no forts were ever built on islands—they had an unhappy habit of disappearing without warning!

The flitterboat rode hard, at this speed, despite the insulating system of springs and shock absorbers. After a ride in one of these "spankers"—the irreverent name the soldiers had for them—a man needed arnica if not a chiropractor. Scott shifted his weight on the soft air cushions under him, which felt like cement.

Under his breath he hummed:

"It ain't the 'eavy 'aulin' that 'urts the 'orses' 'oofs,
It's the 'ammer, 'ammer, 'ammer on the 'ard 'ighway!"

* * *

The flitterboat scooted on, surrounded by monotonous sea and cloud, till finally the rampart of the coast grew before the bow, bursting suddenly from the fog-veiled horizon. Scott glanced at his chronometer and sighed with relief. They had made good time, in spite of the slight delay caused by the subsea volcano.

The fortress of the Mob was a huge metal and stone castle on the tip of the peninsula. The narrow strip that separated it from the mainland had been cleared, and the pockmarks of shell craters showed where guns had driven back onslaughts from the jungle—the reptilian, ferocious giants of Venus, partially intelligent but absolutely untractable because of the gulf that existed between their methods of thinking and the culture of mankind. Overtures had been made often enough; but it had been found that the reptile-folk were better left alone. They would not parley. They were blindly bestial savages, with whom it was impossible to make truce. They stayed in the jungle, emerging only to hurl furious attacks at the forts—attacks doomed to failure, since fang and talon were matched against lead-jacketed bullet and high explosive.

As the flitterboat shot in to a jetty, Scott kept his eyes straight ahead—it was not considered good form for a Free Companion to seem too curious when visiting the fort of another Company. Several men were on the quay, apparently waiting for him. They saluted as Scott stepped out of the boat.

He gave his name and rank. A corporal stepped forward.

"Cinc Mendez is expecting you, sir. Cinc Rhys telaudioed an hour or so back. If you'll come this way—"

"All right, corporal. My pilot—"

"He'll be taken care of, sir. A rubdown and a drink, perhaps, after a spanker ride."

Scott nodded and followed the other into the bastion that thrust out from the overhanging wall of the fort. The sea gate was open, and he walked swiftly through the courtyard in the corporal's wake, passing a door-curtain, mounting an escalator, and finding himself, presently, before another curtain that bore the face of Cinc Mendez, plump, hoglike, and bald as a bullet.

Entering, he saw Mendez himself at the head of a long table, where nearly a dozen officers of the Mob were also seated. In person Mendez was somewhat more prepossessing than in effigy. He looked like a boar rather than a pig—a fighter, not a gourmand. His sharp black eyes seemed to drive into Scott with the impact of a physical blow.

He stood up, his officers following suit. "Sit down, Captain. There's a place at the foot of the table. No reflections on rank, but I prefer to be face to face with the man I'm dealing with. But first—you just arrived? If you'd like a quick rubdown, we'll be glad to wait."

Scott took his place. "Thank you, no, Cinc Mendez. I'd prefer not to lose time."

"Then we'll waste none on introductions. However, you can probably stand a drink." He spoke to the orderly at the door, and presently a filled glass stood at Scott's elbow.

His quick gaze ran along the rows of faces. Good soldiers, he thought—tough, well trained, and experienced. They had been under fire. A small outfit, the Mob, but a powerful one.

Cinc Mendez sipped his own drink. "To business. The Doonemen wish to hire our help in fighting the Helldivers. Virginia Keep has bought the services of the Helldivers to attack Montana Keep." He enumerated on stubby fingers. "You offer us fifty thousand cash and thirty-five percent of the korium ransom. So?"

"That's correct."

"We ask fifty percent."

"It's high. The Doones have superior manpower and equipment."

"To us, not to the Helldivers. Besides, the percentage is contingent. If we should lose, we get only the cash payment."

Scott nodded. "That's correct, but the only real danger from the Helldivers is their submarine corps. The Doones have plenty of surface and air equipment. We might lick the Helldivers without you."

"I don't think so." Mendez shook his bald head. "They have some new underwater torpedoes that make hash out of heavy armor plate. But *we* have new sub-detectors. We can blast the Helldivers' subs for you before they get within torpedo range."

Scott said bluntly, "You've been stalling, Cinc Mendez. We're not that bad off. If we can't get you, we'll find another outfit."

"With sub-detectors?"

"Yardley's Company is good at undersea work."

A major near the head of the table spoke up. "That's true, sir. They have suicide subs—not too dependable, but they have them."

Cinc Mendez wiped his bald head with his palms in a slow circular motion. "Hm-m-m. Well, captain, I don't know. Yardley's Company isn't as good as ours for this job."

"All right," Scott said, "I've *carte blanche.* We don't know how much korium Virginia Keep has in her vaults.

How would this proposition strike you: the Mob gets fifty percent of the korium ransom up to a quarter of a million; thirty-five percent above that."

"Forty-five."

"Forty, above a quarter of a million; forty-five below that sum."

"Gentlemen?" Cinc Mendez asked, looking down the table. "Your vote?"

There were several ayes, and a scattering of nays. Mendez shrugged.

"Then I have the deciding vote. Very well. We get forty-five percent of the Virginia Keep ransom up to a quarter of a million; forty percent on any amount above that. Agreed. We'll drink to it."

Orderlies served drinks. As Mendez rose, the others followed his example. The cinc nodded to Scott.

"Will you propose a toast, Captain?"

"With pleasure. Nelson's toast, then—a willing foe and sea room!"

They drank to that, as Free Companions had always drunk that toast on the eve of battle. As they seated themselves once more, Mendez said, "Major Matson, please telaudio Cinc Rhys and arrange details. We must know his plans."

"Yes, sir."

Mendez glanced at Scott. "Now how else may I serve you?"

"Nothing else. I'll get back to our fort. Details can be worked out on the telaudio, on tight beam."

"If you're going back in that flitterboat," Mendez said sardonically, "I strongly advise a rubdown. There's time to spare, now we've come to an agreement."

Scott hesitated. "Very well. I'm . . . uh . . . starting to

ache." He stood up. "Oh, one thing I forgot. We've heard rumors that Starling's outfit is using atomic power."

Mendez's mouth twisted into a grimace of distaste. "Hadn't heard that. Know anything about it, gentlemen?"

Heads were shaken. One officer said, "I've heard a little talk about it, but only talk, so far."

Mendez said, "After this war, we'll investigate further. If there's truth in the story, we'll join you, of course, in mopping up the Starlings. No court-martial is necessary for *that* crime!"

"Thanks. I'll get in touch with other Companies and see what they've heard. Now, if you'll excuse me—"

He saluted and went out, exultation flaming within him. The bargain had been a good one—for the Doonemen badly needed the Mob's help against the Helldivers. Cinc Rhys would be satisfied with the arrangement.

An orderly took him to the baths, where a rubdown relaxed his aching muscles. Presently he was on the quay again, climbing into the flitterboat. A glance behind him showed that the gears of war were beginning to grind. There was little he could see, but men were moving about through the courtyard with purposeful strides, to the shops, to administration, to the laboratories. The battlewagons were anchored down the coast, Scott knew, in a protected bay, but they would soon move out to their rendezvous with the Doones.

Kane, at the controls of the flitterboat, said, "They repaired the auxiliary unit for us, sir."

"Courtesies of the trade." Scott lifted a friendly hand to the men on the quay as the boat slid toward open water. "The Doone fort, now. Know it?"

"Yes, sir. Are . . . are the Mob fighting with us, if I may ask?"

"They are. And they're a grand lot of fighters. You're going to see action, Kane. When you hear battle stations next, it's going to mean one of the sweetest scraps that happened on Venus. Push down that throttle—we're in a hurry!"

The flitterboat raced southwest at top speed, its course marked by the flying V of spray.

"One last fight," Scott thought to himself. "I'm glad it's going to be a good one."

4

WE EAT AND DRINK OUR OWN DAMNATION.

—THE BOOK OF COMMON PRAYER

The motor failed when they were about eight miles from the Doone fort.

It was a catastrophe rather than merely a failure. The overstrained and overheated engine, running at top speed, blew back. The previous accident, at the subsea volcano, had brought out hidden flaws in the alloy which the Mob's repairmen had failed to detect when they replaced the smashed single unit. Sheer luck had the flitterboat poised on a swell when the crack-up happened. The engine blew out and down, ripping the bow to shreds. Had they been bow-deep, the blast would have been unfortunate for Scott and the pilot—more so than it was.

They were perhaps a half mile from the shore. Scott was deafened by the explosion and simultaneously saw the horizon swinging in a drunken swoop. The boat turned turtle, the shell smacking into water with a loud cracking sound. But the plastic held. Both men were tangled together on what had been their ceiling, sliding forward as the flitter-boat began to sink bow first. Steam sizzled from the ruined engine.

Kane managed to touch one of the emergency buttons. The shell was, of course, jammed, but a few of the segments slid aside, admitting a gush of acrid sea water. For a moment they struggled there, fighting the cross-currents till the air had been displaced. Scott, peering through cloudy green gloom, saw Kane's dark shadow twist and kick out through a gap. He followed.

Beneath him the black bulk of the boat dropped slowly and was gone. His head broke surface, and he gasped for breath, shaking droplets from his lashes and glancing around. Where was Kane?

The boy appeared, his helmet gone, sleek hair plastered to his forehead. Scott caught his eye and pulled the trigger on his life vest, the inflatable undergarment which was always worn under the blouse on sea duty. As chemicals mixed, light gas rushed into the vest, lifting Scott higher in the water. He felt the collar cushion inflate against the back of his head—the skull-fitting pillow that allowed shipwrecked men to float and rest without danger of drowning in their sleep. But he had no need for this now.

Kane, he saw, had triggered his own life vest. Scott hurled himself up, searching for signs of life. There weren't any. The gray-green sea lay desolate to the misty horizon. A half mile away was a mottled chartreuse wall that marked the jungle. Above and beyond that dim sulphurous red lit the clouds.

Scott got out his leaf-bladed smatchet, gesturing for

Kane to do the same. The boy did not seem worried. No doubt this was merely an exciting adventure for him, Scott thought wryly. Oh, well.

Gripping the smatchet between his teeth, the captain began to swim shoreward. Kane kept at his side. Once Scott warned his companion to stillness and bent forward, burying his face in the water and peering down at a great dim shadow that coiled away and was gone—a sea snake, but, luckily, not hungry. The oceans of Venus were perilous with teeming, ferocious life. Precautions were fairly useless. When a man was once in the water, it was up to him to get out of it as rapidly as possible.

Scott touched a small cylinder attached to his belt and felt bubbles rushing against his palm. He was slightly relieved. When he had inflated the vest, this tube of compressed gas had automatically begun to release, sending out a foul-smelling vapor that permeated the water for some distance around. The principle was that of the skunk adjusted to the environment of the squid, and dangerous undersea life was supposed to be driven away by the Mellison tubes; but it didn't work with carrion eaters like the snakes. Scott averted his nose. The gadgets were named Mellison tubes, but the men called them Stinkers, a far more appropriate term.

Tides on Venus are unpredictable. The clouded planet has no moon, but it is closer to the Sun than Earth. As a rule the tides are mild, except during volcanic activity, when tidal waves sweep the shores. Scott, keeping a weather eye out for danger, rode the waves in toward the beach, searching the strip of dull blackness for signs of life.

Nothing.

He scrambled out at last, shaking himself like a dog, and instantly changed the clip in his automatic for high explosive. The weapon, of course, was watertight—a necessity on Venus. As Kane sat down with a grunt and deflated his vest, Scott stood eyeing the wall of jungle thirty feet away. It stopped there abruptly, for nothing could grow on black sand.

The rush and whisper of the waves made the only sound. Most of the trees were liana-like, eking out a precarious existence, as the saying went, by taking in each other's washing. The moment one of them showed signs of solidity, it was immediately assailed by parasitic vines flinging themselves madly upward to reach the filtered sunlight of Venus. The leaves did not begin for thirty feet above the ground; they made a regular roof up there, lying like crazy shingles, and would have shut out all light had they not been of light translucent green. Whitish tendrils crawled like reaching serpents from tree to tree, tentacles of vegetable octopi. There were two types of Venusian fauna: the giants who could crash through the forest, and the supple, small ground-dwellers—insects and reptiles mostly—who depended on poison sacs for self-protection. Neither kind was pleasant company.

There were flying creatures, too, but these lived in the upper strata, among the leaves. And there were ambiguous horrors that lived in the deep mud and the stagnant pools under the forest, but no one knew much about these.

"Well," Scott said, "that's that."

Kane nodded. "I guess I should have checked the motors."

"You wouldn't have found anything. Latent flaws—it would have taken black night to bring 'em out. Just one of those things. Keep your gas mask handy, now. If we get anywhere near poison flowers and the wind's blowing this way, we're apt to keel over like that." Scott opened a waterproof wallet and took out a strip of sensitized litmus, which he clipped to his wrist. "If this turns blue, that means gas, even if we don't smell it."

"Yes, sir. What now?"

"We-el—the boat's gone. We can't telaudio for help." Scott fingered the blade of his smatchet and slipped it into the belt sheath. "We head for the fort. Eight miles. Two hours, if we can stick to the beach and if we don't run into trouble. More than that if Signal Rock's ahead of us, because we'll have to detour inland in that case." He drew out a collapsible single-lenser telescope and looked southwest along the shore. "Uh-huh. We detour."

A breath of sickening sweetness gusted down from the jungle roof. From above, Scott knew, the forest looked surprisingly lovely. It always reminded him of an antique candlewick spread he had once bought Jeana—immense rainbow flowers scattered over a background of pale green. Even among the flora competition was keen; the plants vied in producing colors and scents that would attract the winged carriers of pollen.

There would always be frontiers, Scott thought. But they might remain unconquered for a long time, here on Venus. The Keeps were enough for the undersea folk; they were self-sustaining. And the Free Companions had no need to carve out empires on the continents. They were fighters, not agrarians. Land hunger was no longer a part of the race. It might come again, but not in the time of the Keeps.

The jungles of Venus held secrets he would never know. Men can conquer lands from the air, but they cannot hold them by that method. It would take a long, slow period of encroachment, during which the forest and all it represented would be driven back, step by painful step—and that belonged to a day to come, a time Scott would not know. The savage world would be tamed. But not now—not yet.

At the moment it was untamed and very dangerous. Scott stripped off his tunic and wrung water from it. His clothing would not dry in this saturated air, despite the winds. His trousers clung to him stickily, clammy coldness in their folds.

"Ready, Kane?"

"Yes, sir."

"Then let's go."

They went southwest, along the beach, at a steady, easy lope that devoured miles. Speed and alertness were necessary in equal proportion. From time to time Scott scanned the sea with his telescope, hoping to sight a vessel. He saw nothing. The ships would be in harbor, readying for the battle; and planes would be grounded for installation of the new telaudio device Cinc Rhys had mentioned.

Signal Rock loomed ahead, an outthrust crag with eroded, unscalable sides towering two hundred feet and more. The black strip of sand ended there. From the rock there was a straight drop into deep water, cut up by a turmoil of currents. It was impossible to take the sea detour; there was nothing else for it but to swerve inland, a dangerous but inevitable course. Scott postponed the plunge as long as possible, till the scarp of Signal Rock, jet black with leprous silvery patches on its surface, barred the way. With a quizzical look at Kane he turned sharply to his right and headed for the jungle.

"Half a mile of forest equals a hundred miles of beach hiking," he remarked.

"That bad, sir? I've never tackled it."

"Nobody does, unless they have to. Keep your eyes open and your gun ready. Don't wade through water, even when you can see bottom. There are some little devils that are pretty nearly transparent—vampire fish. If a few of those fasten on you, you'll need a transfusion in less than a minute. I wish the volcanoes would kick up a racket. The beasties generally lie low when that happens."

Under a tree Scott stopped, seeking a straight, long limb. It took a while to find a suitable one, in that tangle of coiling lianas, but finally he succeeded, using his smatchet blade to hack himself a light five-foot pole. Kane at his heels, he moved on into the gathering gloom.

"We may be stalked," he told the boy. "Don't forget to guard the rear."

The sand had given place to sticky whitish mud that plastered the men to their calves before a few moments had passed. A patina of slickness seemed to overlay the ground. The grass was colored so much like the mud itself that it was practically invisible, except by its added slipperiness. Scott slowly advanced keeping close to the wall of rock on his left where the tangle was not so thick. Nevertheless he had to use the smatchet more than once to cut a passage through vines.

He stopped, raising his hand, and the squelch of Kane's feet in the mud paused. Silently Scott pointed. Ahead of them in the cliff base, was the mouth of a burrow.

The captain bent down, found a small stone, and threw it toward the den. He waited, one hand lightly on his gun, ready to see something flash out of that burrow and race toward them. In the utter silence a new sound made itself heard—tiny goblin drums, erratic and resonant in a faraway fashion. Water, dropping from leaf to leaf, in the soaked jungle ceiling above them. *Tink, tink, tink-tink, tink, tink-tink—*

"O. K.," Scott said quietly. "Watch it, though." He went on, gun drawn, till they were level with the mouth of the burrow. "Turn, Kane. Keep your eye on it till I tell you to stop." He gripped the boy's arm and guided him, holstering his own weapon. The pole, till now held between biceps and body, slipped into his hand. He used it to probe the slick surface of the mud ahead. Sinkhole and quicksands were frequent, and so were traps, camouflaged pits built by mud-wolves—which, of course, were not wolves, and belonged to no known genus. On Venus, the fauna had more subdivisions than on old Earth, and lines of demarcation were more subtle.

"All right now."

Kane, sighing with relief, turned his face forward again. "What was it?"

"You never know what may come out of those holes," Scott told him. "They come fast, and they're usually poisonous. So you can't take chances with the critters. Slow down here. I don't like the looks of that patch ahead."

Clearings were unusual in the forest. There was one here, twenty feet wide, slightly saucer-shaped. Scott gingerly extended the pole and probed. A faint ripple shook the white mud, and almost before it had appeared the captain had unholstered his pistol and was blasting shot after shot at the movement.

"Shoot, Kane!" he snapped. "Quick! Shoot at it!"

Kane obeyed, though he had to guess at his target. Mud geysered up, suddenly crimson-stained. Scott, still firing, gripped the boy's arm and ran him back at a breakneck pace.

The echoes died. Once more the distant elfin drums whispered through the green gloom.

"We got it," Scott said, after a pause.

"We did?" the other asked blankly. "What—"

"Mud-wolf, I think. The only way to kill those things is to get 'em before they get out of the mud. They're fast and they die hard. However—" He warily went forward. There was nothing to see. The mud had collapsed into a deeper saucer, but the holes blasted by the high-x bullets had filled in. Here and there were traces of thready crimson.

"Never a dull moment," Scott remarked. His crooked grin eased the tension. Kane chuckled and followed the captain's example in replacing his half-used clip with a full one.

The narrow spine of Signal Rock extended inland for a quarter mile before it became scalable. They reached that point finally, helping each other climb, and finding themselves, at the summit, still well below the leafy ceiling of the trees. The black surface of the rock was painfully hot, stinging their palms as they climbed, and even striking through their shoe soles.

"Halfway point, Captain?"

"Yeah. But don't let that cheer you. It doesn't get any better till we hit the beach again. We'll probably need some fever shots when we reach the fort, just in case. Oh-oh. Mask, Kane, quick." Scott lifted his arm. On his wrist the band of litmus had turned blue.

With trained accuracy they donned the respirators. Scott felt a faint stinging on his exposed skin, but that wasn't serious. Still, it would be painful later. He beckoned to Kane, slid down the face of the rock, used the pole to test the mud below, and jumped lightly. He dropped in the sticky whiteness and rolled over hastily, plastering himself from head to foot. Kane did the same. Mud wouldn't neutralize the poison flowers' gas, but it would absorb most of it before it reached the skin.

Scott headed toward the beach, a grotesque figure. Mud dripped on the eye plate, and he scrubbed it away with a handful of white grass. He used the pole constantly to test the footing ahead.

Nevertheless the mud betrayed him. The pole broke through suddenly, and as Scott automatically threw his weight back, the ground fell away under his feet. He had time for a crazy feeling of relief that this was quicksand, not a mud-wolf's den, and then the clinging, treacherous stuff had sucked him down knee-deep. He fell back, keeping his grip on the pole and swinging the other end in an arc toward Kane.

The boy seized it in both hands and threw himself flat. His foot hooked over an exposed root. Scott, craning his neck at a painfully awkward angle and trying to see through the mud-smeared vision plate, kept a rattrap grip on his end of the pole, hoping its slickness would not slip through his fingers.

He was drawn down farther, and then Kane's anchorage began to help. The boy tried to pull the pole toward him, hand over hand. Scott shook his head. He was a good deal stronger than Kane, and the latter would need all his strength to keep a tight grip on the pole.

Something stirred in the shadows behind Kane. Scott instinctively let go with one hand, and, with the other, got out his gun. It had a sealed mechanism, so the mud hadn't harmed the firing, and the muzzle had a one-way trap. He fired at the movement behind Kane, heard a muffled tumult, and waited till it had died. The boy, after a startled look behind him, had not stirred.

After that, rescue was comparatively easy. Scott simply climbed along the pole, spreading his weight over the surface of the quicksand. The really tough part was pulling his legs free of that deadly grip. Scott had to rest for five minutes after that.

But he got out. That was the important thing.

Kane pointed inquiringly into the bushes where the creature had been shot, but Scott shook his head. The nature of the beast wasn't a question worth deciding, as long as it was apparently *hors de combat.* Readjusting his mask, Scott turned toward the beach, circling the quicksand, and Kane kept at his heels.

Their luck had changed. They reached the shore with no further difficulty and collapsed on the black sand to rest. Presently Scott used a litmus, saw that the gas had dissipated, and removed his mask. He took a deep breath.

"Thanks, Kane," he said. "You can take a dip now if you want to wash off that mud. But stay close inshore. No, don't strip. There's no time."

The mud clung like glue and the black sand scratched like pumice. Still, Scott felt a good deal cleaner after a few minutes in the surf, while Kane stayed on guard. Slightly refreshed, they resumed the march.

An hour later a convoy plane, testing, sighted them, telaudioed the fort, and a flitterboat came racing out to pick them up. What Scott appreciated most of all was the stiff shot of uisqueplus the pilot gave him.

Yeah. It was a dog's life, all right!

He passed the flask to Kane.

Presently the fort loomed ahead, guarding Doone Harbor. Large as the landlocked bay was, it could scarcely accommodate the fleet. Scott watched the activity visible with an approving eye. The flitterboat rounded the sea wall, built for protection against tidal waves, and shot toward a jetty. Its almost inaudible motor died; the shell swung back.

Scott got out, beckoning to an orderly.

"Yes, sir?"

"See that this soldier gets what he needs. We've been in the jungle."

The man didn't whistle sympathetically, but his mouth pursed. He saluted and helped Kane climb out of the flitterboat. As Scott hurried along the quay, he could hear an outburst of friendly profanity from the men on the dock, gathering around Kane.

He nodded imperceptibly. The boy would make a good Free Companion—always granted that he could stand the gaff under fire. That was the acid test. Discipline was tightened then to the snapping point. If it snapped—well, the human factor always remained a variable, in spite of all the psychologists could do.

He went directly to his quarters, switching on the telaudio to call Cinc Rhys. The cinc's seamed, leathery face resolved itself on the screen.

"Captain Scott reporting for duty, sir."

Rhys looked at him sharply. "What happened?"

"Flitterboat crack-up. Had to make it in here on foot."

The cinc called on his God in a mild voice. "Glad you made it. Any accident?"

"No, sir. The pilot's unharmed, too. I'm ready to take over, after I've cleaned up."

"Better take a rejuvenation—you probably need it. Everything's going like clockwork. You did a good job with Mendez—a better bargain than I'd hoped for. I've been talking with him on the telaudio, integrating our forces. We'll go into that later, though. Clean up and then make general inspection."

"Check, sir."

Rhys clicked off. Scott turned to face his orderly.

"Hello, Briggs. Help me off with these duds. You'll probably have to cut 'em off."

"Glad to see you back, sir. I don't think it'll be necessary to cut—" Blunt fingers flew deftly over zippers and clasps. "You were in the jungle?"

Scott grinned wryly. "Do I look as if I'd been gliding?"

"Not all the way, sir—no."

Briggs was like an old bulldog—one of those men who proved the truth of the saying: "Old soldiers never die; they only fade away." Briggs could have been pensioned off ten years ago, but he hadn't wanted that. There was always a place for old soldiers in the Free Companies, even those who were unskilled. Some became technicians; others, military instructors; the rest, orderlies. The forts were their homes. Had they retired to one of the Keeps, they would have died for lack of interests.

Briggs, now—he had never risen above the ranks, and knew nothing of military strategy, ordnance, or anything except plain fighting. But he had been a Dooneman for forty years, twenty-five of them on active service. He was sixty-odd now, his squat figure slightly stooped like an elderly bear, his ugly face masked with scar tissue.

"All right. Start the shower, will you?"

Briggs stumped off, and Scott, stripped of his filthy, sodden garments, followed. He luxuriated under the stinging spray, first hot soapy water, then alcomix, and after that plain water, first hot, then cold. That was the last task he had to do himself. Briggs took over, as Scott relaxed on the slab, dropping lotion into the captain's burning eyes, giving him a deft but murderous rubdown, combining osteopathic and chiropractic treatment, adjusting revitalizing lamps, and measuring a hypo shot to nullify fatigue toxins. When the orderly was finished, Scott was ready to resume his duties with a clear brain and a refreshed body.

Briggs appeared with fresh clothing. "I'll have the old uniform cleaned, sir. No use throwing it away."

"You can't clean that," Scott remarked, slipping into a singlet. "Not after I rolled in mud. But suit yourself. I won't be needing it for long."

The orderly's fingers, buttoning Scott's tunic, stopped briefly and then resumed their motion. "Is that so, sir?"

"Yeah. I'm taking out discharge papers."

"Another Company, sir?"

"Don't get on your high horse," Scott told the orderly. "It's not that. What would you do if it were? Court-martial me yourself and shoot me at sunrise?"

"No, sir. Begging your pardon, sir, I'd just think you were crazy."

"Why I stand you only the Lord knows," Scott remarked. "You're too damn independent. There's no room for new ideas in that plastic skull of yours. You're the quintessence of dogmatism."

Briggs nodded. "Probably, sir. When a man's lived by one set of rules for as long as I have, and those rules work out, I suppose he might get dogmatic."

"Forty years for you—about twelve for me."

"You came up fast, captain. You'll be cinc here yet."

"That's what you think."

"You're next in line after Cinc Rhys."

"But I'll be out of the Doones," Scott pointed out. "Keep that under your belt, Briggs."

The orderly grunted. "Can't see it, sir. If you don't join another Company, where'll you go?"

"Ever heard of the Keeps?"

Briggs permitted himself a respectful snort. "Sure. They're fine for a binge, but—"

"I'm going to live in one. Montana Keep."

"The Keeps were built with men and machines. I helped at the building of Doone fort. Blood's mixed with the plastic here. We had to hold back the jungle while the technicians were working. Eight months, sir, and never a day passed without some sort of attack. And attacks always meant casualties then. We had only breastworks. The ships laid down a barrage, but barrages aren't impassable. That was a fight, Captain."

Scott thrust out a leg so that Briggs could lace his boots. "And a damn good one. I know." He looked down at the orderly's baldish, brown head where white hairs straggled.

"You know, but you weren't there, Captain. I was. First we dynamited. We cleared a half circle where we could dig in behind breastworks. Behind us were the techs, throwing up a plastic wall as fast as they could. The guns were brought in on barges. Lying offshore were the battlewagons. We could hear the shells go whistling over our heads—it sounded pretty good, because we knew things were O. K. as long as the barrage kept up. But it couldn't be kept up day and night. The jungle broke through. For months the smell of blood hung here, and that drew the enemy."

"But you held them off."

"Sure, we did. Addison Doone was cinc then—he'd formed the Company years before, but we hadn't a fort. Doone fought with us. Saved my life once, in fact. Anyhow—we got the fort built, or rather the techs did. I won't forget the kick I got out of it when the first big gun blasted off from the wall behind us. There was a lot to do after that, but when that shell was fired, we knew we'd done the job."

Scott nodded. "You feel a proprietary interest in the fort, I guess."

Briggs looked puzzled. "The fort? Why, that doesn't mean much, Captain. There are lots of forts. It's something more than that; I don't quite know what it is. It's seeing the fleet out there—breaking in the rookies—giving the old toasts at mess—knowing that—" He stopped, at a loss.

Scott's lips twisted wryly. "You don't really know, do you, Briggs?"

"Know what, sir?"

"Why you stay here. Why you can't believe I'd quit."

Briggs gave a little shrug. "Well—it's the Doones," he said. "That's all, Captain. It's just that."

"And what the devil will it matter, in a few hundred years?"

"I suppose it won't. No, sir. But it isn't our business to think about that. We're Doonemen, that's all."

Scott didn't answer. He could easily have pointed out the fallacy of Briggs's argument, but what was the use? He stood up, the orderly whisking invisible dust off his tunic.

"All set, sir. Shipshape."

"Check, Briggs. Well, I've one more scrap, anyhow. I'll bring you back a souvenir, eh?"

The orderly saluted, grinning. Scott went out, feeling

good. Inwardly he was chuckling rather sardonically at the false values he was supposed to take seriously. Of course many men had died when Doone fort had been built. But did that, in itself, make a tradition? What good was the fort? In a few centuries it would have outlived its usefulness. Then it would be a relic of the past. Civilization moved on, and, these days, civilization merely tolerated the military.

So—what was the use? Sentiment needed a valid reason for its existence. The Free Companions fought, bitterly, doggedly, with insane valor, in order to destroy themselves. The ancient motives for war had vanished.

What was the use? All over Venus the lights of the great forts were going out—and, this time, they would never be lit again—not in a thousand lifetimes!

5

AND WE ARE HERE AS ON A DARKLING PLAIN
SWEPT WITH CONFUSED ALARMS OF STRUGGLE AND FLIGHT,
WHERE IGNORANT ARMIES CLASH BY NIGHT.

—ARNOLD, CIRCA 1870

The fort was a completely self-contained unit, military rather than social. There was no need for any agrarian development, since a state of complete siege never existed. Food could be brought in from the Keeps by water and air.

But military production was important, and, in the life of the fort, the techs played an important part, from the experimental physicist to the spot welder. There were always replacements to be made, for, in battle, there were always casualties. And it was necessary to keep the weapons up-to-date, continually striving to perfect new ones. But strategy and armament were of equal importance. An outnumbered fleet had been known to conquer a stronger one by the use of practical psychology.

Scott found Commander Bienne at the docks, watching the launching of a new sub. Apparently Bienne hadn't yet got over his anger, for he turned a scowling, somber face to the captain as he saluted.

"Hello, Commander," Scott said. "I'm making inspection. Are you free?"

Bienne nodded. "There's not much to do."

"Well—routine. We got that sub finished just in time, eh?"

"Yes." Bienne couldn't repress his pleasure at sight of the trim, sleek vessel beginning to slide down the ways. Scott, too, felt his pulses heighten as the sub slipped into the water, raising a mighty splash, and then settling down to a smooth, steady riding on the waves. He looked out to where the great battlewagons stood at anchor, twelve of them, gray-green monsters of plated metal. Each of them carried launching equipment for gliders, but the collapsible aircraft were stowed away out of sight as yet. Smaller destroyers lay like lean-flanked wolves among the battleships. There were two fast carriers, loaded with gliders and flitterboats. There were torpedo boats and one low-riding monitor, impregnable, powerfully armed, but slow. Only a direct hit could disable a monitor, but the behemoths had their disadvantages. The battle was usually over before they lumbered into sight. Like all monitors, this one—the *Armageddon*—was constructed on the principle of a razorback hog, covered, except for the firing ports, by a tureen-shaped shield, strongly braced from within. The *Armageddon* was divided into groups of compartments and had several auxiliary engines, so that, unlike the legendary *Rover,* when a monitor died, it did *not* die all over. It was, in effect, a dinosaur. You could blow off the monster's head, and it would continue to fight with talons and lashing tail. Its heavy guns made up in mobility for the giant's unwieldiness—but the trouble was to get the monitor into battle. It was painfully slow.

Scott scowled. "We're fighting over Venus Deep, eh?"

"Yes," Bienne nodded. "That still goes. The Helldivers are already heading toward Montana Keep, and we'll intercept them over the Deep."

"When's zero hour?"

"Midnight tonight."

Scott closed his eyes, visualizing their course on a mental chart. Not so good. When battle was joined near island groups, it was sometimes possible for a monitor to slip up under cover of the islets, but that trick wouldn't work now. Too bad—for the Helldivers were a strong outfit, more so since their recent merger with O'Brien's Legion. Even with the Mob to help, the outcome of the scrap would be anyone's guess. The *Armageddon* might be the decisive factor.

"I wonder—" Scott said. "No. It'd be impossible."

"What?"

"Camouflaging the *Armageddon.* If the Helldivers see the monitor coming, they'll lead the fight away from it, faster than that tub can follow. I was thinking we might get her into the battle without the enemy realizing it."

"She's camouflaged now."

"Paint, that's all. She can be spotted. I had some screwy idea about disguising her as an island or a dead whale."

"She's too big for a whale and floating islands look a bit suspicious."

"Yeah. But if we *could* slip the *Armageddon* in without scaring off the enemy—Hm-m-m. Monitors have a habit of turning turtle, don't they?"

"Right. They're top-heavy. But a monitor can't fight upside down. It's not such a bright idea, Captain." Briefly Bienne's sunken eyes gleamed with sneering mockery. Scott grunted and turned away.

"All right. Let's take a look around."

The fleet was shipshape. Scott went to the shops. He learned that several new hulls were under way, but would not be completed by zero hour. With Bienne, he continued to the laboratory offices. Nothing new. No slipups; no surprises. The machine was running smoothly.

By the time inspection was completed, Scott had an idea. He told Bienne to carry on and went to find Cinc Rhys. The cinc was in his office, just clicking off the telaudio as Scott appeared.

"That was Mendez," Rhys said. "The Mob's meeting our fleet a hundred miles off the coast. They'll be under our orders, of course. A good man, Mendez, but I don't entirely trust him."

"You're not thinking of a double cross, sir?"

Cinc Rhys made disparaging noises. "Brutus is an honorable man. No, he'll stick to his bargain. But I wouldn't cut cards with Mendez. As a Free Companion, he's trustworthy. Personally—Well, how do things look?"

"Very good, sir. I've an idea about the *Armageddon.*"

"I wish I had," Rhys said frankly. "We can't get that damned scow into the battle in any way I can figure out.

The Helldivers will see it coming, and lead the fight away."

"I'm thinking of camouflage."

"A monitor's a monitor. It's unmistakable. You can't make it look like anything else."

"With one exception, sir. You can make it look like a disabled monitor."

Rhys sat back, giving Scott a startled glance. "That's interesting. Go on."

"Look here, sir." The captain used a stylo to sketch the outline of a monitor on a convenient pad. "Above the surface, the *Armageddon*'s dome-shaped. Below, it's a bit different, chiefly because of the keel. Why can't we put a fake superstructure on the monitor—build a false keel on it, so it'll seem capsized?"

"It's possible."

"Everybody knows a monitor's weak spot—that it turns turtle under fire sometimes. If the Helldiver saw an apparently capsized *Armageddon* drifting toward them, they'd naturally figure the tub was disabled."

"It's crazy," Rhys said. "One of those crazy ideas that might work." He used the local telaudio to issue crisp orders. "Got it? Good. Get the *Armageddon* under way as soon as the equipment's aboard. Alterations will be made at sea. We can't waste time. If we had them made in the yards, she'd never catch up with the fleet."

The cinc broke the connection, his seamed, leathery face twisting into a grin. "I hope it works. We'll see."

He snapped his fingers. "Almost forgot. President Crosby's nephew—Kane?—he was with you when you cracked up, wasn't he? I've been wondering whether I should have waived training for him. How did he show up in the jungle?"

"Quite well," Scott said. "I had my eye on him. He'll make a good soldier."

Rhys looked keenly at the captain. "What about discipline? I felt that was his weak spot."

"I've no complaint to make."

"So. Well, maybe. Starling's outfit is bad training for anyone—especially a raw kid. Speaking of Starling, did Cinc Mendez know anything about his using atomic power?"

"No, sir. If Starling's doing that, he's keeping it plenty quiet."

"We'll investigate after the battle. Can't afford that sort of thing—we don't want another holocaust. It was bad enough to lose Earth. It decimated the race. If it happened again, it'd wipe the race out."

"I don't think there's much danger of that. On Earth, it was the big atomic-power stations that got out of control. At worst, Starling can't have more than hand weapons."

"True. You can't blow up a world with those. But you know the law—no atomic power on Venus."

Scott nodded.

"Well, that's all." Rhys waved him away. "Clear weather."

Which, on this perpetually clouded world, had a tinge of irony.

After mess Scott returned to his quarters, for a smoke and a brief rest. He waved away Briggs's suggestion of a rubdown and sent the orderly to the commissary for fresh tobacco. "Be sure to get Twenty Star," he cautioned. "I don't want that green hydroponic cabbage."

"I know the brand, sir." Briggs looked hurt and departed. Scott settled back in his relaxer, sighing.

Zero hour at twelve. The last zero hour he'd ever know. All through the day he had been conscious that he was fulfilling his duties for the last time.

His mind went back to Montana Keep. He was living again those other-worldly moments in the cloud-wrapped Olympus with Ilene. Curiously, he found it difficult to visualize the girl's features. Perhaps she was a symbol—her appearance did not matter. Yet she was very lovely.

In a different way from Jeana. Scott glanced at Jeana's picture on the desk, three-dimensional and tinted after life. By pressing a button on the frame, he could have given it sound and motion. He leaned forward and touched the tiny stud. In the depths of the picture the figure of Jeana stirred, smiling. The red lips parted.

Her voice, though soft, was quite natural.

"Hello, Brian," the recording said. "Wish I were with you now. Here's a present, darling." The image blew him a kiss, and then faded back to immobility.

Scott sighed again. Jeana was a comfortable sort of person. But—Oh, hell! She wasn't willing to change. Very likely she couldn't. Ilene perhaps was equally dogmatic, but she represented the life of the Keeps—and that was what Scott wanted now.

It was an artificial life Ilene lived, but she was honest about it. She knew its values were false. At least she didn't pretend, like the Free Companions, that there were ideals worth dying for. Scott remembered Briggs. The fact that men had been killed during the building of Doone fort meant a lot to the old orderly. He never asked himself—*why?* Why had they died? Why was Doone fort built in the first place? For war. And war was doomed.

One had to believe in an ideal before devoting one's life to it. One had to feel he was helping the ideal to survive—watering the plant with his blood so eventually it would come to flower. The red flower of Mars had long since blown. How did that old poem go?

One thing is certain, and the rest is lies;
The flower that once has blown forever dies.

It was true. But the Free Companions blindly pretended that the flower was still in blazing scarlet bloom, refusing to admit that even the roots were withered and useless, scarcely able now to suck up the blood sacrificed to its hopeless thirst.

New flowers bloomed; new buds opened. But in the Keeps, not in the great doomed forts. It was the winter cycle, and, as the last season's blossoms faded, the buds of the next stirred into life. Life questing and intolerant. Life that fed on the rotting petals of the rose of war.

But the pretense went on, in the coastal forts that guarded the Keeps. Scott made a grimace of distaste. Blind, stupid folly! He was a man first, not a soldier. And man is essentially a hedonist, whether he identifies himself with the race or not.

Scott could not. He was not part of the undersea culture, and he could never be. But he could lose himself in the hedonistic backwash of the Keeps, the froth that always overlies any social unit. With Ilene, he could, at least, seek happiness, without the bitter self-mockery he had known for so long. Mockery at his own emotional weaknesses in which he did not believe.

Ilene was honest. She knew she was damned, because unluckily she had intelligence.

So—Scott thought—they would make a good pair.

* * *

Scott looked up as Commander Bienne came into the room. Bienne's sour, mahogany face was flushed deep red under the bronze. His lids were heavy over angry eyes. He swung the door-curtain shut after him and stood rocking on his heels, glowering at Scott.

He called Scott something unprintable.

The captain rose, an icy knot of fury in his stomach. Very softly he said, "You're drunk, Bienne. Get out. Get back to your quarters."

"Sure—you little tinhorn soldier. You like to give orders, don't you? You like to chisel, too. The way you chiseled me out of that left-wing command today. I'm pretty sick of it, Captain Brian Scott."

"Don't be a damned fool! I don't like you personally any more than you like me, but that's got nothing to do with the Company. I recommended you for that command."

"You lie," Bienne said, swaying. "And I hate your guts."

Scott went pale, the scar on his cheek flaming red. Bienne came forward. He wasn't too drunk to coordinate. His fist lashed out suddenly and connected agonizingly with Scott's molar.

The captain's reach was less than Bienne's. He ducked inside of the next swing and carefully smashed a blow home on the point of the other's jaw. Bienne was driven back, crashing against the wall and sliding down in a limp heap, his head lolling forward.

Scott, rubbing his knuckles, looked down, considering. Presently he knelt and made a quick examination. A knock-out, that was all.

Oh, well.

Briggs appeared, showing no surprise at sight of

Bienne's motionless body. The perfect orderly walked across to the table and began to refill the humidor with the tobacco he had brought.

Scott almost chuckled.

"Briggs."

"Yes, sir?"

"Commander Bienne's had a slight accident. He—slipped. Hit his chin on something. He's a bit tight, too. Fix him up, will you?"

"With pleasure, sir." Briggs hoisted Bienne's body across his brawny shoulders.

"Zero hour's at twelve. The commander must be aboard the *Flintlock* by then. And sober. Can do?"

"Certainly, sir," Briggs said, and went out.

Scott returned to his chair, filling his pipe. He should have confined Bienne to his quarters, of course. But—well, this was a personal matter. One could afford to stretch a point, especially since Bienne was a valuable man to have aboard during action. Scott vaguely hoped the commander would get his thick head blown off.

After a time he tapped the dottle from his pipe and went off for a final inspection.

At midnight the fleet hoisted anchor.

By dawn the Doones were nearing the Venus Deep.

The ships of the Mob had already joined them, seven battleships and assorted cruisers, destroyers, and one carrier. No monitor. The Mob didn't own one—it had capsized two months before, and was still undergoing repairs.

The combined fleets sailed in crescent formation, the left wing, commanded by Scott, composed of his own ship, the *Flintlock,* and the *Arquebus,* the *Arrow,* and the

Misericordia, all Doone battlewagons. There were two Mob ships with him, the *Navaho* and the *Zuni,* the latter commanded by Cinc Mendez. Scott had one carrier with him, the other being at right wing. Besides these, there were the lighter craft.

In the center were the battleships *Arbalest, Lance, Gatling,* and *Mace,* as well as three of Mendez's. Cinc Rhys was aboard the *Lance,* controlling operations. The camouflaged monitor *Armageddon* was puffing away valiantly far behind, well out of sight in the mists.

Scott was in his control room, surrounded by telaudio screens and switchboards. Six operators were perched on stools before the controls, ready to jump to action when orders came through their earphones. In the din of battle spoken commands often went unheard, which was why Scott wore a hush-mike strapped to his chest.

His eyes roved over the semicircle of screens before him.

"Any report from the gliders yet?"

"No, sir."

"Get me air-spotting command."

One of the screens flamed to life; a face snapped into view on it.

"Report."

"Nothing yet, Captain. Wait." There was a distant thunder. "Detectors clamped on a telaudio tight-beam directly overhead."

"Enemy glider in the clouds?"

"Apparently. It's out of the focus now."

"Try to relocate it."

A lot of good that would do. Motored planes could easily be detected overhead, but a glider was another matter. The only way to spot one was by clamping a detector focus directly on the glider's telaudio beam—worse than a needle in a haystack. Luckily the crates didn't carry bombs.

"Report coming in, sir. One of our gliders."

Another screen showed a face. "Pilot reporting, sir. Located enemy."

"Good. Switch in the telaudio, infra. What sector?"

"V. D. eight hundred seven northwest twenty-one."

Scott said into his hush-mike, "Get Cinc Rhys and Commander Geer on tight-beam. And Cinc Mendez."

Three more screens lit up, showing the faces of the three officers.

"Cut in the pilot."

Somewhere over Venus Deep the glider pilot was arcing his plane through the cloud-layer, the automatic telaudio-camera, lensed to infrared, penetrating the murk and revealing the ocean below. On the screen ships showed, driving forward in battle formation.

Scott recognized and enumerated them mentally. The *Orion,* the *Sirius,* the *Vega,* the *Polaris*—uh-huh. Lighter ships. Plenty of them. The scanner swept on.

Cinc Rhys said, "We're outnumbered badly. Cinc Mendez, are your sub-detectors in operation?"

"They are. Nothing yet."

"We'll join battle in half an hour, I judge. We've located them, and they've no doubt located us."

"Check."

The screens blanked out. Scott settled back, alertly at ease. Nothing to do now but wait, keeping ready for the unexpected. The *Orion* and the *Vega* were the Helldivers's biggest battleships, larger than anything in the line of the Doones—or the Mob. Cinc Flynn was no doubt aboard the *Orion.* The Helldivers owned a monitor, but it had not showed on the infrared aerial scanner. Probably the behemoth wouldn't even show up in time for the battle.

But even without the monitor, the Helldivers had an overwhelming surface display. Moreover, their undersea fleet was an important factor. The sub-detectors of Cinc Mendez might—probably would—cut down the odds. But possibly not enough.

The *Armageddon,* Scott thought, might be the point of decision, the ultimate argument. And, as yet, the camouflaged monitor was lumbering through the waves far in the wake of the Doones.

Commander Bienne appeared on a screen. He had frozen into a disciplined, trained robot, personal animosities forgotten for the time. Active duty did that to a man.

Scott expected nothing different, however, and his voice was completely impersonal as he acknowledged Bienne's call.

"The flitterboats are ready to go, Captain."

"Send them out in fifteen minutes. Relay to left wing, all ships carrying flitters."

"Check."

For a while there was silence. A booming explosion brought Scott to instant alertness. He glanced up at the screens.

A new face appeared. "Helldivers opening up. Testing for range. They must have gliders overhead. We can't spot 'em."

"Get the men under cover. Send up a test barrage. Prepare to return here. Contact our pilots over the Helldivers."

It was beginning now—the incessant, racking thunder that would continue till the last shot was fired. Scott cut in to Cinc Rhys as the latter signaled.

"Reporting, sir."

"Harry the enemy. We can't do much yet. Change to R-8 formation."

Cinc Mendez said, "We've got three enemy subs. Our detectors are tuned up to high pitch."

"Limit the range so our subs will be outside the sphere of influence."

"Already did that. The enemy's using magnetic depth charges, laying an undersea barrage as they advance."

"I'll talk to the sub command." Rhys cut off. Scott listened to the increasing fury of explosions. He could not yet hear the distinctive *clap-clap* of heat rays, but the quarters were not yet close enough for those undependable, though powerful, weapons. It took time for a heat ray to warm up, and during that period a well-aimed bullet could smash the projector lens.

"Casualty, sir. Direct hit aboard destroyer *Bayonet.*"

"Extent of damage?"

"Not disabled. Complete report later."

After a while a glider pilot came in on the beam.

"Shell landed on the *Polaris,* sir."

"Use the scanner."

It showed the Helldivers's battlewagon, part of the superstructure carried away, but obviously still in fighting trim. Scott nodded. Both sides were getting the range now. The hazy clouds still hid each fleet from the other, but they were nearing.

The sound of artillery increased. Problems of trajectory were increased by the violent winds of Venus, but accurate aiming was possible. Scott nodded grimly as a crash shook the *Flintlock.*

They were getting it now. Here, in the brain of the ship, he was as close to the battle as any member of a firing crew. The screens were his eyes.

They had the advantage of being able to use infrared, so that Scott, buried here, could see more than he could have on deck, with his naked eye. Something loomed out of the murk and Scott's breath stopped before he recognized the lines of the Doone battlewagon *Misericordia.* She was off course. The captain used his hush-mike to snap a quick reprimand.

Flitterboats were going out now, speedy hornets that would harry the enemy fleet. In one of them, Scott remembered, was Norman Kane. He thought of Ilene and thrust the thought back, out of his mind. No time for that now.

Battle stations allowed no time for wool gathering.

The distant vanguard of the Helldivers came into sight on the screens. Cinc Mendez called.

"Eleven more subs. One got through. Seems to be near the *Flintlock.* Drop depth bombs."

Scott nodded and obeyed. Shuddering concussions shook the ship. Presently a report came in: fuel slick to starboard.

Good. A few well-placed torpedoes could do a lot of damage.

The *Flintlock* heeled incessantly under the action of the heavy guns. Heat rays were lancing out. The big ships could not easily avoid the searing blasts that could melt solid metal, but the flitterboats, dancing around like angry insects, sent a rain of bullets at the projectors. But even that took integration. The rays themselves were invisible, and could only be traced from their targets. The camera crews were working overtime, snapping shots of the enemy ships, tracing the rays' points of origin, and telaudioing the information to the flitterboats.

"Helldivers's *Rigel* out of action."

On the screen the big destroyer swung around, bow pointing forward. She was going to ram. Scott snapped orders. The *Flintlock* went hard over, guns pouring death into the doomed *Rigel.*

The ships passed, so close that men on the *Flintlock*'s decks could see the destroyer lurching through the haze. Scott judged her course and tried desperately to get Mendez. There was a delay.

"QM—QM—emergency! Get the *Zuni!*"

"Here she answers, sir."

Scott snapped, "Change course. QM. Destroyer *Rigel* bearing down on you."

"Check." The screen blanked. Scott used a scanner. He groaned at the sight. The *Zuni* was swinging fast, but the *Rigel* was too close—too damned close.

She rammed.

Scott said, "Hell." That put the *Zuni* out of action. He reported to Cinc Rhys.

"All right, Captain. Continue R-8 formation."

Mendez appeared on a screen. "Captain Scott. We're disabled. I'm coming aboard. Have to direct sub-strafing operations. Can you give me a control board?"

"Yes, sir. Land at Port Sector 7."

Hidden in the mist, the fleets swept on in parallel courses, the big battlewagons keeping steady formation, pouring heat rays and shells across the gap. The lighter ships strayed out of line at times, but the flitterboats swarmed like midges, dogfighting when they were not harrying the larger craft. Gliders were useless now, at such close quarters.

The thunder crashed and boomed. Shudders rocked the *Flintlock.*

"Hit on Helldivers's *Orion.* Hit on *Sirius.*"

"Hit on Mob ship *Apache.*"

"Four more enemy subs destroyed."

"Doone sub *X-16* fails to report."

"Helldivers's *Polaris* seems disabled."

"Send out auxiliary flitterboats, units nine and twenty."

Cinc Mendez came in, breathing hard. Scott waved him to an auxiliary control unit seat.

"Hit on *Lance.* Wait a minute. Cinc Rhys a casualty, sir."

Scott froze. "Details."

"One moment—Dead, sir."

"Very well," Scott said after a moment. "I'm assuming command. Pass it along."

He caught a sidelong glance from Mendez. When a Company's cinc was killed, one of two things happened—promotion of a new cinc, or a merger with another Company. In this case Scott was required, by his rank, to assume temporarily the fleet's command. Later, at the Doone fort, there would be a meeting and a final decision.

He scarcely thought of that now. Rhys dead! Tough, unemotional old Rhys, killed in action. Rhys had a free-wife in some Keep, Scott remembered. The Company would pension her. Scott had never seen the woman. Oddly, he wondered what she was like. The question had never occurred to him before.

The screens were flashing. Double duty now—or triple. Scott forgot everything else in directing the battle.

It was like first-stage anaesthesia—it was difficult to

judge time. It might have been an hour or six since the battle had started. Or less than an hour, for that matter.

"Destroyer disabled. Cruiser disabled. Three enemy subs out of action—"

It went on, endlessly. At the auxiliaries Mendez was directing substrafing operations. Where in hell's the *Armageddon?* Scott thought. The fight would be over before that overgrown tortoise arrived.

Abruptly a screen flashed QM. The lean, beak-nosed face of Cinc Flynn of the Helldivers showed.

"Calling Doone command."

"Acknowledging," Scott said. "Captain Scott, emergency command."

Why was Flynn calling? Enemy fleets in action never communicated, except to surrender.

Flynn said curtly, "You're using atomic power. Explanation, please."

Mendez jerked around. Scott felt a tight band around his stomach.

"Done without my knowledge or approval, of course, Cinc Flynn. My apologies. Details?"

"One of your flitterboats fired an atomic-powered pistol at the *Orion.*"

"Damage?"

"One seven-unit gun disabled."

"One of ours, of the same caliber, will be taken out of action immediately. Further details, sir?"

"Use your scanner, Captain, on Sector Mobile 18 south *Orion.* Your apology is accepted. The incident will be erased from our records."

Flynn clicked off. Scott used the scanner, catching a Doone flitterboat in its focus. He used the enlarger.

The little boat was fleeing from enemy fire, racing back

toward the Doone fleet, heading directly toward the *Flintlock,* Scott saw. Through the transparent shell he saw the bombardier slumped motionless, his head blown half off. The pilot, still gripping an atomic-fire pistol in one hand, was Norman Kane. Blood streaked his boyish, strained face.

So Starling's outfit did have atomic power, then. Kane must have smuggled the weapon out with him when he left. And, in the excitement of battle, he had used it against the enemy.

Scott said coldly, "Gun crews starboard. Flitterboat *Z-19-4.* Blast it."

Almost immediately a shell burst near the little craft. On the screen Kane looked up, startled by his own side firing upon him. Comprehension showed on his face. He swung the flitterboat off course, zigzagging, trying desperately to dodge the barrage.

Scott watched, his lips grimly tight. The flitterboat exploded in a rain of spray and debris.

Automatic court-martial.

After the battle, the Companies would band together and smash Starling's outfit.

Meantime, this was action. Scott returned to his screens, erasing the incident from his mind.

Very gradually, the balance of power was increasing with the Helldivers. Both sides were losing ships, put out of action rather than sunk, and Scott thought more and more often of the monitor *Armageddon.* She could turn the battle now. But she was still far astern.

Scott never felt the explosion that wrecked the control room. His senses blacked out without warning.

He could not have been unconscious for long. When he opened his eyes, he stared up at a shambles. He seemed to be the only man left alive. But it could not have been a direct hit, or he would not have survived either.

He was lying on his back, pinned down by a heavy crossbeam. But no bones were broken. Blind, incredible luck had helped him there. The brunt of the damage had been borne by the operators. They were dead, Scott saw at a glance.

He tried to crawl out from under the beam, but that was impossible. In the thunder of battle his voice could not be heard.

There was a movement across the room, halfway to the door. Cinc Mendez stumbled up and stared around, blinking. Red smeared his plump cheeks.

He saw Scott and stood, rocking back and forth, staring. Then he put his hand on the butt of his pistol.

Scott could very easily read the other's mind. If the Doone captain died now, the chances were that Mendez could merge with the Doones and assume control. The politico-military balance lay that way.

If Scott lived, it was probable that he would be elected cinc.

It was, therefore, decidedly to Mendez's advantage to kill the imprisoned man.

A shadow crossed the doorway. Mendez, his back to the newcomer, did not see Commander Bienne halt on the threshold, scowling at the tableau. Scott knew that Bienne understood the situation as well as he himself did. The commander realized that in a very few moments Mendez would draw his gun and fire.

Scott waited. The cinc's fingers tightened on his gun butt.

Bienne, grinning crookedly, said, "I thought that shell had finished you, sir. Guess it's hard to kill a Dooneman."

Mendez took his hand off the gun, instantly regaining his poise. He turned to Bienne.

"I'm glad you're here, Commander. It'll probably take both of us to move that beam."

"Shall we try, sir?"

Between the two of them, they managed to shift the weight off Scott's torso. Briefly the latter's eyes met Bienne's. There was still no friendliness in them, but there was a look of wry self-mockery.

Bienne hadn't saved Scott's life, exactly. It was, rather, a question of being a Dooneman. For Bienne was, first of all, a soldier, and a member of the Free Company.

Scott tested his limbs; they worked.

"How long was I out, Commander?"

"Ten minutes, sir. The *Armageddon's* in sight."

"Good. Are the Helldivers veering off?"

Bienne shook his head. "So far they're not suspicious."

Scott grunted and made his way to the door, the others at his heels. Mendez said, "We'll need another control ship."

"All right. The *Arquebus.* Commander, take over here. Cinc Mendez—"

A flitterboat took them to the *Arquebus,* which was still in good fighting trim. The monitor *Armageddon,* Scott saw, was rolling helplessly in the trough of the waves. In accordance with the battle plan, the Doone ships were leading the Helldivers toward the apparently capsized giant. The technicians had done a good job; the false keel looked shockingly convincing.

Aboard the *Arquebus,* Scott took over, giving Mendez

the auxiliary control for his sub-strafers. The cinc beamed at Scott over his shoulder.

"Wait till that monitor opens up, captain."

"Yeah . . . we're in bad shape, though."

Neither man mentioned the incident that was in both their minds. It was tacitly forgotten—the only thing to do now.

Guns were still bellowing. The Helldivers were pouring their fire into the Doone formation, and they were winning. Scott scowled at the screens. If he waited too long, it would be just too bad.

Presently he put a beam on the *Armageddon.* She was in a beautiful position now, midway between two of the Helldivers's largest battleships.

"Unmask. Open fire."

Firing ports opened on the monitor. The sea titan's huge guns snouted into view. Almost simultaneously they blasted, the thunder drowning out the noise of the lighter guns.

"All Doone ships attack," Scott said. "Plan R-7."

This was it. *This was it!*

The Doones raced in to the kill. Blasting, bellowing, shouting, the guns tried to make themselves heard above the roaring of the monitor. They could not succeed, but that savage, invincible onslaught won the battle.

It was nearly impossible to maneuver a monitor into battle formation, but, once that was accomplished, the only thing that could stop the monster was atomic power.

But the Helldivers fought on, trying strategic formation. They could not succeed. The big battlewagons could not get out of range of the *Armageddon*'s guns. And that meant—

Cinc Flynn's face showed on the screen.

"Capitulation, sir. Cease firing."

Scott gave orders. The roar of the guns died into humming, incredible silence.

"You gave us a great battle, cinc."

"Thanks. So did you. Your strategy with the monitor was excellent."

So—that was that. Scott felt something go limp inside of him. Flynn's routine words were meaningless; Scott was drained of the vital excitement that had kept him going till now.

The rest was pure formula.

Token depth charges would be dropped over Virginia Keep. They would not harm the Dome, but they were the rule. There would be the ransom, paid always by the Keep which backed the losing side. A supply of korium, or its negotiable equivalent. The Doone treasury would be swelled. Part of the money would go into replacements and new keels. The life of the forts would go on.

Alone at the rail of the *Arquebus,* heading for Virginia Keep, Scott watched slow darkness change the clouds from pearl to gray, and then to invisibility. He was alone in the night. The wash of waves came up to him softly as the *Arquebus* rushed to her destination, three hundred miles away.

Warm yellow lights gleamed from ports behind him, but he did not turn. This, he thought, was like the cloud-wrapped Olympus in Montana Keep, where he had promised Ilene—many things.

Yet there was a difference. In an Olympus a man was like a god, shut away completely from the living world. Here, in the unbroken dark, there was no sense of alienage.

Nothing could be seen—Venus has no moon, and the clouds hid the stars. And the seas are not phosphorescent.

Beneath these waters stand the Keeps, Scott thought. They hold the future. Such battles as were fought today are fought so that the Keeps may not be destroyed.

And men will sacrifice. Men have always sacrificed, for a social organization or a military unit. Man must create his own ideal. "If there had been no God, man would have created Him."

Bienne had sacrificed today, in a queer, twisted way of loyalty to his fetish. Yet Bienne still hated him, Scott knew.

The Doones meant nothing. Their idea was a false one. Yet, because men were faithful to that ideal, civilization would rise again from the guarded Keeps. A civilization that would forget its doomed guardians, the watchers of the seas of Venus, the Free Companions yelling their mad, futile battle cry as they drove on—as this ship was driving—into a night that would have no dawn.

Ilene.

Jeana.

It was no such simple choice. It was, in fact, no real choice at all. For Scott knew, very definitely, that he could never, as long as he lived, believe wholeheartedly in the Free Companions. Always a sardonic devil deep within him would be laughing in bitter self-mockery.

The whisper of the waves drifted up.

It wasn't sensible. It was sentimental, crazy, stupid, sloppy thinking.

But Scott knew, now, that he wasn't going back to Ilene.

He was a fool.

But he was a soldier.